LAST CALL

+ AT THE +

NIGHTSHADE
LOUNGE

LAST CALL
+ AT THE +
NIGHTSHADE LOUNGE

A NOVEL OF MAGIC AND MIXOLOGY

PAUL KRUEGER

QUIRK BOOKS
PHILADELPHIA

Library of Congress Cataloging in Publication
Number: 2014909455

ISBN: 978-1-59474-759-5

Printed in the United States of America
Typeset in Bembo Std

Designed by Timothy O'Donnell
Cover photographs:
(woman) © szefei/shutterstock;
(bar) © Chris Goodman
Cupbearer's Court logo designed by
Katie Savage
Production management by John J. McGurk

Quirk Books
215 Church Street
Philadelphia, PA 19106
quirkbooks.com

10 9 8 7 6 5 4 3 2 1

*To the bartenders, baristas, and waiters
who pour the world a stiff drink and keep 'em comin'*

PROLOGUE

It was another Friday night, not that it mattered to Officer Jim Regan of the Chicago PD. There were fifty-two Fridays in a year, and he'd been around for fifty-two years. That meant the number of Fridays he'd lived through was . . . was . . . The hell with it. He wasn't gonna do the math.

After all, it was Friday.

His usual routine was to get off his beat, squeeze back into his civvies, then head down to the Loose Cannon with the rest of the Twentieth Precinct and drink the night away. But tonight he'd gone solo and wandered south into Ravenswood, to the Nightshade Lounge. It was a neighborhood joint his partner mentioned once upon a time, a place where no one would give a shit that he'd flunked his sergeant's exam for the fifth time.

Jim slurped down the last of his boilermaker and slammed the entire thing on the counter, the empty shot glass rattling inside the equally empty beer glass. "Good stuff," he boomed to everybody within thirty feet, which was pretty much nobody. It was past one a.m. and the bar had mostly emptied. He clapped a meaty hand on the counter. "I'll take one for the road."

The bartender studied him from behind a pair of square eye-glasses. "I think you're good, man," he said.

Jim studied him back. He was young—practically a kid—and wore a white dress shirt with rolled-up sleeves and a tucked-in tie like an old-timey barkeep. Little punk.

"Come on," Jim said, pulling out his wallet. "It's for the road. Give me a break, huh?"

The bartender shook his head. "Our drinks aren't going anywhere. How about you come back tomorrow night, and your first one's on me? I'll call you a cab." The kid whipped out his phone before he was even done speaking. Jim waved him off.

"S'all right," he said. "Don't hafta worry about getting busted. I'm a cop."

The kid grinned. "Knowing what the city pays you, I'll make it two rounds then. But for now, let's get you that cab."

Jim waved him off again. "Keep the damn cab," he said, scowling. "I can walk." He lurched to his feet, then looked back. Maybe because he'd been pickling his brain in bourbon and beer since getting off work, but he only just noticed that Mr. Shirt-and-Tie was alone behind the bar. "Hey," he said, "what happened to the girl?" The friendly-looking redhead with a pretty face and not too terrible figure had been happy to serve him.

The kid mimed smoking an invisible cigarette.

Jim grimaced. Now that was a bad habit he'd never picked up. Walking the beat was risky enough. He dropped a fiver on the bar but couldn't focus well enough to give the kid the dirty look he deserved. "Well, tell her thanks for doing *her* job."

"Get home safe, Officer."

And so Jim Regan staggered out, muttering darkly with each step.

Officer. It wasn't like he was gunning to be the next commissioner, for chrissake; he just wanted the stripes on his sleeve. But these days everything was run by up-jumped little shits like that punk bartender.

Summertime Chicago was sweltering. Jim got only three blocks before blotches of sweat darkened his shirt. He stopped and reevaluated. New plan: screw walking and take the bus. The nearest stop was just over the Montrose Street Bridge in Horner Park, a quick trip even for him.

As he heaved across the two-lane bridge, Jim eyed the rusted pedestrian railings. *What a goddamn surprise*, he thought; something around town needed fixing up. He'd seen six mayors come and go since he first put on the uniform, and if there was one thing each generation of paper pushers downtown was good at, it was coming up with new ways to fuck up something that was already pretty thoroughly fucked.

The streetlights flickered overhead. Something was rustling behind him—not a car; didn't sound like wheels. More like footfalls.

Jim turned and froze.

God, no. Jesus, Mary, Joseph, no.

Not the DTs. Not now. Jim might be a drunk—an *alcoholic,* he was supposed to say—but he knew when to stop. Stopping was all that kept him from turning out like his old man, a real drunk's drunk: the thrashing, then trembling, sweating through his undershirts. Moaning and clawing at the air, at things that weren't there. Things like this.

Jim blinked, but the thing didn't go away.

It wasn't huge—the size of a big dog, maybe—but it was a horrible skinless pink color, as if made of flayed muscle. And it was crawling forward.

Jim glanced around wildly. "Stop," he said as the thing took one ponderous step closer. "Police!" But the thing just blinked a yellow eye and took another step. He tried again: "Stop! Police!"

The ugly bastard didn't even falter. Sped up even, scuttling toward him like a fleshy crab as the streetlights flicked faster. Its head was barely a stub, with lit-up catlike eyes and a horrible, tooth-ringed, flesh-flapped mouth. Jesus, the thing had *fangs.*

Jim ran.

Gym membership, he thought between puffs, *first goddamn thing tomorrow. Show those*—puff, puff—*shaved-chest pretty-boy rookies what a real man can do.*

The thing was still coming. *Zigzag,* he thought. *That's what you're supposed to do to get away from bears or crocs or whatever, right?* He threw his left foot over his right . . .

. . . and fell face-first. He dug his fingers into the ground. The world was spinning at an unmerciful tilt and a sickening groan was tearing through the night air: metal dragging on asphalt, like a loose car muffler. But there were no cars. Just the streetlamps of Montrose Avenue and the scrabbling sounds of the thing behind him and distant sparks—

Sparks. Jim shoved himself to his feet. Something was barreling toward him, grating out sparks in its wake.

"Police!" he yelled with what little breath he had left. "Clear the street! Police!" He might've been in his fifties and still not making sergeant, but if he was going to die, at least he would die a cop.

It was a person—black female, tall, dreadlocks—and she was dragging a stop sign, a chunk of concrete still attached to the bottom. She hefted it as she sprinted, even though there was no way her skinny arms could've lifted it, and the sparks and the noise stopped.

"Pol—" Jim couldn't even get the word out before she jumped—*right over his head*—and sliced the stop sign through the thing's neck like an executioner's ax.

The head bounced into the darkness as the girl landed with a soft thump. The thing's body swayed, collapsed onto its haunches, and then exploded in a burst of thick, ugly smoke.

Jim fell to his knees and puked.

Five boilermakers and a half-digested piece of pizza splattered like acid onto the side of the road. He flinched as something grazed his shoulder, but it was just the girl. The stop sign clanged to the ground next to him.

"On your feet." Her tone was sharp enough to shave with.

"How'd you—" He shook his throbbing head, tried to keep his voice from squeaking. "—the fuck is that thing?"

The girl—woman, Jim supposed—glanced impassively at the burned spot in the road. "Tremens."

Jim shook his head. "No way, lady. That ain't no pink elephant."

"Not exactly, no."

"That was—it was real." Jim said it tentatively, testing, but the woman didn't disagree. The thing was not a hallucination. Not something his sauced-up brain had invented. "That's—that's *dangerous*." He looked around wildly. The scorched spot where the tremens had disappeared still sizzled. "Could be more of 'em. Gotta call my captain—"

"There *are* more of them," she said. "But don't worry."

"But—"

"Officer," she said, "where were you drinking just now? At the Nightshade?"

"How'd you—"

"I'm a bartender," she said. "I know things." She held out a hand. "Come with me. Let me pour you a drink and I'll explain everything."

Officer—not Sergeant—Jim Regan swallowed. He had priorities. This thing had to be identified, and Captain Harding at the Twentieth needed to know about it. Animal control would have to be dispatched. They might even need to cordon off the bridge.

But for the first time that day one of these kids was treating him with a little respect, and that was too much for him to ignore.

THE

DEVIL'S WATER

DICTIONARY

————

AN ARCHIVE ABOUT
ALCOHOLIC ARCANA AND ALCHEMY.

————

The knowledge contained herein has two applications. The first is to arm humanity against the forces of darkness, which manifest in the shadows and conspire to undo all that we have built and cherish. If the few brave souls who learn the mixological arts stand like a wall between the happy whole of humanity and its complete ruination, the wisdom of these pages is the mortar that holds its bricks together.

The second application is to provide humanity with some rather tasty inebriates to make the whole thing more enjoyable.

The recipes that follow will yield cocktails that, while transcendent in flavor, are nonetheless ordinary in their conjuring. Yet under specific circumstances, when made with precisely the right ingredients, these drinks can become something far more extraordinary. And they may transform their drinker into the same.

Those who read on will learn how to do the impossible: To fade from sight. To exert control over distant objects with only one's mind. To justify the existence of the olive, which is the most loathsome of all fruits. It is the position of *The Devil's Water Dictionary* that almost all which humanity deems impossible can be achieved—with the liberal application of alcohol.

If you seek to defend the people of the world in the name of the Cupbearers Court, then you will find no greater ally than this book. And if you are merely a curious bystander who now finds him- or herself a little thirsty, then by all means enjoy this book anyway. In all likelihood, an operative of the Court has already been dispatched to modify your memory (see: *OBLIVINUM*), so you may as well enjoy a stiff drink while you await your absolution.

To your continued good health—
BIBO ERGO SUM

CHAPTER ONE

Bailey Chen was taking care of some serious business.

"Hello?" She plugged a finger into her non-cell-phone ear. "Jess? Are you still there? I was just saying that I think Divinyl's doing some really interesting things with their business model—"

"Yup!" said a perky-sounding female. "That's great! So you probably know we're—"

"'A revolutionary return to revolving music,'" Bailey recited. "'The company that's bringing the retro sound of vinyl to the convenience of a mobile platform.' I think that's really, uh—" She cast around for the right word. *Cool? Awesome?* What could you really say about an audio-filter app that took sharp, clear mp3s and re-rendered them into record-styled hiss- and pop-filled playback?

Anything, she reminded herself, anything as long as it landed her an interview.

" . . . really innovative," Bailey said. "And I'd love to come in and talk with you."

She heard a crackle on the line, and Bailey wondered for a split second if it was an intentional throwback designed into Divinyl's corporate phone system or just a side effect of her shitty cell reception.

"Totally!" Jess said. "God, can you believe we haven't talked since, like, high school? We have *so* much to catch up on."

"Oh," Bailey said. "Um, yeah!"

Bailey could believe they hadn't talked since, like, high school because they hadn't talked that much *in* high school. But maybe Jess was one of those people who had dramatically changed in college. Besides, if Bailey landed the job, Jess would probably be her first office friend. They could do business-lady things, like go out for chopped salads. Or, even better, make an intern bring them chopped salads, which they would eat in their spacious, window-filled corner offices while planning total domination of their market sector. (And maybe online-shopping for statement necklaces, because it was, after all, their lunch break.)

Bailey smiled. If she'd ever had a mental picture of success, that was it: lunch delivery, ruthless business sense, and power jewelry.

"Bailey?"

"Sorry, Jess, I'm here. So do you have any time coming up this week or—"

"Bailey!"

This time her name was not coming from the phone. Zane Whelan's shaggy-haired head appeared over the end of the bar, his square eyeglasses gleaming. "There you are!"

Shit. "Um, gotta go," Bailey chirped into her phone, "but *callmebackwhenyougetach*—"

Zane frowned. "Are you . . . talking to someone?"

"Hydrangeas," Bailey said quickly.

"Huh?"

"Hydrangeas, wisterias, oleander, rhododendron, and anthurium," Bailey said, nodding to the trivia emcee gamely grinning down at a clipboard from behind her microphone. "Five of, uh, the most common poisonous plants."

"Anthurium?" Zane blinked. "That sounds like something from a B movie."

Bailey pocketed her phone. "Well, it's real."

The emcee paced the bar floor, shooting pleading glances at

each team. "Come on, guys," she said, with microphone-added reverb. "I only need five. You've still got twenty seconds left to—yes! You."

The captain of a team of yuppies had leapt to his feet. "Oleander, poinsettia, dandel—"

But just as he said "dandelion," a buzzer drowned him out.

"Duh," Bailey said under her breath. "Dandelions are edible."

"Really?" Zane said.

"They're good in salads."

"Sorry." The emcee shook her head like a rueful gameshow host. "Dandelions may not taste great, but they are not poisonous. They're actually—"

Bailey mouthed the rest of the sentence: "—edible and good in salads."

"Wow." Zane tapped out a few polite claps. "I'm impressed."

"Oh, um, don't be," Bailey said, praying he wouldn't ask about the phone call. "Poinsettias aren't toxic to humans unless you eat, like, five hundred leaves. She should have called him on that one."

"Hey, ease up. Not everyone in this bar's an Ivy League graduate."

Bailey flushed. "I didn't mean—"

But Zane was grinning. "Because *that* distinction is the exclusive territory of our smartest barback."

He patted her shoulder, and Bailey tried not to cringe.

"Right," she said. "Thanks."

"And as the smartest barback at the Nightshade Lounge"—Zane went on—"you really should know better than to go sit on the floor during a busy shift."

"I'm sorry, I'm sorry," Bailey rushed to say. "I just had to, uh, the music—"

"Music?" Zane shook his head. "Bailey, that jukebox has probably been here since the sixties. It totally doesn't work. You know that."

"Right," Bailey said. Sometimes it felt like nothing worked at the Nightshade Lounge except Bailey. And Zane, of course.

Zane gave the jukebox a fond pat on its cracked glass. "Anyway. Don't slack on me, okay?"

"I'm not," Bailey protested. If there was one thing she *wasn't*, it was a slacker. "I'm just—"

"Look, Bailey, I told my uncle you could do this job with no experience," Zane said. "And you *can* do it. But if you *don't* . . . " He cleared his throat and continued in a low voice. "I don't want to have to fire you the first week."

Bailey could only nod. She wanted to explain—*Sorry, Zane, that I'm not only looking for the first opportunity to ditch the job you pulled major strings to get me but also doing it while on the clock*—but instead gave him the truncated version: "Sorry. Yup."

"Good." Zane smiled. He'd shown up to work wearing what he always wore: a slim old three-piece suit, complete with loosely knotted tie and rumpled dress shirt, which made him look like a Swinging London modster about to zip off on a candy-colored scooter. "And in return, I'll continue to pay you and act as your beneficent overlord."

"More glasses!" Trina, the redheaded bartender who was Zane's counterweight that night, yelled at them from the other end. "Sometime this century, please?" she added. "Not *those* glasses, Zane. You already made that joke, like, five minutes ago."

Zane crammed his spectacles back onto his face. "I still think it's funny."

"On it," Bailey said, glad for the abrupt end to the conversation. She scooted along in the narrow space behind them, calling out, "On your back! On your back!" as she passed. After depositing a freshly cleaned stack of old fashioned glasses by Trina's side, she glanced at the garnish tray.

"Thanks," Trina said. "I'm low on—"

"Cucumbers," Bailey said with a nod. "On it. On your back, on your back . . ."

"Bailey—" Zane said as she passed.

"More towels?" Bailey knew Zane could never have enough towels.

"Damn, you're good." He plunged a spoon into his shaker and stirred the contents into a froth.

On the one hand, Bailey was well suited to the job of barback. Her small stature meant she could navigate the cramped bar with ease. Her sharp eye for details and logistics allowed her to solve problems before they became problems—a shortage of cucumber slices, for instance. Her Ivy League education . . . well, the really nice UPenn bottle opener she'd gotten sure came in handy. And though she liked people well enough, she wasn't always the best when dealing with them. But as a barback she didn't have to. She just had to keep shuttling supplies and ensuring the line moved smoothly.

On the other hand, barbacking was a terrible job.

The Ravenswood neighborhood had plenty of bars, but the Nightshade was an institution (which, in Chicago, more or less meant a place that stubbornly refused to close). The dark drapes, low lights, and worn-down emerald-colored booth cushions evoked a kind of comfortably faded Second City swank—emphasis on *faded,* because Bailey was pretty sure the cushions hadn't been replaced since at least the Carter administration. But while the place wasn't trendy enough to serve fourteen-dollar cocktails, it wasn't crappy enough to sell only cheapie cans of light lager, either.

Even though it seemed to Bailey like Garrett Whelan had no business savvy whatsoever, the Nightshade did a brisk business selling mixed drinks to mixed company. So in theory her duties as barback should have been:

1. Keep bartenders supplied with a steady stream of clean glasses while removing the used ones.

2. Make sure each garnish tray is well stocked at all times.

3. Regularly check the garbage, taking it out before it overflows.

(Bailey did her best work when she could prioritize everything, preferably in list form.)

At the height of a rush, however, her list was far more likely to look like this:

1. DO EVERYTHING.

2. RIGHT **NOW.**

3. OR ELSE.

All night, every night she never stopped moving. No matter how on top of the situation she was, there was always another fire to put out.

And then there were the customers. They started the evening pleasant enough. But a few rounds had the same effect as a trip to Pinocchio's Pleasure Island: anyone could turn into an ass.

"So that'll be a martini for me," one of the hard-core trivia enthusiasts slurred at her awhile later. She leaned over the bar and gazed down at Bailey with glassy eyes.

Bailey greeted the girl with a patient smile. "I'm sorry, but I'm just a barback," she said. "I can't make—"

"—two glasses of whiskey with ice," the girl continued. "And for Trev—hey, Trev! What do you want?"

A few paces away, Trev muttered.

"Oh, yeah," said the girl. "A Long Island iced tea." With her lazy, boozy diction, the order came out *lawn-ilan-icy.*

Bailey doubled down on her outward customer friendliness, even as her internal patience evaporated. "I'm sorry, ma'am," she said again, "but I—"

Zane appeared like magic. "Ladies," he said smoothly, positioning himself between his barback and members of the "Wreck Your Privilege" trivia team. "I know a thing or two about making a decent Long Island. Why don't you leave it to me?"

His performance felt increasingly unreal as Bailey watched. The Zane she'd always known had been clumsy and awkward, but apparently a lot changed when you hadn't seen someone for five years. This version of Zane effortlessly charmed his customers, entertaining them while he mixed their drinks with the showy vigor of a stage magician.

Speaking of people who've changed since high school, she thought, and then squashed the notion as quickly as it appeared. Yes, high school Zane had been the kind of guy who couldn't admit to his feelings for his best friend Bailey until a couple of beers at Luke Perez's graduation party had loosened his tongue . . . and Bailey's pants. Yes, talking to Zane two weeks ago had been a catch-up session even more awkward than her theoretical upcoming "please give me a job" chat with Jess. But no, overall, things were fine. Zane and Bailey were friends again, and it wasn't too awkward (which was good). He'd even given her a job to help get her parents off her back (which was even better). And if the only side effect was her own sudden, terminal uncoolness, well, so be it. She probably deserved it.

"You know," Bailey said, "it'd probably help if you taught me how to make drinks. Just for when you or Trina are too busy." The bar lifestyle had wreaked havoc on her sleep schedule and her social life, and the pay truly sucked, but calling herself a bartender was at least kind of cool and would sound less embarrassing when she got around to having friends again.

Zane shook his head. "No dice," he said. "No offense, but you're not ready."

"Not ready?" Bailey was incredulous. "What happened to *smartest barback?*"

"You're also our only barback," Zane said. "And right now that's where I need you. Okay?"

Bailey tried not to scowl. "Okay."

Zane nodded his head toward the blank spot behind him that Trina should've been occupying. "It's gonna be a little busy for a bit," he said. "Trina's stepping out for a smoke."

Ah, yes, Bailey thought. *Wouldn't be an evening at the Nightshade without one of the staff taking a suspiciously long smoke break right at the height of the rush.* All the bartenders, even Zane, usually excused themselves during shifts, leaving Bailey and the remaining bartender to hold down the fort—which, fine, drinking and smoking did kind of go hand in hand. But as far as she could tell, none of the lounge's staff smoked: no tobacco smell, no yellow teeth, no pack-size faded spots on their pockets.

"Zane," she asked slowly, "do you have a light?"

"Huh? No. Why?"

Interesting, Bailey thought. "No reason," she said. "What do you need me to do?"

Zane winced. "I'm sorry to ask—"

Bailey's heart sank. Zane had no poker face. Whatever he was about to say, it wasn't going to be pretty. But unfortunately, "not pretty" was her job.

"What is it?" she said. "Spit it out."

"Funny you should use that phrasing," Zane said. "Someone must've been feeling a little, ah, soft-boiled. Women's bathroom—"

"How bad?"

Zane smiled weakly. "She almost made it."

"Hey! Suit guy!" yelled a Cubs fan. "We're thirsty over here!"

Zane nodded to him. "Sorry," he said. "Really, sorry." And then he was off, grabbing a shaker and glass of ice as he went.

Bailey spent a half hour scrubbing the bathroom to a service-able shine, though she knew full well someone would undo all her work the second she put the mop and bucket away. She probably could've gotten to the bar faster by half-assing the job, but being detail oriented was so entwined in her DNA that she couldn't leave things unfinished, no matter how stupid or gross they were. By the time she rejoined Zane on the line, that goddamn bathroom sparkled.

The trivia game was winding down as Bailey slipped behind the bar, and even though she'd flitted in and out all night, she still mentally answered more questions than most of the teams, faltering only in classic literature. *So I haven't read every book,* Bailey thought. Trivia was just a test of fact retention, and her brain was as absorbent as a sponge.

Also, she thought as she replenished the plastic straws with-out being asked, *I'm a self-starter. Think of what I could do in the right environment.*

With a bang that rattled the glasses on the shelves, Trina re-turned from her smoke break (decidedly *not* smelling of cigarettes, Bailey noted), and more people filtered out. By a half hour from closing, only a few customers remained. Zane sent Trina home early, leaving just him and Bailey to close up.

"That was fun," he said, as if they'd just stepped off the best roller coaster ever.

Bailey looked at him sidelong, estimating whether sufficient distance separated her from his insanity.

"Oh, come on," he said. "You didn't have a fun night in the trenches?" He playfully dropped into a boxer's crouch and swiped at the air.

"They didn't box in the trenches," she said. "They used long-range bombardment weapons. Can you mime a howitzer?"

"As soon as I learn what that is," he said. "You're telling me you don't get anything out of the rush times? Not even a trickle of adrenaline?"

"Zane, adrenaline's something your body makes to stop you from dying horribly." She plunked down a martini glass, which he snatched right up and dried off. In tandem they worked with assembly-line efficiency. "And no," she said, "it's not fun. Jobs aren't supposed to be. That's why they're jobs."

"They're not supposed to be, but that doesn't mean they *can't* be, right?"

Bailey grunted.

"Well, hey," he said. "You wanna come out tonight? Me and some of the other bartenders around town like to stop in at Nero's Griddle—you remember Nero's, right?"

Bailey barely had time to nod.

"And you've gotta meet this buddy of mine who works down in Boystown, and, more important, my girlf—"

At that Bailey snapped to attention, but Zane was frowning at his phone. Whatever he was reading had snuffed out his smile.

"What is it?" she said, more curious about his trailed-off sentence than whatever was on his phone. Only one word started with *girlf,* and it wasn't one she'd ever heard Zane use about himself.

"I have to go." Zane crammed his phone back into his pocket. He looked serious, even grim, as if he were barely aware that Bailey was still there, and then reached for supplies: lime juice, triple sec, a bottle of tequila that he produced from under the counter.

"Hey!" Bailey cried. "We just cleaned those—"

"I need you to close up, Bailey." Zane slapped the lid on his now-full shaker, which he started to shake with a weirdly exact rhythm, rattling the ice cubes against the metal sides in a seven-point beat.

He grabbed a margarita glass, dipped the rim in water, and then jammed it into the salt dish and twisted. He strained the contents of the shaker into the salt-rimmed glass, then dropped in one of the last remaining lime wedges. The lime bobbed a bit against the cubes, and in the low bar light, the glass seemed to be glowing green.

Zane snatched up the drink, took a few deep gulps, and squeezed his eyes against what looked like a brain freeze. "You know the drill," he said. "Set the dishwasher, clean out the trays, and give the counters a good polish. The rest of it we can handle when we open tomorrow night. Just lock up when you're done and get home safe, okay?"

Bailey frowned. "What's going on?"

"Don't worry about it. We'll do breakfast another midnight."

"But—"

Zane was already vaulting over the bar and headed for the door. When he yanked it open, Bailey caught a glimpse of someone standing outside, an angular woman with dreadlocks. The moment the woman saw Zane, she took off running, and the two of them sped off into the night.

The doors swung shut again, leaving Bailey alone in the quiet, empty bar.

Confused, a little pissed off, and realizing it was too late to call Jess to pin down an interview, she slammed the dishwasher shut, rattling every glass and cup inside. She trudged back to the front to polish off the counter, seriously ready to call it a night. Starting at Zane's end, she moved her rag in small circles, systematically eliminating any hint of grime or spillage. Everywhere her towel went, it stayed until the surface beneath was a varnished brown mirror.

As she made her way to Trina's end, something caught her eye: a small hole in the space beneath the counter. As she approached, she realized it wasn't just a hole; it was a gap between panels that looked like it could slide open. She pushed it wide open—it must have been designed to stay flush with the wall when closed—and found a row of six small bottles: four clearish, two pale browny. All the elementary liquors—vodka, tequila, gin, rum (light and dark), and whiskey—and all with the same label—not Jack Daniel's or Seagram's or anything she recognized, but one with no name and a logo of two interlocked *C*s.

She reached for one, popped the cork, and took a sniff: vodka. The good stuff as far as she could tell. Her first instinct was to put it right back; after all, it was Nightshade inventory, and hidden in a secret compartment besides. Instead, she grabbed a spare glass, some ice, and the carton of orange juice in the mini-fridge under the sink. Zane had a strict no-drinking policy while on the job, but this hardly counted. And after tonight she'd fucking earned it.

Not ready yet, she thought as the ice cracked under her measured shot of vodka. What was to be ready for? *Look at me now, Zane. I'm making a drink, and I'm managing.* Having filled the glass with orange juice, she stuck in a straw, gave it a quick stir, and replaced the bottle, shutting the secret compartment and promising herself she'd ask Zane or Trina tomorrow what the hell that was about. Then she turned and admired the fruit of her labors: a freshly made screwdriver.

The drink gleamed cheerfully on the counter, just as Zane's margarita had. Bailey squinted upward. Maybe a bulb was out or one of the neon signs was leaking (could they leak?), making the tainted air cast everything in an extra-glittery glow. Whatever. Drinks were for drinking, not for gawking at, and so that's exactly what Bailey did.

Bailey had had screwdrivers before. Usually they were slapdash concoctions, little more than orange juice and vodka splashed together inside a red Solo cup. But this one was no dorm room special; rather than clash, the vodka and orange juice harmonized. The drink was sweet and tangy and cold, and the liquid burned just the right amount on the way down. Bailey had intended to take only small sips, but when she pulled the glass away from her lips, she was surprised to see she'd already downed half.

Well, she thought as the delicious feeling spread from her stomach to her toes, *I'll have to drink more screwdrivers.*

When she swung out the front door ten minutes later, she felt even warmer inside. Warm, but not tipsy or clumsy. Refreshed. *Curiously* refreshed. Probably the best she'd ever felt postshift. She jammed her key into the door to lock up like the dutiful employee she was. Except somehow she really jammed it because when she turned the key, it stuck. She'd completely bent it.

"Shit."

Bailey stared at her hand, wondering how she'd manage to warp a solid piece of metal when she had trouble opening twist-off beers. Prepared to struggle, she dug in her heels and yanked, but the key came out so easily she stumbled backward. Stunned and a little woozy, she stared at the crooked key in her palm, then daintily took it in her fingertips and slowly, tentatively, bent it upward. The metal yielded to her hands. The key was utterly straight and good as new.

No harm done, Bailey told herself. She dropped her keys into a jacket pocket and started to stroll home, wishing she knew how to whistle so she could complete the picture.

Ravenswood had been a rough little neighborhood on the North Side when her parents moved in, but gentrification set in during the twenty-odd years since. Now it felt like a suburb that had been swallowed, whole and unchewed, by a big city. Damen Avenue, where the Nightshade Lounge sat on the corner of Leland, was as business district-y as the neighborhood got, lined with closed-for-the-night shops, a few parked cars, and the occasional tree. In the distance a late-night Brown Line train trundled along its elevated track. Sunnyside Avenue, where she was headed and where she now lived—again—with her parents, was quiet, with squat houses set behind small well-kept lawns and raised front porches. Everywhere, people hung up the city flag of Chicago—two blue stripes on white, with four red stars in the middle—as if city hall was afraid that people this far north would forget where they were living.

As Bailey turned onto Leland, she felt the hairs prick on the back of her neck. She wasn't weird about walking by herself—this was her home turf after all, and she possessed an above-average amount of street smarts thanks to a mandatory girls-only session during orientation week called "Sisters Self-Defendin' It for Ourselves." But while Damen was the main drag, with streetlights and shop windows and potential witnesses, Leland was more secluded, especially after last call. Despite the warm September night, she shivered and quickened her pace, glancing over her shoulder. *No one's there,* she told herself. *Just a few more blocks.*

But the more she walked, the more certain she was that she was hearing something: a skittering noise down the block, something rustling through the leaves on the ground. Bailey thought it was probably a rat or a raccoon, but then again, she wasn't sure she knew this neighborhood anymore. Maybe there were muggers now. Vaguely recalling her instructor's method for self-defendin' it, Bailey whipped out her keys, brandishing them like tiny daggers between her knuckles.

"I can hear you," she said a little shakily. "I know you're there."

Confidence lets your attacker know you're not an easy target! the instructor had told them. *Remember the acronym S-A-F-E: stay alert, announce, f-something.*

Shit, what was *F*? Focus? Well, she was trying to. Bailey pivoted but saw nothing distinct enough to focus on.

But she could *hear* it.

And then it came out of the darkness. Whatever was following her wasn't just another hungover coed in gym shorts. It didn't even look human: too low to the ground, eyes too yellow. Glowing yellow.

"Good boy," Bailey said, keys held high. "Nice b—"

But it wasn't a dog. It was something awful that she'd never seen before.

Before she could scream, something rammed into her, hard and dense, like a cannonball to the ribs. Her head smacked the pavement, her elbow skinned across asphalt. The not-a-dog was heavy on top of her: a horrible, squirming, four-legged *thing* the size of a German shepherd, with a head like a protruding tumor and limbs covered in naked ropes of salmon-colored muscle.

Bailey scrambled under it, the world spinning from alcohol and adrenaline. The thing was pawing at her with stubby feet and she couldn't keep it off, couldn't wrestle away, couldn't escape.

Oh, God, she thought. *I'm going to die.* Here, on the streets of Ravenswood, less than half a mile from where she'd grown up, less than half a block from where she'd just scrubbed a toilet.

No, Bailey thought. *No. No.* The slimy weight on her chest was too heavy for her to draw breath for a scream, and the world was going fuzzy around her. God, no. This was how it ended, not with a bang but with a minimum-wage job and a heap of student debt. Bailey cringed, and with all her dizzied, nauseated might, she mustered up one stupid, single, and probably final thought:

Fuck. That. Shit.

And she kicked. Hard.

It worked. She pushed the thing away with the soles of her sneakers and, before she had time to think, sprang to her feet, closed her eyes, and threw the hardest punch of her life.

It was ugly and clumsy, and her fist hooked around the thing's side instead of slamming it head-on. But her knuckles met flesh, and in a spray of black blood, its head caved in like a rotted pumpkin.

"Shit!" Bailey yelped, and leapt back. The remains of the animal-thing's body splatted to the concrete. Smoke curled up from the edges of its limbs, as if it were a leaf catching fire, and the night air filled with a thick chemical stench. Bailey coughed, shielding her eyes, and before she even had time to worry about how to scrape the nasty mess off the pavement, the thing's body collapsed with an abrupt squelch.

Bailey jumped back from the puddle, out of the street, and glanced around wildly for something else: A pack? A flock? Another pair of yellow eyes? But she saw nothing. Just a quiet street and a fizzing pool of dead-smelling . . . something.

She clamped her bloodstained hands over her mouth and smothered a scream. The screwdriver roiled inside her. Her arms and legs shook like it was below freezing, and her heart squeezed painfully with every breath.

She wasn't safe. She wasn't safe, and she was going to be sick.

Terrified and trembling, Bailey did what she apparently did best: she fled back home.

The Screwdriver

A drink to lend gravitas to the beginner bartender

1. *Fill a highball glass with ice.*

2. *Pour glass one-third full of vodka.*

3. *Fill remaining two-thirds of glass with orange juice.*

4. *Stir once and serve.*

The screwdriver is one of bartending's most basic and useful cocktails. Though one cannot oversell the importance of a quick mind and a good heart in the life of a bartender, occasions arise when the best tonic is pure brawn. In this department, the screwdriver remains unmatched.

Bartenders favor this cocktail for myriad reasons. Its ingredients are few, cheap, and easily obtainable in all but the most remote places. It can be mixed quickly, in the event that one has been caught flat-footed while also being conveniently within arm's reach of a fully stocked bar. And though the abilities granted by the proper preparation of other libations may require years of steady practice to master, drinkers of the screwdriver have found that hitting things very hard in the face until they die is rather straightforward.

VODKA.

Unfortunately, records of vodka in the pre-Blackout era are sparse; however, its use is known to date back to at least the 1400s, when its existence was first attested in Polish court documents. Vodka (diminutive of the Russian *voda*, "water") was then—anecdotally—the only thing known to convince Slavic men to leave their homes in the dead of winter, let alone to hunt prowling tremens. Traditionally distilled from sugar-rich cereal grains or potatoes, vodka also found a secondary medicinal use as a restorative aqua vitae, its strengthening properties being mistaken for healing ones.

Post-Blackout, vodka found its way to American shores in the saddlebags of the Polish cavalier Casimir Pulaski, who encouraged its bibulation amongst the cavalrymen he trained to fight in the American Revolution. Though he expressly forbade its use in open battle, his horsemen would frequently be dispatched with rations of vodka to patrol the fringes of his encampments and root out lurking tremens.

ORANGE JUICE.

The logistical difficulty of producing mass quantities of orange juice sidelined its use for many years as a bartending curiosity and little else. It wasn't until the mid-twentieth century and the advent of widespread refrigerated trucking systems that bartenders were able to incorporate it regularly into their repertoires. For best results, fresh-squeezed juice is recommended; if none is available, canned orange juice, with its higher vitamin C content, is preferable to standard grocery bottles or cartons. It is unknown who created this particular combination, but the name "screwdriver" was coined by Frederick Leeds, a Florida bartender who claimed that he used the drink to help him remove from his boat hitch a screw that had rusted into place.

CHAPTER TWO

Bailey woke to the sound of snapping jaws, causing her to yelp and nearly fall out of bed. No—*breathe*—she was alone. Gingerly she pushed herself to a sitting position and brought a careful hand to her chest. Her heart was beating like a jackhammer, and the scrapes on her elbow still stung. But she was definitely alone, and alive.

She blinked until her surroundings came into focus. Her childhood bedroom was an untouched shrine to her teenage self. Normally she resented waking up to posters of heartthrobs whose careers had long since lost their pulse or to her stack of For Dear Life CDs. Today she couldn't have been gladder to see them. They were things that made sense. They were *normal*.

But somewhere under her bed, she remembered, were her blood-clotted clothes. And forty feet down the hall from them were her parents, expecting their normal daughter to rise and shine.

With a deep breath, she swung out of bed. She'd replaced her work outfit with the first things she could grab when her limbs had stopped shaking: a baggy T-shirt she'd stolen from her ex (and ex-TA) Dan and the ugliest flannel pajama pants she owned. She slipped her feet into owl-headed slippers and then padded out into the world.

Everything in the hallway was normal: family portraits on the walls and the familiar scents of lemon cleaner, jasmine rice, and fresh flowers from her dad's shop.

Maybe everything *was* normal. Maybe she *had* imagined it.

"Please tell me there's breakf—" Bailey said as she emerged into the kitchen, but then she stopped in horror.

The room was a tableau of tasks interrupted: Water running over the dishes in the sink, the crossword abandoned on the table. And her parents. Who had just broken apart from what appeared to be a very passionate make-out session.

"Gross!" Bailey yelped. "God, my eyes! Gross!"

"Beetle," her dad said, unhanding his wife. He was a squat man—not fat, but just a bit round, like he'd stayed svelte just long enough to get married and then let himself go in spectacular fashion. Or at least so Bailey assumed; the earliest pictures she'd managed to unearth of her parents were from her second birthday party. Now her dad was leaning back against the kitchen counter, failing to look at all casual.

Bailey squeezed her eyes shut and for just a moment forgot about the nightmares of the last few hours. "*Ohmygod,*" she said. "Is this what you two do in the kitchen when I'm sleeping?"

"I'm sorry your father and I love each other," her mom said, squeezing her husband tighter. She was skinny, with long straight hair, and, despite her husband's significantly greater mass, she appeared to have been attempting to envelop him.

"Yeah," said her dad, beaming. "Maybe if we hated each other, we could've given you the neglectful childhood you always wanted." He kissed his wife on the cheek.

"Not our Bailey," her mom said with a smile before her expression hardened a shade. "Did you talk to Jess about the job? When's your interview?"

"Wow," Bailey said. "Did you maybe want to let me have coffee first?"

"I'm only asking," her mother said. "And it's a pretty simple question."

Bailey dumped coffee into a WORLD'S SEXIEST FLORIST mug.

"That's been out for a while," her dad said helpfully. "Hope you don't mind room temperature."

The only way the stone-cold coffee could have been *room temperature* was if the room in question had been a meat locker, but Bailey chugged it like it was a healing elixir.

"What's wrong, Bailey?" Her mom, an accountant, had an irritatingly sharp eye for detail. Bailey turned and struggled to remember what a normal facial expression looked like.

"Nothing," she croaked, clearing her throat. "Um, nothing. Just . . . hungry?"

Her mom looked unconvinced. Her dad looked at the fridge.

"Plenty of leftovers in there, Beetle," he said. "Help yourself."

"Did you even *call* Jess yesterday?"

"*Mom.*" Bailey pulled a container of lasagna out of the fridge, even though her stomach felt like a concrete brick.

Her dad grinned. "Our girl just probably had a rough night."

You have no idea, Bailey thought. "No, no," she said, aiming for chipper but missing. "Just a late one. You know how bars get at closing time." They didn't, of course. Hell, after last night, even Bailey barely understood what happened after hours. Her parents exchanged a look as she forced a smile. "I'm fine, you guys. You don't need to interrogate me."

"We know, Beetle," her dad said.

"It's not an interrogation," said her mom. "We just want to make sure *you're* happy and not"—she paused before deciding on the proper word—"settling."

"I'm not," Bailey said, surprised by her own certainty. "Bartending's just . . . a job."

"That's right," her mom said. "A job, not a career. You didn't go to business school just to sling drinks and up the death toll of Chicago's brain-cell community." She cracked a smile and Bailey's dad chuckled, but Bailey gritted her teeth.

"I *know,* Mom," she said. "And I'm working on it."

"So you *did* talk to Jess."

"Yes," Bailey said, a bit too slowly. "But I'm, ah, waiting for her to call me back."

It wasn't technically a lie.

"Well, don't wait too long," her mother said with a crisp nod. "That position sounds like a dream job for you."

"A dream job with dental benefits," her dad added.

"She'll call me when she calls me." Bailey slammed the microwave door with more force than necessary. "I've kinda got a lot on my mind right now, okay?"

To Bailey's immense relief, the doorbell rang in the front hall. "I'll get it," said her dad. "Dearest Laura?"

"Yes, dearest Sandy?"

"You're still on top of me."

"Oh. So I am."

While her parents disentangled themselves and her dad lumbered out, Bailey stared intently at the lasagna revolving in the microwave and tried to get a grip. She was exhausted, *and* she was supposed to go in for a shift.

No. Ugh, no. She gave her pounding head a little shake. She'd definitely call in sick, and maybe for the next shift, too. Call Jess back, she decided. Figure out if she, Bailey, was crazy or just . . . crazy. And then find a way to let Zane know that maybe working a night job wasn't the best thing right now. That what she really needed was to take a step back and get some—

"Well, good morning, Zane!" her dad practically sang from the front hall.

—distance.

"Hi, Mr. Chen," Zane said. "Can Bailey come out to play?"

"Yes." Bailey jogged down the hallway and pushed her dad out of the way. With a rattle, the front door slammed behind her, leaving her alone with Zane on the porch. She started in on her half-formed lie. "So, Zane, I think I'm sick and—"

"Sick?" Zane said. "Or you're recovering from an attack last night?"

"—shouldn't be working if I'm coming down with—" Bailey froze. "What?"

Zane, who had traded last night's gray suit for a black one, looked over Bailey's mismatched PJ situation like he was trying to figure out the best joke to make.

"What did you say?" Bailey said again, her voice quavering.

He jerked his head toward the street. "Walk with me?"

"How about you come inside and tell me?"

Zane craned his neck past her, toward the inside of the house, and lowered his voice. "This isn't anything your folks need to hear."

Bailey frowned. The silence of the last four years notwithstanding, Zane had been close enough to Bailey's parents to practically be family. The same had been true of Bailey to Zane—well, to his uncle Garrett, anyway, who was basically Zane's father. Secrets weren't really a thing they did.

Unless . . .

She looked Zane in the eyes, the one part of him that seemed unchanged since first grade. Behind his glasses, they were that same cool gray, always on the verge of sparking with excitement about something. Like right now.

"My place," Zane said. "Come on. I think I've got a box of doughnuts or something."

Bailey considered.

"Fine." She opened the door a crack. "I'm going out! Be back, uh, soon!"

They headed down Sunnyside toward Welles Park, where together they had spent a lot of time climbing around the playground or running through the fields, pretending to be dinosaurs or cowboys or robots, depending on what movie had just come out. But they weren't kids anymore, and Bailey didn't feel like playing. Suddenly every rustling leaf was the two-second warning of another skinless hellbeast, about to drag her to the ground and devour her from the inside out.

"You all right?" Zane asked. "You look scared."

"Fine," Bailey said, a little too quickly. "Fine."

"You're safe during the day. Tremens don't like the light—burns those weird muscles of theirs. And there's fewer drunk people for them to feed off of."

"Tremens?" said Bailey with the nonchalance she imagined cool people used to greet everything, even descriptions of skinless not-a-dog demon things.

"The thing you saw—killed, rather." He nodded. "I caught the end of it. You did well."

Bailey's fake coolness evaporated. "You *what?*" She stopped abruptly, and Zane overshot her by two steps. Her voice was shaking. "You saw me there and you didn't *help?*"

Zane put up his hands. "I showed up just in time to see you punch it. And I didn't approach you afterward because you had superstrength and none of the training to use it. You would've been a danger to anyone near you. Even me."

"Superstrength," she said. "I have superstrength."

"Had," he corrected. "But if you want to take a moment to try flexing your guns, be my guest."

Bailey didn't have time for this. Zane was being too cryptic. "Well, did you catch the other one or—"

"There was no other one. Tremens hunt solo. They're too greedy to share. And too stupid to work together. Come on."

Zane led her out of the park and up to Wilson, then hung a left until they reached the blocky sand-colored apartment building where Zane lived—just Zane, alone, like an actual adult. The place was classic Chicago style: three floors, high ceilings, and sunrooms that stuck out toward the sidewalk and made Bailey twitchy with envy. In her price range, natural light was as easy to come by as reliable hot water.

"Zane," she said, because he was humming to himself as he rummaged for his keys, "you promised you'd explain. Stop fucking around."

"I'm not—" He stopped humming and sighed. "Look, this whole thing is best shown, not told. You trust me, right?"

Once upon a time Bailey would've trusted Zane to do anything, whether it was keeping quiet when she'd gotten that C+ or keeping his back turned while she changed out of her bathing suit. But that was before he tried to tell her that skinless demons stalked the streets of Chicago. Nothing, in other words, was what it seemed.

Unfortunately she didn't really have a choice.

"Right," she said, and she followed him up the stairs.

Zane's apartment was a far cry from the jungle of books and papers that had been his childhood bedroom. His records, once scattered across his floor like bizarro vinyl tiling, were now neatly color-coded on a wall shelf. His furniture was *furniture*: not the secondhand puke-stained IKEA crap that had filled Bailey's rathole of a college apartment, but a plump red couch and real armchairs with throw pillows covering the worn spots. His windows even had *curtains,* for God's sake. This was somewhere a grown-up lived.

Along one of the brick walls, Zane had built himself a makeshift bar from plywood paneling. He'd left it unpainted, all the screws still visible, but the raw look somehow only added to its charm. Bailey settled herself on a battered stool that looked as if it, like Zane's suits, had been picked up in a thrift shop. Zane sidled behind the counter and in short order produced two green bottles, a jar of olives, and a martini glass. Then he grabbed a gleaming cocktail shaker and walked over to the fridge.

"Isn't it a little early for a cocktail?" she said.

Zane chuckled. "Okay. You know how when you've had just enough to drink, you feel like you can do pretty much anything?"

You mean, like the time I tried to steal a concrete birdbath from my English professor's front yard? Bailey thought. *Or the time I walked home in a snowstorm wearing only that very much too short minidress with the orange sequins? Or the time I hit on my decidedly gay lab partner in front of his boyfriend?*

But all she said was: "Yeah."

"Well, what if I were to tell you that was literally true?" He plinked crushed ice into the shaker.

Slowly Bailey connected the dots.

"You're telling me I turned into Bailey the—the *whatever* slayer last night because I had a drink?"

"Not just any drink," Zane said, opening a bottle of something that smelled like Christmas. Gin. "What you had was a screwdriver: chilled orange juice and vodka." He poured a shot of the gin, then carefully eyed the height of his hand before dumping it onto the ice. "But using just the right vodka"—he poured only half a shot of the other bottle; it had a scent Bailey didn't recognize—"and served in just the right proportions, in just the right glass . . . well, drink that, and you can kick a tank across a lake."

"You can't be serious."

"Well, maybe not *the* lake, what with its being Great and all."

"You know what I mean."

"Sure," he said. "And yeah, you get to be pretty damn strong."

"Zane," Bailey said slowly, "you're joking. How stupid do you think I am?"

"Not very." Zane stirred the mixture with the vigor of a human blender. "Not at all, actually. You're not scrambling to justify the crazy shit that happened to you last night. We both know you're smarter than that. You're here because you're looking for answers. Because you want to learn, to figure it out. And I want to help you. But like I told you earlier"—he clapped a strainer on the shaker and tipped its contents into the glass—"this is something better shown than told."

The liquid was clear enough that Bailey could see Zane through it without distortions, as if it were somehow even clearer than the glass that held it.

"Final touch." Zane popped open the jar of olives, plucked one out, and let it roll to the bottom of the drink. As it did, something changed. The way light hit the cocktail, sitting there on the counter, made it look like a small, clear lantern.

Zane held it up like it was Excalibur.

"This," he said, "is a perfect martini."

Bailey eyed the liquid. "So you're gonna drink it, then Hulk out in your apartment?"

He chuckled. "Does this look like a screwdriver to you? No. Different cocktails produce different effects."

Bailey leaned forward on the stool, curiosity tingling the back of her neck. "So . . . what does a martini do?"

"You'll see," Zane said. "Or, really, I guess you won't." He took a sip of the drink and then pulled a face. "Oh, right, this thing's almost pure gin. Gross."

"Should've thought that through before you—"

Bailey stopped. Zane was gone.

She jumped off the stool. He hadn't ducked under the bar or hidden behind the couch. The spot where he'd been standing a moment ago was empty. She whipped her head around and then circled the whole living room, but all she could see was Zane's fancy couch and Zane's semi-shabby carpet and Zane's coffee table with Zane's coasters. But no Zane.

She called his name.

Silence.

"This isn't funny," Bailey said. "Where'd you go? Zane," she called again. It wasn't a question this time, but the answer was still silence.

Feeling a tinge of panic, Bailey took a breath. *Reality isn't playing by the rules anymore,* she reminded herself. *Or else you've sunk into an elaborate fugue state. Either way, anything is possible.* Stepping across to the kitchen, she slowly crossed possibilities off her mental checklist: smoke and mirrors, a trapdoor, even something as mundane as him hiding behind the couch (she checked again, for good measure).

The kitchen was empty. So were the bathroom and Zane's bedroom, which, she couldn't help noticing, was still a mess and smelled like him. Back in the living room, Bailey pulled an olive out of the jar and rolled it in her palm like a dull green eyeball.

"Zane," she called one last time as she headed toward the couch, "come on."

Nothing. Of course. Bailey tossed the olive, caught it, and then hurled it at the space behind the bar.

"Ow!"

Bailey jerked back with a squeak. Instead of bouncing off the back wall, the olive thunked off something in the air.

"You've got a killer arm," said a voice. Zane's voice.

"You—you're invisible?" Bailey said, reclaiming her seat.

"You noticed." Though she couldn't see him, she knew he was grinning. "Or didn't notice, as the case may be."

She shook her head. "Nope. I don't believe it. Being drunk does not give you superpowers."

"Bailey," Zane said, "you can see for yourself."

And with that, he faded back into sight.

"Jesus!" Bailey almost fell off the stool.

"Got me good," Zane said, polishing olive juice off his glasses. "Which I guess I deserved."

Bailey gaped.

"So . . . wait, hang on. This is insane. You mean anyone can just up and make a martini like that?" she said. "Some idiot might just trip over the right combination one day and end up invisible? That's crazy dangerous."

"Not without the right stuff," Zane said, patting the bottle of gin. For the first time Bailey noticed the label, a pair of interlocking Cs that formed the rough shape of a goblet. Beneath was a motto in ornate text: "*Bibo ergo sum.*"

"I picked the martini because it's a good way to show you this is the real deal without risking my deposit." He went on. "But there's a lot you can do, depending on the liquor. A tequila slammer lets you make these awesome force fields. Drink a White Russian, and you can walk on air. And if you've ever wanted to know what it's like to breathe underwater, I make a sick Tom Collins."

Bailey's mind was in overdrive. "So you're saying someone can just get hammered and turn into a one-girl army?"

"No amount of cosmos will make me a one-girl anything," Zane said. "And no, actually. So there's this energy inside you, right?"

Bailey wrinkled her nose. "Sounds New Agey."

"Nah," he said. "I mean, we're alive, right? And that's pretty incredible. There's this little bit of magic, and everybody has it. But for magic to do something, it needs a focus and a territory. For us, the focus is a drink. The territory's you. The alcohol frees up that spark, and the other ingredients shape how you can use it. Make sense?"

Bailey nodded slowly.

"Okay. So imbibe too much alcohol, and you'll lose your hold on that spark, just like any other reflex. You might end up having a pretty good night, but it won't be a magical one. Not literally anyway." Zane shrugged. "But yeah, that's pretty much it. Magic."

"Magic," she repeated.

"Magic." He wiggled his fingers.

Bailey stared. "You're telling me the secret to magic, something humankind's obsessed over since, I don't know, *forever*, is . . . booze?"

Zane grinned. "Booze is universal, it brings people together, and a lot of times it results in the creation of more people. What could be more magical than something that does all that?"

Bailey had to admit he had a point. Also, he'd just reappeared before her eyes.

"Okay. Okay, fine," she said. "So you guys drink magic cocktails at work. And then what? You go out and play superhero on your smoke breaks since none of you smoke?"

"We're not playing anything." Zane's grin faded. "Do you know why bars exist?"

"To fulfill a need created by the demands of a willing market?"

His smile returned a little. "Okay, smartest barback. And what's that need?"

Bailey could think of a lot of obvious answers—the need to celebrate, the need to savor fancy cocktails, the need to obliterate reality—but she suspected none of those was what Zane was looking for. She shrugged.

"Human beings are animals," Zane said. "That means we get all the perks: moving around, eating, doing more than just sitting wherever our roots are, or bumping along as single cells. But that also means we have to deal with the baggage. And a big piece of baggage, one that people don't think about too often anymore, is predators."

Bailey blinked. "That thing was trying to eat me?"

"Not eat," he said. "It was trying to *drink* you. That same magic spark I was talking about—your animus? That's their nectar. And pound for pound, you can't find a better source than Homo sapiens. Especially a Homo sapiens who's had a few," he added, miming drinking from a glass.

"Okay." Bailey's slow understanding of this new reality didn't make it any easier to swallow. "So you're saying that bars were invented to herd us all together?"

"Exactly." Zane's eyes glinted with approval. "Pack them all in where it's easy for a qualified bartender to keep an eye on them and defend them if need be. And what better place to defend them—"

"—than somewhere with all the necessary supplies." She finished his thought. It was utterly ridiculous, yet the pieces fit, like she was playing Scrabble and learning that her opponent's twelve-letter play made entirely of *X*s and *J*s was a real word. "Why magic, though? Why not use guns or something?"

"Guns are great for killing stuff that follows the laws of biology. Do skinless demons that nosh on your life force sound like something you can classify with binomial nomenclature?"

"Right," Bailey said. "So all those 'smoke breaks' . . . "

"We're lifeguards," he said, "if lifeguards killed demons. Or shepherds, except the sheep are people and the wolves are night-dwelling hellbeasts. Or—"

"I get it."

"Right. Right." He was bouncing again. The somberness had faded and his usual Zane energy was coming back. "Well, now you know the truth. I'm sorry I kept it from you."

Bailey shook her head. "It's fine. I'm not mad. *Really*," she added in reply to his skeptical glance. "I appreciate you telling me the truth."

"You're welcome." His glasses had squirmed down his nose, and he hastily jammed them back into place, making Bailey smile. It was an awkward motion, the kind she would've expected from the old Zane, not the new one. She was about to change the subject, but she saw he wasn't smiling with her.

"What's wrong?"

He pursed his lips. "It's just . . . you're a civilian who had an encounter, and you weren't immediately triaged by a bartender. When that happens, there are rules to follow."

"Triaged?" She didn't like the sound of that. "Rules?"

"I have to bring you before the Cupbearers Court. You—"

"Whoa," she said, putting up her hands. "I don't want to go to court. I've never even gotten a parking ticket."

"It's not that kind of court, Bailey," he said. "If I don't, I could be disbarred for not following procedure."

"Procedure," she repeated.

"Yeah," he said. "You know my uncle Garrett? He's not just the owner of the Nightshade. He's a Tribune in our bartender government. I can't just—" He chewed his lip. "I wasn't even supposed to tell you all that," he said softly. "But I couldn't lie to my friend."

Bailey's stomach twisted queasily, but she threw Zane a smile that was more confident than she felt. "Sure," she said. "Whatever you say." She eyed her pajamas. "But please tell me I can change first."

The Martini
A libation to lend the drinker a glasslike disposition

1. *Fill a shaker with ice.*

2. *Pour in two ounces of gin and one-half ounce of dry vermouth and stir vigorously.*

3. *Strain mixture into a chilled cocktail glass.*

4. *Garnish with a single green olive and serve.*

The martini's utility for fieldwork is not readily apparent. Bartenders' role as the world's sword and shield is decidedly at odds with a potion that makes its drinker difficult to find.

However, to assess it as such is to sell short the martini's potential. Because tremens rely entirely on sight, a bartender thusly equipped is a most dangerous foe.

GIN.

While America largely spent the Great Hangover acquainting itself with the power of whiskey, across the Atlantic, gin (from the French *genièvre*, "juniper") became the chief spirit of England's fascination. Quality varied historically; much gin was privately produced in residential homes, often flavored with turpentine and other additives unsuitable for spellcraft. During Prohibition, cheap bootlegger products occasionally contaminated sanctioned bartending stockpiles. For this reason, gin-based cocktails have lost some popularity in favor of the more direct power offered by drinks made of vodka, whiskey, or rum.

The botanical nature of gin, flavored with juniper berries and originally used as herbal medicine, renders it both versatile and dangerous. Nonetheless, gin has its supporters. The American bartender Philip Barnes was a particularly tireless advocate of its use; most famously at the fifth National Symposium of Cupbearers Courts in 1913, he was reported to have used a gin-based drink to stretch his arm so that he could flick his rival, Amos C. Stubbs of Skokie, Illinois, on the nose.

DRY VERMOUTH.

A fortified wine that, like the gin paired with it, has gained little traction for fieldwork. Its origins can be traced to ancient China, where healers added herbs to wine to make it medicinal.

The innovation of mixing vermouth with gin is credited to the nineteenth-century bartender Bertram Fish, whose bar was left stocked with only those two ingredients and a jar of olives (see below) as an April Fool's prank played by his brothers. Fish spent the next month invisible, successfully convincing both his brothers that their houses were being haunted by a ghost with a curious affinity for their wives' undergarments.

OLIVE.

Once famously criticized by the French bartending legend Hortense LaRue for "tasting like rotten seawater," the humble olive has nonetheless distinguished itself as the proper garnish for a martini. The light brine flavor of this pickled fruit counteracts the floral perfume of liquors. LaRue spent many years attempting to find a replacement garnish. Her failure was said to be her greatest regret.

CHAPTER THREE

The Nightshade Lounge, as might be expected, looked different during the day. For one thing, it was way too bright. The lights that were on during evening shift made the furniture look dark brown; the sun made them gleam almost purple and showed exactly how chipped and scarred everything was. The walls looked farther away from one another and the ceiling seemed higher. Seeing it like this—clean, empty, smelling more like Pine-Sol than bargoer sweat—Bailey felt a pang of preemptive nostalgia. She was fond of the Nightshade. It really wasn't *that* bad a place to work.

Then she caught sight of the closed bathroom door. Okay, mostly not a bad place.

Three bartenders stood behind the counter. They weren't wearing black robes, but they looked like judges anyway. A large burgundy flag hung behind them, with the cup-shaped logo of the interlocked *C*s stitched in glinting gold thread. On the right was a wiry black woman whose bald scalp gleamed. On the left was a lumpy man whose shape and coloring reminded Bailey of a pile of mashed potatoes. Standing between them was Zane's uncle and the lounge's owner, Garrett Whelan.

Garrett was even smaller than Bailey, and Bailey was pretty small. (Her college friends called her a midget; she preferred *waifish*, or, when she'd had a few beers and was trying to chat up some beef-brained econ major, *fun-sized*.) The way she remembered Garrett, his energy was as outsize as his body was petite. He didn't walk so much as bounce, moving with the noodle-limbed energy of a depression-era cartoon. His slicked-back hair was gray, but only just; in another year or two, it'd be full-on white. His mustache was a shade darker and curled up at the corners like a hairy smile. Growing up, Bailey had seen Garrett forever parked behind the Nightshade's counter—because when Zane was your best friend, playdates involved reading comics by a jukebox while slurping down free Shirley Temples—but now he mostly left the bar to Zane.

Bailey wasn't sure whether the circumstances called for her to be overtly cheerful or just coolly friendly, but she hazarded a wave either way. Garrett gave her a generous nod.

"Miss Chen. A pleasure, as always."

Bailey smiled. Garrett wasn't her uncle, but he'd always been generous with the soda gun. Plus he had let her take a job at the Nightshade with no questions asked. (Well, besides "When can you start?")

"Haven't seen you around here much these days!" she said.

"Idle hands, Ms. Chen." Garrett clucked his tongue and shook his head. "There's little for me to do around here with young Zane at the helm. I'm occupied with establishing enterprises elsewhere."

"Enterprises," Bailey repeated. "Like a new bar?"

"Garrett, if you don't mind." The bald woman interrupted, her voice clear, high, and ever so slightly annoyed. "Let's begin."

Garrett took a shot glass that bore the same double-C symbol and banged it on the counter like a gavel. "I call to order this convention of the Chicago chapter of the Cupbearers Court," he said to his audience of four. "*Bibo ergo sum.*"

"*Bibo ergo sum,*" everyone except Bailey replied.

"The members of the Tribunal will identify themselves for the record," Garrett continued.

"Standing for the South Side, Ida Jane Worth," said the woman.

"Standing for the West Side, Oleg Petrovich Kozlovsky," said the lumpy man with a clipped accent.

"Standing for the North Side, Garrett Duncan Whelan," said Zane's uncle. He turned to Bailey. "And we of course are familiar, but if you would kindly oblige the Court?"

"Oh, right," Bailey said. "Um, Bailey Chen. No middle name."

He nodded. "And keeping the Court record for this session is . . ."

Zane raised his hand, which was holding his phone. "Got it."

A frown creased Garrett's already wrinkled brow. "Zane."

"Come on," Zane said. "I type way faster than I write. You can't even read my handwriting. Plus this way we can keep the records digitally, instead of cramming up another file cabinet down in the—"

"Zane." Garrett's said firmly. "The humble pen and paper have sufficed since the days of the *Annals of Clonmacnoise*. And if it was good enough for Conall Mac Eochagáin to translate the record of intoxicating effects of aqua vitae on an Irish chieftain—"

"It's good enough to do the same way for six hundred damn years," Zane muttered.

"What's that?"

"Nothing," Zane said more loudly, fishing a small notebook out of his pants pocket. "Ready when you are."

"Excellent. Now that my amanuensis has ceased his truculence, we can begin."

Garrett turned to Bailey. "Young Ms. Chen, it has been brought to our attention that you've had an encounter with a specimen of the extraplanar abomination that our vernacular has designated 'tremens.' Would you consider this an accurate summation of the events as they occurred?"

"Um." It took Bailey a second to parse his meaning. "I would." Despite her not quite clean jeans and hastily combed hair, she found herself speaking more properly than usual. Only a night ago she'd been cleaning scuzz out of this place's darkest corners, but as an ad hoc courthouse the bar suddenly felt as if it commanded her respect.

"Zane, were your dexterous fingers equal to the task of transcription?" Garrett said.

"Yeah, yeah," said Zane, flipping to a fresh page. "Got it."

Garrett nodded. "Very well then," he said, pleased. "We'll consider the matter concluded and move on to the administration of your oblivinum."

Concluded? "Actually, um." Bailey raised her hand but then lowered it. She wasn't in class. "What about the part where I killed the . . . it?"

Everyone stared.

"Yeah." Zane looked up and set down his pencil stub. Bailey could see that, indeed, his handwriting was just as terrible as it had been in third grade. "Uncle Garrett, you left out the part where she punched the tremens into demon dregs."

Garrett blinked. "Is this true, Ms. Chen?"

"I . . . yeah," Bailey said. "I killed it, and I'm pretty sure there was another one with it, but it was too scared to come near me. Or something."

"Impossible," Kozlovsky boomed.

"Tremens move independently," Worth said crisply. "The energy they produce is like a magnetic field—powerfully repellent. They simply can't band together, least of all after feeding." She smiled kindly over the edge of the bar, as if Bailey were a kindergartner holding up a finger painting for approval. Bailey blushed.

Okay, so she had been bragging. But even postgraduation, she couldn't squash her innate need for hard work and recognition. "Underpromise and overdeliver": that was her motto. She wanted everyone listening—the Tribunal, Zane's friends, Zane himself—to know exactly how awesome it had been. How awesome *she'd* been.

For the first time since leaving school, she'd managed to succeed at something that wasn't slicing limes or scrubbing barf. *Of course,* she thought, *I finally do something cool out of college, and it's got nothing to do with my major.*

"And just how," Garrett said slowly, "did you manage, as my dear nephew so colorfully put it, to punch it into demon dregs?"

"I made a cocktail," Bailey said. "I thought that's how this whole thing worked."

The room went dead still.

"Impossible," Kozlovsky repeated. He leaned over to Worth and spoke in what he must've thought was a whisper. "There is no way."

"Not impossible." Worth was regarding Bailey with interest. "Just talent."

Talent. The word sent a warm wave of pride down Bailey's spine. Zane wasn't looking up, but he smiled to himself as he scribbled out a few last flourishes.

"I'm afraid this simply cannot be true." Garrett fiddled with an empty shot glass, his composure seeming to dissolve. "She's never— she hasn't—"

"It's totally true." Zane said. "All due respect, Uncle Garrett, but you know I know better than to leave a fully loaded screwdriver just lying around the bar. Bailey mixed that up herself. First try: nailed the proportions. She's a natural."

"Well," Garrett blustered, "well. I suppose that *does* change things, but—"

"Change things?" said Zane. "Dude—I mean, Uncle Garrett— she threw together a perfect screwdriver without even—"

"What proof?" Kozlovsky said. "What proof that she did?"

"Hey . . ."

Bailey's small voice couldn't cut through the rising chatter. If there was one thing she hated, it was being talked over.

"Hey!"

Everyone shut up and stared at her. Again.

"If you need me to prove it, I'll do it again," Bailey said.

She straightened, a distinct, uncomfortable pride burgeoning in her chest. She was no show-off, but when she did a good job, she wanted her A+, dammit. And if she literally and figuratively kicked ass at bartending, she wanted them to know it.

After a pause Garrett spread his hands agreeably. "I merely wished to expedite proceedings, my dear."

"Yeah, sure." Zane rolled his eyes and made a show of shaking out his writing hand, but Garrett continued smoothly.

"You remain a dear and old friend of the Whelan family, and I thought it a kindness, considering the harrowing nature of your experience. But if you wish to . . . reenact your feat of the other night—"

"Make her!" said Kozlovsky. "See what the little one can do!"

"Do you want to try, Bailey?" Worth said.

Bailey thought for only half a second. "Yes. I mean, yes, please. Um, thank you." She nodded at the bar. "I'll need, um, some supplies."

The bartenders quickly assembled the necessary ingredients for the screwdriver. With shaking fingers, Bailey repeated her motions of the night before: enough vodka to set the ice cracking lightly, a glug and a half of orange juice to the rim, a quick stir. Miraculously, the drink began to glow.

"*Prosit!*" Kozlovsky beamed, his eyes wide. "This," he said slowly, "is why I drink vodka."

He offered her a meaty hand, which Bailey shook awkwardly, crushed in his grip.

"Yes, very impressive, young lady," said Worth.

"Impressive indeed," Garrett said briskly. "But we must proceed."

Garrett turned to Worth and offered up the shot glass he'd been using as a gavel, and Worth began dripping ingredients into it: something clear, something brown, a bunch of somethings that smelled sharp, noxious, and herbal by turns.

"Now what?" Bailey whispered to Zane. "I sign some kind of NDA and I'm scot-free?"

Zane's mouth twisted. "Not exactly. An NDA's just a piece of paper. And if the Court sues you for breaking it, all the magic stuff goes into the public record."

"Oh." It seemed sensible enough—Chicago had enough violence without people flinging around fireballs and ice beams or whatever—but something still wasn't sitting right. "So how do you keep people quiet, then?"

"Oblivinum." He said the word like it tasted bad.

"Obli-what?"

Zane nodded to where the Tribunal stood. After a final eye-dropper's worth of something pungent and cinnamony, Worth tapped the side of the little glass, which obediently glowed a bright purple, and slid the completed shot across the counter.

"Ms. Chen, this drink will reduce the last twenty-four hours of your life to a haze," she said. "After you drink it, you will lose consciousness."

"We'll bring you home, though," Zane said. "Don't worry."

"Yes," Worth said. "And once you wake up, that will be that. No worse for the wear other than a terrible hangover."

Bailey's stomach flipped. "Do I have to?" she said at last, her voice irritatingly small. "What if I just promise not to tell?"

"I empathize with your trepidation, Ms. Chen," Garrett said, "but I'm afraid that all civilians must take the oblivinum."

"Civilians?"

"Nonbartenders," said Garrett. "Of course, those initiated don't require modified recollection—"

"Until you retire," Zane said. "Then even Uncle Garrett will have to drink it."

Garrett's mustache twitched. "Ah, retirement. The changing of the guard. Can't be trusted to wield power once I've gone gray and fusty, and the memories of all things demonic and magical must therefore be expunged." He gave a short, cold laugh. "But yes, unless you are a bartender, you must. It would be an honor to have you as my forebear in this particular regard. I invite you to, please, drink."

Bailey froze. Losing memories wasn't exactly untraveled territory. She'd done practically the exact same thing many a night in college; only this time she wouldn't have a pair of puke-splattered shoes or cute but hung-over Dan, the TA, in her bed to corroborate her patchwork recollections. And yet, when she tried to take a step toward the bar, her feet felt glued in place.

"Oblivinum and its magical effects were first attested to by the Dionysian cults of ancient Greece when mixing white wines with salt, vetch flour, sweet clover, and spikenard," Zane said. "Naturally, they didn't leave us an exact recipe. And that particular formulation had the unfortunate side effect of sending drinkers into a murderous frenzy. So today we use a complex but essentially harmless combination of low-alcohol distilled fruit wines to much the same effect." He pushed his glasses up his nose. "*And* it tastes like licorice. Or so I've heard."

If Zane was trying to make her feel better, it was only half working. Bailey smiled but still didn't move.

"She doesn't require a history lesson, Zane," Garrett said. "Just let her drink." He closed his eyes. "'Wine goes in, secrets go out.' Babylonian Talmud."

Bailey gave Zane an "is he for real?" look, but Zane didn't seem to notice.

"Bailey." Zane's shoulders were slumped and his eyes shone with regret. "It was nice to share the truth with you, if only for a couple hours."

"Yeah," she said, "it was."

"Let's still hang out when you're back to, uh, normal."

"Yeah," Bailey said. "Normal."

She'd always liked normal. Normal was everything she'd ever wanted: steady paycheck, cute one-bedroom apartment, cream-colored business cards that she could use for networking or winning free lunches. But here, now, compared to everything she'd just heard and said, *normal* sounded . . . *boring.*

"You impressed the hell out of me. You really could've made—"

"Surely"—Garrett interrupted—"surely, Zane, you're not intimating that your petite friend be inducted into our particular, peculiar way of life?"

"I don't know. Maybe I am." Zane looked at Bailey, eyebrows raised. "What do you say, Bailey? You've got the brains for it." Earnestness radiated from him like heat. "You've got the guts. I mean, you accidentally mixed a perfect screwdriver on your first try. Hell, you'd probably be able to make some major breakthroughs in theoretical magic. You could help us try to mix the—"

"Zane," Garrett barked. "Your friend more than likely has alternative, less dangerous plans for employment." He looked at Bailey expectantly.

"What, that computer stuff?" Zane said.

"It's an app, actually," Bailey said. "For music."

"You see? There." Garrett smiled. "Very . . . exciting."

"Divinyl's a really hot start-up right now," Bailey said to no one in particular. "And I'd get, um, dental benefits and stuff."

Garrett laughed. "Well, that we can't provide, I'm afraid. Frankly, Ms. Chen, this isn't a career for everyone. It's not for the, ah, delicate or faint of heart."

Bailey tightened her jaw. She looked at Zane, but he'd gone tight-lipped and silent under his uncle's gaze.

"Yeah," he said softly. "Cheers, Bailey."

It wasn't a toasting cheers; it was a "see you later" cheers. That was it. Just a good-bye. Not even a scrap of recognition for what she'd done, how goddamn well she'd killed that demon.

Underpromise, overdeliver. No one had expected her to survive a tremens, let alone kill it. And yet here she was, alive and well and about to knock out cold any memories of the one time she'd been really, naturally good at something.

That did not sit well with Bailey Chen. Bailey Chen was not delicate. Or fainthearted.

She picked up the shot glass, immediately put it down, and knew she wouldn't pick it up again.

"Is something the matter, Ms. Chen?" Garrett said.

"Yes." She whirled back to face the bar. "I mean, no. Kind of. I don't think I want to forget this." She was barely able to believe her own mouth. "I guess this is probably unorthodox for these kinds of things, Your, um, Honors"—she gave the figures behind the bar a weird half curtsy—"but I've thought a lot about this in the last thirty seconds, and I've got a question."

Garrett raised an eyebrow. Zane rocked forward on the balls of his feet. Bailey took a deep breath.

Underpromise, overdeliver.

"How much does a novice bartender make a week in this joint?"

Zane grinned.

CHAPTER FOUR

And so, at two that same night—or the next morning, depending—
Bailey set off for Nero's Griddle on Belmont for what Zane had
promised would be "an indoctrination session, but with pancakes."

"You okay?" Zane peered at her as they descended from the
Brown Line El. "You look kind of—"

"I'm fine," Bailey said. But she couldn't help casting a look
down the two-way street and around all corners, looking for something . . . lurking.

"The streets are safe, Bailey," he said. "Especially around these
parts. Bartenders' beats overlap by at least half a block in every
direction."

"I've killed a tremens," she said. "I'm not afraid." Still, she'd
been immensely glad to see him when they met up at the train stop.
He'd changed his tie and looked in better spirits than he had a few
hours earlier.

"I'm not saying you're afraid," he said with a small smile. "I'm
just saying you're safe."

In spite of herself, Bailey shivered. Zane noticed.

"So I'm going to offer you my coat," he said. "And we're gonna
skip the part where you're stubborn and say n—"

"*God*, yes," said Bailey, reaching for it greedily. "Give it here."

Clearly amused, he removed it, leaving him in just his shirt and
vest. "I thought you weren't one for chivalry," he said.

"Chivalry is dumb," she said. "But so's being cold."

Zane chuckled. Without his coat, his clothes traced the contours of his body quite nicely; amazing what could happen when a guy traded up from oversize band T-shirts to things with collars and buttons. "The East Coast made you weak. We'll have to toughen you up."

"I can go back to the cold, no problem," she said. "You don't forget that kind of thing."

"Just like riding a bike."

"I don't think you actually know what riding a bike is like."

"Of course not. I ride the El. What am I, a savage?"

Bailey laughed, and despite the autumn chill, she felt warm.

As they approached Nero's, she saw a couple waiting outside. One was a small, handsome young man with an acid-green mohawk. His eyebrows, lips, and ears were studded with metal, and a bright silver ring dangled from the middle of his nose, fogging with each breath. He wore a heavy leather jacket, and Bailey felt that if he were to take it off, she'd see arms covered in tattoos.

The other was a woman a little older than Bailey. She was angular and dark, with sharp cheeks and sharper eyes. Pretty. She wore her hair in black dreads that fell down the sides of her face. With a jolt, Bailey realized she was the person who'd been standing outside the Nightshade the night before, the one Zane had sprinted to meet. The woman peeled herself off the wall as Bailey and Zane approached. The mohawk guy followed a step behind.

"Glad you could make it, babe," Zane called to them, and it was all Bailey could do not to make a face. *Babe?* "I thought you had to work."

"I work where I'm needed," said the woman with dreadlocks. She almost smiled. "So I'm here now."

Then she drew Zane close and kissed him.

Bailey gaped. She'd believed in alcohol magic, soul-drinking demons, even memory obliteration in a shot glass, but Zane Whelan with a girlfriend? Did not compute. For most of their lives Zane had shown no interest in girls. She'd even wondered briefly if he was gay—not that there was anything wrong with that. But then came the graduation party incident, and he'd definitely shown interest in a girl, and it had been way too much.

But apparently not so much that he couldn't get over her after four years. And make out with this gorgeous-looking stranger woman.

The mohawk guy coughed to grab her attention. "They're better about it than a lot of the couples I've met," he said. Something about the lilt of his voice sounded distinctly out-of-towny.

Bailey thought of her parents that morning and shivered. "Yeah," she said faintly. *No*, she reminded herself, *this is good*. She didn't want her grown-up friendship with grown-up Zane to be tainted with the remnants of his childhood crush. If only they made some kind of cocktail to make you feel better about stupid-bad romantic decisions.

Well, they do, Bailey thought. *It's called "any cocktail ever," if you drink enough.*

The mohawk guy stuck out a hand. "Bucket," he said.

"Haven't got one," she said.

He laughed. "No. That's my name. I work up in Boystown."

"Oh." Bucket was rather a strange name for a person, but then again if anyone were to be named Bucket, it'd be this guy. "Wait. Boystown . . . " Bailey's brain clicked. "Zane mentioned you."

"Only good things, I hope," Bucket said.

"Oh, of course," Bailey said. "I just didn't realize there was a whole midnight breakfast club." Her voice had a little edge, and she shot Zane a sideways glance. Just to remind him that, *ahem*, midnight breakfast used to be their thing. As in, just the two of them.

Zane must've noticed, or he just got tired of kissing, because he broke away from his *girlfriend* and puffed out his chest. "Actually, we call ourselves the Alechemists."

"The Alechemists?" Bailey said with a snort. "Do you guys even use ale?"

"I told you," said the girl. His girlfriend. Her.

"I still think it's a cool name," Zane muttered. "And yup, that's Bucket. He's at Long & Strong in Boystown."

"Not 'Long' like that, eh?" Bucket said quickly. "It's the owner's last name. But I also accidentally saw him naked once, so, yeah. Long like that, too."

"And this is my girlfriend, Mona," Zane said. "She works out on the West Side."

Mona's smile was faint as a fingerprint on glass. "How do you do?"

"Well," Bailey said, "I just narrowly avoided gentle brain damage at a bar. So I guess not that different from a normal evening, right?"

Bailey grinned and cocked her head, but Mona didn't laugh. She didn't even look Bailey in the eye, instead gazing slightly lower at the coat draped over Bailey's shoulders.

Zane gave Bailey a light punch, which annoyed her for some reason. Like he was suddenly her big brother or something.

"Oops." He retracted his hand and held up his buzzing phone. "One second."

"Zane—" Mona started to say, but Zane shook his head.

"It's Garrett. I have to."

"Can't he just send you a textual missive?"

Bailey frowned but apparently Zane didn't notice Mona's weird phrasing. He stepped to the edge of the sidewalk, his finger in his ear.

"So," Bailey said, "how do you begin my training? Do you start with, like, types of drinks or do you just try to figure out a personal combat style or—"

"Whoa, there," said Bucket, who, being closest, was the one she'd chosen to barrage with questions. "First of all, Zane's your boss, not me. Secondly of all, Zane, who is your boss, is—"

Bailey followed Bucket's gaze to Zane, who was speaking animatedly and frowning.

"—busy. But I'm sure he'll have an elaborate training regimen already planned. You know Zane."

"Yeah," Bailey said softly, her excitement fizzling as she watched Zane slowly shrink back and fold his arms. Whatever conversation he was having didn't seem particularly warm and fuzzy.

"It's fine," Bucket said cheerfully. "I mean, probably. Garrett runs a tight ship, you know?"

"Old guard," Mona said from Bucket's right. She lit a cigarette. "They don't like being told no."

Bailey frowned; she was hardly old, but *no* wasn't exactly her favorite word either.

"It's probably because Halloween's coming up." Bucket said.

"And Garrett won't let Zane trick or treat?" Bailey said. Bucket laughed.

Mona didn't follow suit. "All Soul's Night is one of the worst of the year for tremens activity," she said, exhaling smoke. "It's not just a holiday for children."

"Children, or ladies dressed as sexy robots or sexy vampires or sexy Statues of Liberty," Bucket said and then frowned. "Anyway, yeah. Costumed revelers drinking, plus extra creepy-crawlies out and about"—he pronounced it *aboat*—"means that we bartenders have extra monster mashing to do. Gotta plan our—"

"Hey," Zane said, pushing past them toward the front doors. "Sorry. Let's get a table."

"Table?" Bailey said. "Don't we have to train in a, you know, bar?"

"We're not training you today."

"Why not? I thought the best way to hit the ground was running." A little jig of excitement coursed through her. She was doing something, finally.

"Have you ever actually tried hitting the ground running?" said Bucket. "Great way to break your ankle. And down here I don't have access to my sweet-ass health care."

Bailey frowned. "'Down here?'"

Zane sighed. Bucket grinned.

"All right, let's just get it over with," Zane said. "As Bucket loves to remind us, he's—"

"I am a proud son of the great nation of Canada!" Bucket trumpeted, pointing a proud finger in the air. Bailey got the impression this was something he did rather often.

Zane hung his head. Mona looked unimpressed.

"Ensurer of health care!" Bucket continued. "Guardian of the Great White North!"

"Bagger of milk," Zane said, a smile returning at last.

Bucket lost a little of his composure. "Okay, why do Yanks get so caught up on this bagged milk thing?"

"In a weird country full of weird things," said Zane, "it's the weirdest thing."

"*Tch*," said Bucket. "It's no different from bagged water."

Bailey blinked. "There's bagged water?"

"There's nothing the Canadians won't bag," said Zane, "which we can discuss more inside."

Despite its Roman-inspired name, the decor of Nero's Griddle was all American. The seats were squashy booths. The floor was a giant chessboard of vinyl tiles, and neon signs hanging in the windows advertised TAS-TEE DO-NUTS. The only thing that stuck out was the jukebox: instead of playing pleasant, harmonic rock 'n' roll from the mid-twentieth century, it pumped angry gravel-voiced death metal into the air like smog.

"What's the deal?" Bailey said, pointing to the jukebox as she sat down.

"Nero's daughter runs the place now," Zane said. He took a seat next to Mona, leaving Bailey to sit with Bucket.

Bailey grimaced. "And she thinks that music is adding to the ambience?"

Mona looked up, as if she could see clouds of jagged notes floating around her head. "Ironic juxtaposition," she said.

"Zee!" From behind the diner counter, an aproned barista gave the table a wave. He was stockier than Zane, wore chunkier glasses, and sported a black apron folded to reveal a T-shirt emblazoned with a picture of a busty anime girl with bright blue hair.

Bailey froze. The barista's eyes lit up.

"And Tokyo Rose!" he continued. "*Ohayou gozaimasu*, Bailey-chan!"

Then he bowed, because *of course* he did.

"Trent Fierro," she said in a voice frigid enough to freeze the hottest latte. "You know I'm still not Japanese, right?"

"Oh, right," said Trent. "*Gomennasai.*" And he bowed again.

Zane spoke before she could jump behind the counter and tear out Trent's stupid neck beard, hair by hair. "Why don't you showcase your espresso skills and whip us up a round of Americanos?"

Trent's grin could've curdled macchiato foam. "For Zee and friends? On the house. That means you, too, Tokyo Rose."

"What's up with you and Trent?" Bucket said. His mohawk had wilted into a green curtain that covered one side of his face.

Bailey didn't even bother answering him. "You brought me to get coffee from my stalker?" she whispered furiously to Zane.

"He didn't stalk you," Zane said. "He just, uh, followed you everywhere." He frowned. "Okay, point taken."

"Loving the Bailey-Zane banter, guys," said Bucket. "Not that helpful, though."

"Trent's really into anime and manga," Zane said. "But hey, everyone needs a hobby, right?" He grinned at Bailey, who didn't return the smile. Instead, she turned to Bucket.

"Sophomore year Trent decided that *I* was the school's other resident expert in Japanese culture and the only one who, like, understood him. Which—two problems: I'm a born-and-raised American. Also, Chinese."

"Ah," Bucket said, wrinkling his pierced nose. "Ew."

"I've never even been to Tokyo," Bailey muttered. "And roses are the fast food of flowers." Her dad had taught her that lesson early on, and it had stuck.

Zane laughed. "Well, I'll keep that in mind next Valentine's Day."

"I—" Bailey's mind skidded briefly off track as Mona's piercing gaze fell on her. She squirmed under its intensity. "Um, anyway, let's never speak of it again," she said.

"I dunno," Bucket said. "There's some pretty excellent Canadian Japanese glam rock if you're into that kind of thing, eh?"

A waitress appeared. "Hi, Zane," she said before nodding to Bailey. "Who's the new girl?"

It took Bailey a moment to realize that she, not Mona, was the newcomer. Which—*seriously?* She'd been coming to this diner since she was fourteen years old. Then again, this waitress, with her earnestly lined eyes and her not quite even eyebrows, probably was fourteen. Now there was a grim thought. Bailey sat back, contemplating her mortality.

Zane remained cheerfully oblivious to her existential horror. "The new girl's an old friend," he said. "This is Bailey. Bailey, this is Diana. She's our regular waitress. Yours, too, now."

Diana peered at Bailey, looking somehow both bored and inquisitive. Bailey, for her part, felt unsure and intrusive, as if she'd been brought to someone else's church and didn't know when to stand, sit, or kneel. The other Alechemists gave their food orders, and it was only after the silence continued that Bailey realized it was her turn.

"Um, pancakes," she said. "Please."

"All righty." Diana clicked her pen. "Coffees are coming right up."

"Thanks."

Bailey wasn't really jonesing for a caffeine fix, but she also didn't want to be the only person not having any. Diana went on her way, and Bailey leaned in before more chitchat could take over. "So, I take it you two, um, survived tonight."

"No," said Mona, deadpan. Zane and Bucket laughed as Bailey flushed.

"They're both healthy and whole," said Zane. "And pleased to have you join us."

Bailey glanced at Mona, who looked not the least bit pleased. Or the least bit anything else, for that matter.

"So we're giving her the full rundown, eh?" said Bucket with a theatrical crack of his knuckles.

Zane nodded and then reached into his pocket. "First thing's first: my gift to you, from master to apprentice." He held a serious face for a moment but then giggled. "Heh. You have to call me master now."

"No way," Bailey said. "No gods, no masters."

Zane frowned. "Isn't that commie talk? What kind of business school student are you?"

An underemployed one, Bailey thought. She reached out a hand. "Gimme."

From his coat pocket Zane pulled a slim black volume and tossed it to Bailey. The silver letters on the spine read: *The Devil's Water Dictionary.*

Bailey studied it, frowning. "So is this a water dictionary owned by the devil, or . . . "

"Ha. Funny." Zane grinned. "Every language has its own nickname for distillates. Aqua vitae. Eau de vie. *Uisce beatha. Yakovita.* Devil's water is just what we here call it. Old-timey American drinkin' lingo at its finest."

"Mmm." Bailey was only half listening. She'd already opened the book and started flipping its pages.

Zane chuckled. "Yeah, I figured you'd like it. It's got almost every one of our secrets: our recipes, our history, the occasional scrap of abstract magical theory."

"Theory?" Bailey repeated.

"Oh, yeah." Zane's eyes lit up. "I mean, there's some pretty basic underlying magical tenets behind your everyday cocktails. But the really exciting stuff is what *isn't* in there."

"Like what? Picklebacks and Jägerbombs?"

Mona shot Bailey a look. "Like legends," she said.

"Like alchemy," said Bucket.

"Like your wildest dreams," Zane said, with a glint in his eye.

Bailey stared at the little book in her hands.

"So, yeah, that's yours," Zane said. "It's your sword, your shield, and your standard-issue frag grenade. A thousand books can tell you how to mix a drink, but only one will teach you how to do it right. This baby's got the entire history of bartending infused within every page."

She flipped the pages and then slipped the book into her purse. She could read it later. Besides, if the telltale gleam in Zane's eye was any indication, he was about to launch into his version of the entire history of bartending-kind.

"Humans have sensed the connection between alcohol and magic for a long, long time," Zane began. "Dionysic wines that granted women superstrength. Ayurvedic arishtas that cured you with fermented herbs. Sake offered to the Shinto gods for ritual purification."

"Those dogs with the barrels around their necks," Bucket added helpfully.

"Right," Zane said. "But mere fermentation could get us only so far. Once Taddeo Alderotti perfected fractional distillation in the thirteenth century—"

Bucket yawned and flapped his hand in a *blah-blah-blah* motion.

Zane coughed. "Anyway, used to be that whatever you wanted, your friendly neighborhood barman—"

"Or barwoman"—Mona interrupted—"though *they* were usually called witches."

"—could whip you up a drink for it." Zane went on. "And I don't mean party tricks, like we do every night. I'm talking etheric travel, incorruptible flesh, alchemy. Ancient bartenders knew how to mix humble liquors and liqueurs to create a solution for every problem that life could throw at you."

Bailey sensed a "but" lurking on the outskirts of the story.

"But," Zane said, "sometime in the eighteenth century, something happened. Overnight all that knowledge just vanished. None of the old texts survived intact, and from what we've been able to piece together, bartenders started dying by the score."

He paused as Diana appeared with a tray of steaming Americanos.

"Food'll be up in a second," she said. Then she glided along to assist a table of surly kids who looked like they shopped exclusively in a leather-filled dungeon.

"We call that time the Blackout," Zane continued as each of them started performing their various coffee rituals. "Since then we've been trying to regain that knowledge."

"And we've gotten a lot of it back," Mona said. "A lot."

"Yeah," Zane said. "Physical experimentation and investigations into theoretical magic, new and better ways of distilling. We're getting there."

"But?" Bailey said. She could sense he was building up to something.

"But," Zane said with gravitas, "there's one big missing piece that no one's been able to crack in more than three hundred years: the secret of the Long Island Iced Tea."

Bailey laughed into her coffee. When she put down her mug, the three Alechemists were staring at her.

"Oh, God," she said. "You're serious. Sorry."

"Nothing could be more serious."

"It hasn't always gone by that name," Mona said. "Nor has it always had the same formulation. We didn't even have cola for most of the nineteenth century, let alone premade sour mix."

Zane leaned forward, the familiar spark again in his eyes. "Magical energy is unlocked with alcohol, but too much alcohol will dilute it past the point of usefulness. If properly mixed, a Long Island Iced Tea could defy the most basic law of magic: multiple liquors working in perfect harmony to unlock the drinker's deepest potential."

"Basically, the philosopher's stone," Bucket said. "With a lemon twist."

"Hang on," said Bailey. "Deepest potential? Philosopher's stone? As in—"

"There are conflicting reports." Zane interrupted. "Well, not even reports. Legends. But they all say things like increased powers, immortality, forbidden knowledge. And other talents that even the best modern drinks could never unlock."

Bailey nodded slowly. "So that's why you call yourselves the Alechemists," she said. "You're trying to re-create the Long Island iced tea."

"Zane's like Nicolas Flamel," Bucket said, "if Nicolas Flamel dressed like a Beatle, had a girlfriend, and also had a really sexy

Canadian sidekick no one ever wrote about. Oh, and, um, a Bailey."

"But why?" a Bailey asked.

Everyone stared at her.

"Why what?" said Zane.

"Why this quest for enlightenment?" Bailey said.

"Are you kidding?" Zane said. "Why not? You've seen the good we can do with the little magic tricks we know. Hell, you're a trainee and you've already done some good yourself. Think of what we could do with even more." He gripped his coffee cup tightly. "If you ask me, the Court's too content with running things the way they always have been. The world is changing, and the court's resources and liquor stockpiles can't last forever. We have to be ready to adapt. To go further."

Bailey looked at Bucket, who'd added enough milk to turn his coffee the color of a manila folder. "You think so, too?"

Bucket shrugged. "I mean, immortality would also be sweet as hell," he said. "You get to see how everything turns out; you get to do all the things you'd never get around to. Spend a century saving up and then splurge on something incredible."

"Like wh—"

"The entire island of Manhattan," Bucket interrupted. "Rented out for a day. One goal uptown, one goal downtown, and every professional hockey player in Canada or the States trying to get a single puck to either one. Not," he added, sipping his coffee-milk, "that I've given it much thought."

Bailey chuckled and then, out of politeness, turned to the remaining Alechemist. "And what about you, Mona?" she asked, trying to keep her tone as pointedly unpointed as possible.

Mona stared back through half-lidded eyes. "I want to know how it tastes."

And then she calmly turned her attention back to her coffee, as if Bailey's question had been an interruption instead of part of the conversation.

Zane flashed Bailey an apologetic look. *Sorry, that's kind of just how she is.*

"Food's here!" Bucket said, perking up as Diana teetered over with a plate-laden tray.

"Thank God," Zane said. "I'm starving."

"Starving enough to eat those greasy worms you Americans dare to call bacon," Bucket said, taking his plate of waffles from Diana. "You know, in the rest of the world, bacon means *Canadian* bacon. It's like the metric system of pork products."

Diana set down the rest of their food—Zane's scrambled eggs, Bailey's pancakes, and Mona's decidedly non-breakfast bowl of gumbo—but only Zane and Bucket seemed eager to dig in. Even when faced with hot, delicious diner food, Mona was—as in all things apparently—reserved. Even with Zane's arm around her shoulders. When he looked at her she'd smile, but otherwise he might as well have been cuddling a tree.

Bailey cut her pancakes into squares. That was no way to act when a guy like Zane Whelan touched you. She could imagine his arm wrapped around her. Its warmth. Its weight, draped across the nape of her neck. The strength hidden in its wiry muscles. The smell infused in every fiber of his sleeve—

"Whoa, B-Chen," said Bucket around a hunk of waffle. "You okay? You've got this whole Asian glow thing going on." He gestured to his cheeks.

"I'm fine," Bailey said. She sounded more breathless than she'd meant to. "Just my, um, early-onset menopause."

It was a dumb and not even logical joke, but the boys laughed. Mona almost smiled. And then she took Zane's free hand.

Bailey decided to concentrate entirely on her pancakes. Sweet, reliable pancakes. Pancakes were delicious. Pancakes were dependable. She'd been eating pancakes her entire life and never got tired of them. They'd been there forever, like an old friend. Pancakes understood her.

Mona threaded her fingers through Zane's, which made Zane hold her a little closer, which made Mona smile just a little bit more.

Gosh, but these are good pancakes, Bailey thought, chewing furiously. Because if she didn't focus all her mental energy on breakfast, there was a chance she'd think the thought she was really thinking. And that thought was

Ohshitohshitohshit.

"Oh, shit."

Bailey looked up. Zane had his phone out, and Mona and Bucket were staring at him.

"What?" Bailey said, setting down her fork.

"SOS," Zane said. "Vanessa, from the Pig and Castle. She's sobering up but saw one on West Henderson. That's—"

"Three blocks over, three blocks up." Mona, now disentangled from Zane, whipped out a small silver flask from the pocket of her leather jacket, poured an exact 1.5-ounce shot of whiskey into her coffee cup, and followed with a dose of cream.

The cup began to glow.

Mona slung back the coffee, tucked away the flask, and leaped over Zane, bolting out of the booth. Bucket dumped a pile of crumpled bills onto the table. Bailey was still putting on her jacket when Zane hauled her out by the elbow.

"What—"

"This is the fun part." Zane pushed open the door and swept them both into the night. "But we've gotta run."

So Bailey ran. She pounded after Zane down Belmont, threading through pedestrians and dodging mailboxes and trees, finally jumping off the curb to jaywalk (jayrun?) up Southport.

"Do you mind," Bailey yelled ahead to Zane, huffing a little, "explaining . . . what's . . . happening?"

"I set up a bartenders' group message that'll ping anyone who's nearby, in case someone spots something they can't handle when they're out on patrol and—"

Ahead of them, Bucket had skidded to a stop, causing Zane and Bailey to practically crash into him.

"Oh," Bailey said, "shit."

Henderson was a small side street—residential and relatively quiet. Or it would have been usually. Mona was crouched on top of a parked SUV, one hand pressed to her temple and the other pointing to where a fat, glistening bulk of muscles was convulsing in the middle of the road. It was the first tremens Bailey had seen since her night of screwdriver bravery, and it was even more horrifying flailing—like a tumor with legs and teeth. Up on the car Mona twitched her fingers, and the tremens squeaked in pain.

"Irish coffee," Zane said in awe. "She's making it hallucinate."

"Nice," Bucket said, and he elbowed Bailey. "Study up, eh?"

Bailey automatically pulled the book from her jacket pocket but then stopped. Neither Zane nor Bucket was doing anything— they were just watching as Mona made the demon thrash and wail.

"Should I go get . . . backup or . . . something?" Bailey said hesitantly. "How's she going to kill it with just"—she glanced at a page in *The Devil's Water Dictionary*—"illusions?"

But before Zane could answer, Mona had closed her hand into a fist and stood up. With one swift movement she ripped a windshield wiper from the car, raised it high, and jumped into the air. When she landed, she sank the wiper into the tremens.

"Like that," Bucket said, "I guess."

The twitching tremens burst, and its black blood sprayed onto Mona. She straightened, flung her hair out of her eyes, and wiped her face with her arm as casually as if she'd simply broken a sweat.

Bucket threw up his arms and let out a whoop. "Yeah! That's the spirit!" He grinned. "Hey, get it? Like spirits?"

He nudged Bailey, who felt like she was going to puke. The first time she'd seen a tremens, she'd been so shocked that she hadn't let the gruesomeness of killing it sink in. She'd been too pumped with the adrenaline rush of not dying to appreciate how gory it was. But this was literally bloody awful.

"Holy shit," Zane said. "Baby, that was—" He hovered reassuringly around Mona, but she didn't look at all like she needed comforting. In fact she looked right at Bailey.

"Bartending," she said. The calm in her voice, while she stood there flecked with blood, made Bailey's skin crawl. She handed the gory windshield wiper to Bailey, who took it without thinking. "It was bartending."

"She knows," Zane said. "She's ready. Aren't you, Bailey?"

Bailey gripped the wiper, the coating of warm tremens blood oozing between her fingers, and stared at her three fellow bartenders. "I'm ready."

Somehow Bailey managed to keep down her midnight breakfast until she got to Ravenswood.

The Irish Coffee
An elixir to induce illusions

1. *Pour three ounces of fresh hot coffee into a glass mug.*

2. *Add one teaspoon of brown sugar and one and a half ounces of Irish whiskey. Stir gently.*

3. *Float one ounce of fresh cream on top of the drink. Serve without stirring or mixing.*

The emergence of a codified Irish coffee dates to the winter of 1940, when severe snowstorms grounded a commercial flight in County Limerick, Ireland. The local bartender, Padraic Kelly, had been attempting to perfect a coffee-based cocktail, but the recent bad weather that week had left him short on supplies and customers alike. When he found his bar unexpectedly full, he saw a golden opportunity to earn back his losses and engineer an alchemical breakthrough at the same time.

Using the cold weather to his advantage, Kelly was able to sell his entire stock of whiskey and coffee to the stranded passengers. Each customer was served a slightly different ratio, allowing Kelly to observe a wide spectrum of results. He soon realized one of his customers had been imbued with the ability to manifest illusions in the minds of the other patrons. Though he later cited his knowledgeable eye for the supernatural, his barback claimed he'd been tipped off by the fact that after a certain point, all his customers had failed to notice they were sipping from now-empty glasses.

COFFEE.

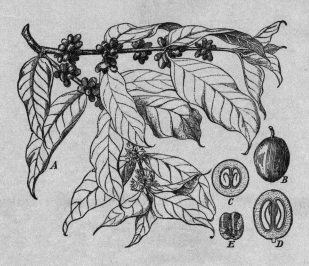

FIG. 23 — *Coffea arabica.*

The discovery of coffee's restorative properties predates that of alcohol, although it is impossible to pin down an exact date; some legendary sources credit the Oromo people, whereas others (such as the *Abd-al-Kadir* manuscript) attribute the beverage's invention to the enterprising Sheikh Omar, who boiled the beans in a last-ditch attempt to survive in the desert. Regardless of origin, the drink's healing abilities have made its practitioners—the *baristi*—natural allies of the bartending community. But where they manipulate coffee in its raw form to *repair* the fibers of the body, the introduction of alcoholic components helps it instead *augment* the body or, in the case of whiskey, the mind. For best results, a pure arabica bean blend is recommended; robusta beans, though hardier and richer in antioxidants, are handicapped by their high pyrazine content, which produces a bitter taste and an aggressive diuretic effect unsuitable for magical potables.

Irish Whiskey.

Thrice distilled, unlike its twice-distilled Scottish counterpart, Irish whiskey is comparatively sweeter and smoother, and it lacks the peaty, smoky flavors in scotch that can destabilize the caffeine compounds. Whiskey (from *uisce beatha*, "water of life") was first attested in the 1400s in the monasteries of Ireland, where one scribe called it "drinkable evidence of a loving and beatific God."

CHAPTER FIVE

"So," Zane said, "ground rules."

"Now there's a name for a coffee shop," said Bailey.

He grinned appreciatively, and Bailey willed herself with all her might not to blush. Which was worse: having a crush on Zane, the best friend she'd already rejected once, or having a crush on Zane, the best friend who was now in love with someone else?

"Very funny," Zane said. "I like a little sassy insubordination in my employees."

Nope. Worst was definitely having a crush on Zane, her *boss*.

"Anyway, rule number one: no moonlighting. While you're an apprentice, this is your one source of income. No second jobs, not even if it's just helping out your dad in the shop for an afternoon."

"Okay, sure." That much she was actually thankful for. She loved her dad, and as a kid she'd loved wandering through the fragrant candy-colored clouds of begonias and alstroemeria. But as soon as she'd reached the age where it was okay for him to put a spray bottle in her hand and set her to work, the fun had evaporated faster than spritzes of plant food. "This is a serious job, and you want my head a hundred percent in the game."

"That's right," he said. "No distractions."

Bailey nodded and tried her best not to be distracted, but the way Zane stayed close, even from across the counter, made it difficult.

They were in the Nightshade Lounge an hour before opening.

Bailey stood behind the bar, poised for action, while Zane sat on a stool, leaning hard on his elbows. She couldn't see, but she knew him well enough to guess that his knees were bouncing anxiously. Zane never had been much for sitting still.

"Next rule," he said. "While you're an apprentice, no magic outside work, and no using it for nonwork purposes. It's the same reason you don't swipe a pair of scissors from an office gig, except it's magic instead of scissors and a bar instead of an office, so in hindsight maybe that wasn't the best comparison."

"Got it. Use my powers only for work-approved good. Anything else?"

He tapped a long finger on his chin. It was a good look for him. "All right," he said. "If I know you, you've already started on your homework."

She rankled at being thought of as predictable. "Not necessarily . . . "

"So if you were to show me your copy of the *Devil's Water Dictionary*, it wouldn't be covered in neon Post-its cross-referencing everything?"

In fact her copy at home was fringed in enough adhesive flags to turn it into an attractive, if offbeat, Christmas wreath.

"I don't have to answer that."

Zane chuckled and then rapped his knuckles twice on the counter. "Well, barkeep, let's say I want a drink with rye, bitters, sugar, and water. I want an—"

"Old fashioned," she said. This she could do. Whether the subject was the Battle of Hastings or the makeup of a magic-inducing cocktail, Bailey had always understood pop quizzes. Read, memorize, regurgitate. Though not literally, in the case of the cocktails. She cast a still-wary glance at the bathroom door.

"Over ice, in an old fashioned glass," she said, finishing the recipe.

"Served with?" Zane raised an eyebrow, almost like he was teasing her, and Bailey briefly forgot what they were talking about.

"Um," she said, "a smile?"

Zane shook his head and mimed a spiral with his finger. Oh, right. The garnish.

"An orange twist," Bailey said, "and nothing else."

"Damn right, nothing else," he said. "So why don't you make me one?"

She turned to the bottles behind her and, ignoring her shaking hands, pulled the appropriate ones, taking the time to check the labels before plunking them on the counter. Glass in place, she built the drink layer by layer—the sugar, the water, the bitters, the Court-issued whiskey—then gave it a stir with a long silver bar spoon and dropped in one of the oversize ice cubes meant specifically for drinks like this. Finally, she shaved a perfect spiral off an orange peel, rubbed it along the rim, and slipped it into the drink.

The peel hit the liquid with a tiny *plink*. Bailey caught her breath and eyed it like the fuse on a bomb, waiting for it to make the drink light up and . . . .

Nothing.

"Dammit." Bailey flicked the glass but it was no good. Bum fuse. The cocktail had been perfectly measured, mixed in the right order, poured into the right glass, and chilled with the right amount of ice. What she created should've been a glassful of magic potion instead of a mere drink.

"Well, I bet it tastes great," Zane said. "Just keep practicing and you'll get the hang of it." He patted her on the shoulder—a friendly pat, Bailey knew, but one that still sent a flutter to her stomach. "Here, why don't you have this?"

He slid her creation over to her. Bailey eyed the six-ounce monument to her failure.

"You said no drinking on the job."

"Yeah, but you're not on the job for another fifteen minutes," Zane said, glancing at his pocket watch (*because of course he has a pocket watch,* she thought). "You might as well enjoy that one."

Bailey looked up from the drink. "But don't I need to make one that, like, works?"

"Baby steps," Zane said. He'd started drifting to the back. "I'm gonna do some quick inventory. Just try to breathe, okay? You're gonna do great."

He left and Bailey exhaled. Of course. Of course tonight wasn't going to be that different from all the nights she'd already endured as a barback. Zane was in charge, and Bailey followed orders. What had she expected to change about that?

Instead of letting herself answer the question, Bailey downed her drink.

It might not have been magical, but it didn't taste half bad: bitter and sweet, with a smack of orange to perk everything up. Good but not perfect, and that's what this business required. Perfection. Precision. People's lives were at stake.

Bailey took another sip and scowled. So much for underpromise, overdeliver.

The door swung open and Trina slipped in, wrapped in a pink coat and matching puffy headphones that clashed fantastically with her red hair. She must not have seen Bailey because no sooner had she shut the door than she struck a rock star pose, one arm in the air, and mouthed along to words that only she could hear.

Bailey stood still and sipping and watched until Trina's eyes flew open.

"Bailey!" She turned almost as red as her hair and tugged her headphones out of her ears. "I—I didn't see you there. Or, um, hear you. Just jamming to Orange Banana's early stuff. As one does." She smiled sheepishly and twiddled her headphone cable.

"Oh," Bailey said, "of course."

"Do you know them?" Trina said, pulling off her coat. "They're Canada's number one J-Rock glam band. I just loaded up their whole discography into my Divinyl."

"Neat," Bailey said quickly. An irritating voice told her she should quiz Trina on her listening habits, how often she used the app, what she thought Divinyl could do for other fans of Canadian Japanese glam rock, but Bailey ignored it. The voice sounded kind of like her mother anyway.

"So, about that cabinet? The other night?" Trina said. "Zane, um, told me I left it unlocked. I'll be more careful in the future." Trina's voice was steady, but her eyes were on the ground.

"You mean the thing that saved my life and bagged me a promotion?" Bailey wasn't much of a hugger, but this seemed like a good occasion to go for it, and she threw her arms around Trina.

"So you really saw a tremens?" Trina said in a muffled voice.

"Yup." Bailey let Trina go and stepped back. "Killed it, actually. All thanks to your lackluster cabinet-locking skills. So, yeah, I don't know how I'll ever find it in me to forgive you."

"Not to worry." Zane emerged from his office, a fresh towel in his hand. "Bailey may not believe in penitence, but I do." He threw the towel to Trina. "We don't have a new barback yet, and tonight Bailey's training. Since it's a job that requires attention to detail, and you can use a refresher—"

"Fine." Trina deflated a little. "But I'll still take first shift patrol?"

"You got it." Zane beamed. "But first, clean up those counters."

"Yeah, yeah," she grumbled, snatching the towel. "I'll get you for this, Whelan."

"Less griping, more wiping," he said, smiling. "I just came up with that one," he added as she squeezed past him. "You like it?"

Trina disappeared into the dishwashing room with a flash of her middle finger.

"That just leaves us in the trench together," he said to Bailey.

"Yup," she said. "Together."

You don't have a crush on Zane, she told herself. *The real Zane wears For Dear Life T-shirts and hasn't figured out how to shave. You just have crush on, I don't know, three-piece suits and a stubble-free upper lip. Get over yourself.*

Maybe that was it. All she had to do was get used to the new Zane, *really* used to him, and things would go back to the way they'd been in high school. There was no way she ever would've gone out with him back then.

Except it wasn't back then. It was now, a bizarro world where Zane had a job and a decent wardrobe and a girlfriend and a doozy of a passion project, and Bailey had nothing to her name but a diploma and a collection of ex-boyfriends' T-shirts. He was a grown-up, and Bailey was just a teenager who'd gotten old.

"Hey." Zane sidled up next to her, and Bailey jumped. "Penny for your thoughts?" He held up a coin from the cash register.

"That's a quarter."

"So keep the change."

She took the quarter and put it back in the drawer. "My thought is that it's almost opening time," she said, "and I want to get working."

"Ah, subservience. Another prized quality in my staff." The light glinted off his glasses. "Let's do this."

On the basis of the high-octane chaos that had accompanied her brief tenure as a barback, Bailey expected her first night as a bartender to put her through the wringer. But the customers stayed orderly, and the drinks stayed simple: scotch neat, draft beer, vodka soda. After spending the past day speed-reading through her shiny new copy of *The Devil's Water Dictionary,* Bailey felt a little let down. She wanted to make martinis, not change for a twenty. Even Trina, reporting back from patrol, said it had been quiet out there.

"Didn't see a single one," she said. "Which is too bad, because

I was jonesing to rock my mojito powers."

Trina glanced around and then waved her hand over an ice cube, which melted to a little puddle. She snapped her fingers, and the puddle instantly froze. She pointed at it, and it instantly re-formed into a perfect cube.

"Wow," Bailey said.

"It's nothing," Trina said, but Bailey could tell she was pleased. "Just the thing I'm awesome at."

The evening slowed down so much that Bailey had to check her phone to make sure time wasn't going backward. But no, it was eleven thirty. Trina was carting in a case of clean glasses from the dishwasher, Zane was handing out credit cards and receipts to their respective owners, and Bailey was bored.

But then, she thought, *better bored than dead. Underpromise, overdeliv—*

"Bailey." Zane clapped her on the shoulder. "Why don't you man the counter solo for a bit?" he said. "Er, woman it. Whatever. I can't get the card machine to take debit, and I'm gonna call the bank. Also, it's changed the display to Spanish for some reason and—"

"Wait. Solo?" she said. "Um, I'm not sure I'm ready—"

"Not ready to do what?" he said. "Babysit Sleepy Ernie over there?"

At a far table a half-conscious man raised his hand in a wave before it flopped down to his side.

"You've got this," he said. "You made it through big, scary college. You can handle an hour or two behind the bar. Trust me, it'll be fun." He coughed. "Also, you kind of have to, um, obey my every command and stuff."

"You just couldn't wait to pull that one, could you?" She tried to glare at him but ended up smiling.

"I deserve a cookie for holding out this long," he said, heading for the office. "Try not to die, okay?"

Bailey listened to his creaky footsteps receding on the old wooden floor. Safe was better than dead, she reminded herself. And if Zane wasn't nearby, she could practice.

In her twenty-two years Bailey had enjoyed a lion's share of beginner's luck. Made valedictorian in high school, got in early decision to her top-choice college, even won a raffle for a week's worth of free pizza in her first week on campus. She didn't get second chances because she didn't need second chances. Practice was for people who weren't good enough to stick the landing the first time. But here she was, stymied. Old fashioned number one had been a failure. A dud. Useless. It was going to take at least a second try. Which was fine. Where old fashioned number one had failed, old fashioned number two would be a glowing concoction that she could proudly point to and say—

"Goddammit." She'd dropped in the orange twist just like the recipe said, but once again she'd made a drink that was pretty, not glowy. She sipped deeply, just to be sure (one never could tell with the lighting in this place). It tasted just as good as the first one, but the flavor wasn't the point. As she'd learned from her speed cramming, each of the five vital liquors had different effects, and whiskey's domain was the mind. But her mind didn't suddenly achieve higher consciousness or flood with new intelligence and power. She didn't even feel the warmth that the screwdriver had produced. This was just booze and ice in a glass.

She dumped out the drink, rinsed the glass, and set it down on the bar. "Third time's the charm," she muttered as she started to drizzle water over a sugar cube to dissolve it. Once again she went through each step precisely as written in *The Devil's Water Dictionary*. And once again she found herself with a very pretty glass of whiskey, citrus, and frozen water. It tasted nice, and she couldn't think of a more devastating compliment for her work. *Nice* was just another way of saying *useless*.

Number four was normal. So was number five. Six looked for a moment as if she'd finally cracked the spell, but then she realized the glowing effect was just light glinting off a piece of ice that had chipped when she dropped it in the glass.

What did you think, Bailey? she mused. *That you'd nail mixing old fashioneds, then stir up the perfect Long Island iced tea while Zane was taking out the trash?*

She glanced at the clock while taking her now customary sip of number six. It was well past midnight. The bar closed at two, but chances were likely they might cut out early, depending on whether they could get Sleepy Ernie out the door in a timely fashion. She'd be able to put her disastrous attempts at magic behind her for the night, get some rest, and start all over again in the morning.

Yeah, Bailey admitted. *And then Zane and I would make out or something.*

The neon CHICAGO CUBS sign buzzed at her from across the room, illuminating one letter at a time. C-H-I-C-A-G-O. C-H-I-C-A-G-O. As she cleaned her glass yet again, her brain, slightly tickled by whiskey, had an amusing, irrelevant thought: *Chicago has seven letters in it. And I've just made six old fashioneds.*

Bailey, another part of her brain thought, *those two facts have no correl—*

Shut up, self.

Before she'd been precise, but now she was slapping the drink together like an essay an hour before it was due. By the time the ice splashed into the whiskey, she wasn't even thinking about getting the recipe right anymore. She was just looking forward to drinking. She was screwing up, but as long as Zane couldn't see those screw-ups, they were less real.

She took the final ingredient—the orange peel, cut as jagged as a cartoon lightning bolt—and nestled it between the ice cube and the glass. The peel pushed the cube, which struck the glass with a soft *clink*.

And just like that, the old fashioned glowed a soft red-brown.

Her jaw dropped. "You've gotta be shitting me."

But no, this one appeared to be on the level, *appeared* being the key word, because Bailey was suddenly having trouble finding her footing. Of the six failed experiments, five had been sampled within the past hour, and even if she'd spaced them out with some water (which she had intended to do but then forgot), the fact was she was a tiny Asian girl with a minimal amount of body fat. Her resistance to alcohol was about as effective as cardboard armor.

Well, she reasoned, she wasn't drunk. Hell, she wasn't even tipsy. She was just feeling a little more loosely wound than usual. Zane had said that too much alcohol in the system would dampen magical effects, but she was already metabolizing the old drinks. She'd drink this one now, then surprise him with her sudden aptitude. *I can't believe it,* he would say, after a sip. *You're amazing.* Then he'd push the glass out of the way, whip off his glasses, and sweep her up against the bar—

"Bailey?"

The door shut with a *click* as Zane headed into the bar.

"Eep," Bailey said. "I mean, um, yes. Present. How was the bank?"

"*No bueno,*" Zane said. "I'll try calling in the morning. Hey, what's that?"

She'd tried to scoot the evidence of her unsanctioned cocktail experimentation behind the forest of beer taps, but apparently he'd already noticed.

"Oh, you finally cracked it?" Zane rushed to her side and stooped to inspect the drink. When he saw the glow in full effect, he nodded slowly in approval. "*Niiiiice.*"

He picked up the glass, held it to the light, and took a big gulp, complete with a little *ahhh* at the end. As Bailey looked on in quiet despair, he took another sip, then another, and then beamed at her. "Tastes great." He raised the glass in a toast. And then he let go of the glass and dropped his hand.

Bailey lunged for it, but the drink didn't drop. The glass was suspended midair, without even a wobble.

"Whoa." Bailey's despair turned to wonder. "What?"

"Come on, Bailey, you studied. You know what."

She closed her eyes and thought of the old fashioned's *Dictionary* entry. "'A potable to lend physicality to the will of the mind,'" she whispered.

"It's kind of a long way to say telekinesis," Zane said. "But then again, telekinesis is kind of a long way to say telekinesis."

She suddenly remembered they weren't alone. "Wait. There are witnesses—"

He waved her off. "Ernie," he called, "you don't see anything, right?"

Ernie, now spread across three chairs, rolled over and scratched himself.

"See?" said Zane. "We're fine. Now grab your coat. Or hell"— he gestured toward the back room—"I'll get it for you."

Her coat reeled into the room as if on an invisible fishing line, depositing itself neatly over her shoulders.

"Trina!" Zane called.

"Scrubbing," Trina said from the bathroom.

"You said it was a pretty quiet night, right?"

Trina poked out her head. "Yup."

"Congratulations," Zane said. "You're promoted back to bartender!"

"Thank God," Trina said.

"You're welcome." Zane gave her a thumbs-up. "Can you handle the post-closing-time patrol? I'll do one final sweep now, but—"

"*We* will," Bailey said firmly. "I'm ready."

The old fashioned glass floated away from Zane's lips, and he frowned.

"What?"

"Put me in, boss," she said with more bravado than she felt. "Let me take my first smoke break."

The Old Fashioned
A potable to lend physicality to the will of the mind

1. *Drop a sugar cube into an old fashioned glass and let dissolve in a little water.*

2. *Add four dashes of Angostura bitters.*

3. *Pour in two ounces of rye.*

4. *Stir well with a bar spoon.*

5. *Add an orange twist and one very large piece of ice. Serve.*

The old fashioned is the premier whiskey cocktail. Its telekinetic properties make it incomparably versatile; a creative bartender can make use of its effects in offensive or defensive contexts and even beyond patrols, particularly in situations concerning high shelves.

The modern old fashioned was codified at the first National Symposium of the Cupbearers Court in 1852. Although this status has previously invited a cultural pushback, young generations of bartenders quickly found principles to be far less practical than moving things with one's mind.

RYE WHISKEY.

American whiskey, which is made with a mash of at least 51 percent rye, was rediscovered in 1790, toward the beginning of the Great Hangover. Credit goes to Joshua Cromley, a Virginia distiller who, while drunkenly attempting to drive off a census taker, accidentally made his own horse explode.

Rye whiskey soon became the preeminent weapon of the fledgling country's defense against the unnatural. Subsequent rediscoveries gradually taught modern man how to temper the liquor's raw power and, in doing so, saved the lives of countless horses.

––––––––––

ANGOSTURA BITTERS.

Special preparations of botanically infused alcohol and water, bitters act as a lens to "refract" energy. Angostura bitters in particular were rediscovered in the 1820s by Johann Gottlieb Benjamin Siegert, a German doctor in Venezuela. Working from fragments of an old text, the doctor thought he had merely invented a new kind of medicine that tasted extremely good. It wasn't until ten years later, when the concoction was displayed in England, that a bartender properly attributed Siegert's discovery to the mixological arts.

––––––––––

ORANGE TWIST.

Fruit garnishes are inherently the freshest part of a finished cocktail. The matter of the old fashioned's garnish was settled at the first National Symposium in 1852. The legendary Hortense LaRue, then merely an amateur bartender who had bluffed her way inside, bested all comers by presenting an old fashioned garnished with an orange peel. When the proponents of the lemon and the cherry protested that she must have cheated, and that as a woman she had no place at the court anyway, LaRue responded by mentally seizing the two objectors and juggling them for nearly a quarter of an hour.

CHAPTER SIX

The mean streets of Ravenswood were hardly mean, but Bailey had never felt more wary of them. Damen was quiet, the lights of the Hibachi restaurant and the insurance company and even the place that sold Italian beef sandwiches all dark for the night. Cars passed, but not many, and when they got to the broad intersection of Lawrence, they crossed under the glare of a red light.

"Are you sure you want to do this, Bailey?" Zane walked purposefully, but he still seemed a little nervous when his gaze fell on her.

"I'm sure," Bailey said, imitating his patrol-swagger walk as best she could. "Why? Are you scared?"

Zane hesitated for only a half second. "No."

"Okay." Bailey nodded crisply. "So teach me."

Zane blew out a breath. "Right. So a bar's typical patrol radius is six blocks in every direction. It's big, but the zones overlap. Better to have too many bartenders prowling than not enough. So Nightshade territory goes—"

"North to Foster, west to Clark, south to Montrose, and west to . . . Western."

Zane blinked. "Right. I forgot you have the home turf advantage here."

Bailey shrugged. "I can find my way around just fine. What I *don't* know how to do is hunt."

"It's not hunting," he said. "But okay. Uh, look for busted lights." He pointed to a neon nail salon sign that flickered between dead and near dead. "Tremens love shadows."

"I thought tremens were sensitive only to sunlight," she said.

"They are," said Zane. "But they also take advantage of darkness. They know how bad our night vision is. Dark helps them get behind you."

"So why don't we all just carry flashlights?" Bailey said, hugging herself. Not that she was scared, because she wasn't. Home turf advantage, after all. "We could send them out with census forms or something."

"The Court tries to keep on top of writing to the city to get more lights installed," Zane said. "All under the guise of concerned citizens, of course. But—"

"But at the end of the day," Bailey finished for him, "we're still in Chicago."

"You're goddamn right we are. Inefficient, recalcitrant, and glorious."

Zane kept walking, but Bailey had stopped on the corner of Ainslie, then she took a sharp right down the side street.

"Uh, Bailey? Where are you going?"

"If tremens hate light, we're not doing any good staying out here," she said, gesturing toward the streetlight bathing them in an unflattering industrial orange. "So let's go where it's dark."

Zane hesitated but followed.

"What else should I be looking for?" Now Bailey was the one walking with purpose. Maybe it was the alcohol pumping in her veins, but she was itching to fight something. Learn the ropes. Kick ass. Although she wished she had something to take notes with.

"Well," Zane said, "hedges with loose branches. Alleyways with debris they could use as shelters. Ectoplasm."

"Really?"

"No," Zane admitted. "Here, look."

They cut up Winchester, checking under cars and in the alcoves of apartment buildings. But nothing was there. They didn't see a single living thing—if tremens counted as living—until they hit Winona, where a cab casually rolled through the stop sign.

"Those are important, too." Zane nodded at the taillights.

"The cabbies?"

"The people," he said. "Don't get so focused on hunting prey that you leave innocents unprotected."

The wind whistled down Winona, and again Bailey shivered. "Is it always this boring?" she said. *Thank you, whiskey.* "I mean, sorry."

But Zane seemed unmiffed. "No, I get you. The grind can get dull: making a drink, getting magic powers, using them to punch tremens until they explode . . . "

"But that's not dull at all."

"No," Zane said with a grin. "It totally isn't. But it's still a routine."

"Ugh." She puffed out a pouty sigh. "I guess I thought this whole patrol business would be more, I don't know, superhero-y."

"You mean, you come out dressed for battle, something snarly and homicidal obliges you and shows up, and you summarily kick its ass?" He laughed. "Not so much. In this case, it's really to your benefit to go looking for trouble."

"Right."

"Mona swears she can sense them. A disturbance in the Force or something. She gets so determined about that stuff. I love it."

Bailey stiffened at the *L* word.

"Anyway, I told her—"

"*So,*" Bailey said before she could stop herself, "you and Mona, huh?" She gave a cursory glance under the bed of a white pickup.

"Yup." Zane gave a little sigh as he peered down a narrow alley. "Me and she, she and me. Jury's still out on what our celebrity-couple name will be. I'm thinking Zona because otherwise it'd be Mane and—"

"How'd that, um, happen?" Bailey interrupted. *Just be chill. Casual. Absorb all this information and make it as normal as possible.* "She doesn't seem like your type."

"I have a type?"

"Well, sure." *Five foot nothing, Chinese American, a little drunk on experimental old fashioneds . . .* When Zane frowned a little, she backpedaled. "Okay, not really. But I see the way you are now . . ."

"Hmm." It wasn't agreement or disagreement, just acknowledgment. "She kind of came out of nowhere, honestly. I was out in Humboldt Park one night, catching up with a guy I know who's stationed out there—at a bar, I mean. Cantina La Estrella? Makes a killer margarita." Bailey shook her head, and Zane kept on. "Anyway, she was working a shift with Hector. He went out to patrol, and things got busy back on the home front."

Bailey blushed but then realized that he really meant *at the bar.* "So you jumped behind the bar and helped out?"

Zane did a palms-up. "I tried. You should've seen her. She didn't need my help. Shaking, stirring, salting rims. She's really good, Bailey. Almost superhuman."

Bailey gave a noncommittal *mmm.*

"And then, when I saw her fight for the first time . . ." He heaved a contented, faintly visible sigh into the chilly air. "I gotta tell you, Bailey, she might be the best bartender I've ever seen. Better than Garrett in his prime."

"Better than you?"

"It's like we're doing two different jobs. She's bartending, and I'm mixing drinks and occasionally killing stuff. She's helped me grow so much as a bartender. And when I told her about my whole pipe dream for the Long Island . . . she didn't think I was crazy. She was right on board. Can you believe it?"

Bailey couldn't believe it, actually. At that moment she'd rather believe in tremens.

"So is it normally this quiet?" She put herself on high alert, scanning the shadowy patches.

"Not really," he said, a bit more businesslike. "But quiet's a good thing. When it comes to tremens, you can always hear them com—"

And just then one darted out in front of them.

"Shit!"

Bailey saw it first. It surged into the dim light from under a Dumpster, its muscles visible with every motion. The slit mouth between its eyes was already open wide, creepy and hungry.

"*Zane!*" Bailey grabbed his forearm but worried she was too late. She remembered how impossibly fast her tremens had moved.

But she'd never seen Zane in action.

He thrust out a hand and jerked the tremens aside with nothing but his psychic powers. It hurtled into the base of a streetlight with a dull *clank,* then spilled to the sidewalk.

"Zane," Bailey said. "Zane!"

The tremens stumbled to its feet, but Zane was ready. A manhole cover ripped out of its resting place and plowed into the tremens's ankles, sweeping it off its feet. And there Zane stood, guiding the metal disk with a determined face and a steady hand.

The manhole cover had overshot, but it braked in the air and then fired back at the tremens. Bailey stared, awed by Zane's control.

The creature wobbled to its feet (or whatever its appendages were), a sitting duck for the careening piece of city property. But at the last possible instant it surged to life and hopped onto the manhole cover as if it was a skateboard.

"Shit," Zane said. With brows tensed, he twisted his wrist and the disk flip-flopped. But rather than slip off, the creature used the momentum to springboard itself and speed into the dark.

"Is it gone?" Bailey said, but she already knew the answer.

"No." Zane's voice was as tight as her grip on his arm. "They don't usually give up when their prey fights back. They—*there!*"

The tremens had reemerged. It circled them, approaching closer with each pass.

Bailey felt like she was going to barf. The tremens moved too quickly, too fluidly, and her *RUN* instinct was blazing in her brain. Zane's apparently wasn't. He was pivoting around her to keep the tremens in his line of sight.

"Just a little closer," he muttered. "A little closer, you skinless bastard . . . "

Don't scream, Bailey told herself. *Don'tscreamdon'tscreamdon'tscream.* The tremens wasn't even touching her, but she could already feel that hopeless, helpless ache churning in the pit of her stomach.

"Gotcha." Zane pointed a finger at the asphalt and levered his thumb as if working the hammer of a gun. A loose bit of pavement pulled away just as the tremens stepped on the spot: a small shift, but enough to send the tremens sprawling and slamming onto the pavement. As it fell, the manhole cover whirled out of the shadows, spinning vertically like a saw blade. Bailey watched as the cover dropped—

—and cut deep into the pavement. The tremens scuttled off.

"Son of a bitch," Zane said, as if narrowly missing a kill shot on a homicidal demon was no more annoying than getting stuck at a red light. The tremens darted back to the Dumpster, but Bailey caught a glimpse of its face: one yellow eye was shut, the flesh around it covered in burns.

She barely had time to look before she realized something was wrong. Maybe she didn't have Mona's sixth sense, but she could *see,* and something was coming. Right for Zane. Only one thought filled her mind: *scream.*

"On your back!"

Zane was too slow. The tremens knocked him to the ground,

wrenching his arm from her grip and sending Bailey to the ground with a *thump*. She scrambled off her stomach, grabbing for her friend, but the tremens had already wrapped its tendrils around him. When it breathed him in, Zane convulsed in pain. His mouth opened to scream, but no sound escaped. Above them the streetlights flickered.

Do something, Bailey thought. But what? She had zero powers and even less combat experience. There was nothing she *could* do.

But if she didn't do something, Zane would die.

Fuck it, Bailey thought.

She sprang to her feet and sprinted away from Zane and the tremens as fast as her legs would carry her. The wind whipped her hair into her eyes. *Hair tie next time,* she thought. *If there is a next time.* When she reached the end of the block, she banked hard and, lungs burning, turned around.

Somewhere she'd read that the average manhole cover weighed approximately 110 pounds, or slightly less than the average Bailey. So she knew she wasn't strong enough to throw a one at the tremens. She was, however, strong enough to throw something else: a Bailey.

The tremens heard her coming; it must have because it turned and trained its terrible yellow eyes right on her. But Bailey kept charging. She plowed into it with a shoulder check that would've gotten her benched from her middle school lacrosse team for aggressive behavior. The tremens fell, and Bailey, her momentum spent, sprawled across Zane's prone form.

"Now! Kill it now!"

Even as she said it, the manhole cover came crashing down like an iron comet. It hit the tremens in the middle of its back, folding it grotesquely in half. Smoke was already rising, its acrid smell snaking down Bailey's throat and reactivating her vomit instincts.

Don't scream don't puke don't—

The cover clanged to its side. The tremens was gone, a puddle of black ooze the only proof it'd been there at all.

"Holy shit."

Bailey coughed, blinked, and felt for broken ribs. She was alive, and Zane was alive—very alive, actually, directly underneath her, still breathing and very warm.

"Yeah." Zane blinked but didn't get up. Didn't move her either. "I guess I learned what a howitzer—"

Bailey leaned down and kissed him.

It wasn't sweet, or planned, or even particularly neat. Bailey was thrumming with rye whiskey and adrenaline, and kissing Zane only added to the excitement. But she was kissing him, and he was kissing *her*, his arms pulling her closer, lips parting, familiar even as the kiss was infused with something new. Something they hadn't had four years ago. This was deeper. Better.

Or it was until Zane yanked away.

"What the hell was that?!" His voice was a full octave higher than usual.

Bailey's chain of thoughts exploded in slow motion. She'd kissed Zane. That was bad. She'd kissed Zane. He had a girlfriend. She'd kissed Zane. She liked it, but that didn't matter, because *that was bad.*

And she was still half on top of him.

"I—jeez. Shit. Sorry. *So* sorry." She scrambled to her feet. "I didn't—"

"I have a girlfriend!"

"I know, I know," Bailey said, squeezing her eyes shut and raising her hands in surrender. She flushed so red that her head felt like it was glowing. "I did a dumb thing that was also wrong and bad, and I know, okay? I know and I'm sorry and I know that I'm sorry." She was babbling, but that had nothing on the never-ending *OH MY GOD WHY DID YOU DO THAT?* loop streaming through her head.

Zane muttered something, and Bailey remembered she should

be listening. "What was that?" she said.

He'd been on the verge of furious a moment ago, but her sudden attention made him dial it back a few degrees. "It's nothing," he said, each syllable overenunciated in a distinctive *back off* way.

"What?" she said again, more softly.

"I said, Where was that four years ago?!"

No. Absolutely not. Anger, not embarrassment, flared in Bailey's chest. "I knew it," she said.

"Knew what?" He was on his feet now, towering over her. His tie was askew and his hair was sticking up, a shadow of the messy Zane she used to know.

"You're still stuck in high school," she said. "You've changed all these things about your outside but—"

"*I'm* stuck in high school?" Zane laughed. He pressed a hand to his mouth, shrugged, and then laughed again. "Jesus. Look around you, Bailey. You didn't hit some big red pause button when you left. I know this'll shock you since your big *college-educated* brain has trouble with subjects other than *you*, but everyone's life went on when you weren't here. Mine included."

Bailey winced. But before she could gather her wits, he spoke again.

"This was a mistake," he said. "If you can't keep your cool when things get intense—"

"I saved your life," she said. "You didn't even see the second one—"

"What second one?" he said. "Weren't you listening? They *always hunt solo.*"

"You scratched up the first one's face and put out its eye. But the second one was fine," said Bailey. "There were two of them."

Zane shook his head. "Impossible. The energy fields—" He folded his arms over his chest, bunching up his suit coat. "You know what? Never mind. I never should've let you push me into taking you out tonight. But typical bossy Bailey—"

"*I* did just fine out here. The problem is you." *Yes,* her brain said. *That's the ticket.* Deflect, deflect, deflect. "You didn't *teach* me how to make my own old fashioned; you just waited until I cracked it by myself. Then you swooped in and drank it and didn't let me make another one for myself—"

"You shouldn't have even engaged!" Zane yelled. "This was just a stupid, I don't know, ride-along!"

"If I hadn't *engaged*, you'd be dead," Bailey said. Now it was her turn to be coldly quiet. "I may not know magic, Zane, but I know teachers, and I know bad ones. Because I've spent most of my life in school, and I've never been called a bad student."

Fallen leaves twitched even though no wind blew. She'd gone too far. She sneaked a look at Zane, who was staring hard at the ground, clenching and unclenching his fist. Making the leaves dance. Avoiding her more than anything.

At last he opened his fist, and the leaves fell still.

"Fine," he said quietly. "I'll get you a new teacher."

Her heart sank into the pit of her stomach.

"So here are my last orders to you as my apprentice," Zane said, putting a nasty emphasis on the last word. "Will you listen to me, for once, and follow them?"

Bailey nodded dumbly.

"Go home," he said. "Get some rest. If you still want to do this, you'll be assigned to a new master in a few days." He looked at her now, right in the eye. "And then you'll be done with me."

CHAPTER SEVEN

The subsection of Chicago's Lakeview neighborhood known as Boystown cheerfully announced itself to pedestrians with impeccably clean sidewalks and fluttering rainbow flags. The shops were quaint, inasmuch as anything could be quaint within the bounds of a sprawling world-class metropolis. But what the apartments and condos of Boystown lacked in that old Chicago gothicness, they more than made up in the kind of sleekness that would've made Frank Lloyd Wright's mouth water.

And then, like a fly in the proverbial soup, there was Long & Strong.

If it was possible to win bars in contests, Long & Strong looked like a consolation prize. The outside boasted zero windows, a chipped brick facade, and an awning covered in fading stripes. Bailey double-checked the address Bucket had texted her, winced, and then triple-checked. North Halsted. This was it.

Well, better this than bumming around at home, Bailey told herself and went inside.

Despite the long hours and thankless scrubbing at the Nightshade, Bailey had liked waking up knowing she had somewhere to be, even if it was just a neighborhood bar with sticky counters. It gave her something to structure her life around. A week of waking up without that structure made her days feel lumpy and misshapen; it took a heroic amount of self-motivation for Bailey to even reach for her phone to order a pizza. She thought she'd be fine interacting with no one aside from her parents and Netflix, but it turned out that too much sitting around drove her nuts. So on the last Friday in September, the fourth day of her between-bars limbo, still in her PJs and still with no word from Zane or any of the Alechemists, she'd screwed up the courage to call Jess for her billionth follow-up on the Divinyl gig. But all she got was voicemail.

"So anyway," Bailey had said, one minute and thirty-eight excruciating seconds into her message, "I'm totally keeping busy, but not too busy to pick up if you call. So, you know . . . call me. Please. Sorry. Um. Bye." Her thumb tapped the end call button.

A moment later she swore loudly, redialed, and left a much shorter follow-up message: "Oh, and I forgot to mention, this is Bailey Chen. Thanks, bye."

Ugh, ugh. Bailey had fallen onto the couch face-first in total despair, wedged her phone under a cushion so she couldn't hear it vibrate, and cranked up the TV just to be sure. By the time her dad got home that evening she still hadn't moved, except to hit "next episode" with the remote.

"No work tonight, Beetle?" he'd said, as if he couldn't tell from her uncombed ponytail and cereal-stained T-shirt that she was not in going-out mode.

"No work for a little bit," said Bailey. Mainlining all six episodes of Britain's longest-running sitcom *Oi! What's All This, Then?* had left plenty of free brain space to perfect her cover story. "I'm being, um, transferred. They're shuffling me to another bar Garrett has a financial stake in, as a way of fostering—"

"Wait. So you're not working with Zane anymore?" Her dad frowned. "I thought that was the whole reason you were tending bar."

Bailey refused to blush. "Actually, I'm pretty good at it," she said, more defiantly than she'd meant. "Bartending, I mean. I don't need Zane's help."

Her dad shrugged. "I'm sure you are, Beetle. Hey, does that mean you'd be free to help me out in the shop for a while?"

She fiddled with the remote. "Uh, how about I get back to you on that?"

"Don't turn your nose up at flower arranging, Beetle. You're a natural. Besides, it's got a lot of crossover with bartending."

"How so?"

Her dad opened his mouth, then closed it.

"The second I think of how so," he'd said, "you'll be the first one I tell."

That night she'd sat on her bed with the door locked, poring over *The Devil's Water Dictionary.* Who cared what Zane thought? He'd never bothered to find out what she was capable of. She could mix these cocktails with her eyes closed. But her gaze drifted from the page to the ink-black night outside the window, and her thoughts followed suit. How many tremens lurked out there right now? How many bartenders were out there, protecting people like her—and her parents—from them? What happened if a bartender *didn't* get there in time?

What would've happened to Zane?

The more questions she asked herself, the more their probable answers gave her the creeps. Especially when she was alone. Alone and in a bedroom whose walls were still painted what Home Depot called Sparkling Mimosa.

Her phone buzzed and Bailey jolted—once from the vibration and again when she saw an unfamiliar 312 number on the display. *Okay, so* not *Divinyl.* But still another nonparent human who wanted to talk to her.

"Hello?"

"Bailey?" said a familiar voice. Before she could identify it, though, it saved her the trouble. "It's Bucket. So, about your reassignment. Are you free tomorrow night?"

"Um," Bailey glanced at the leather-bound day planner she'd bought in a fit of ambition two weeks before graduation and brushed a streak of dust off the cover. "I think so."

"Great. Zane wanted to make sure you had a friendly face around, so he pulled some strings to get you in here. You're gonna be apprenticed to my boss, Vincent Long."

She could practically hear Bucket's smile over the phone. "The Long in Long & Strong?"

"That's the one," said Bucket. "I'll text you the address. It's not far from the Brown Line. Vincent'll want to tell you what's what, so get here at seven, eh?"

And so it was quarter to seven when the door to Long & Strong slammed behind Bailey. The bar's inside was no better than the outside. The place was lit with strings of bright red lights shaped like little chili peppers. The paint peeled in spots. The pool table was scuffed, its balls and cues weathered. Even the rainbow flags in the corners looked halfhearted. All bars existed to serve a need, just like any other business, but as Bailey stepped in, all she could think was: *Who would need a place like this?*

The answer was surprisingly apparent. At only almost seven in the evening, the bar was already packed. The room held an even ratio of older men who'd probably been customers for years and younger men who were probably too poor to afford anywhere else. Neither side seemed to mind. In fact they mingled freely. A few gave her cursory glances when she walked in, but otherwise they ignored her. She smiled. Nervous as she was about being reassigned, that was something she could get used to.

Bucket was behind the bar. His mohawk stood straight up, like some kind of Canadian crested bird. "Bailey!" he called over the music. "Vincent's downstairs in his office! You can go on down!"

"Great!" Bailey shouted back. "Anything I should, uh, know

about him?"

But Bucket had already dashed off to serve a customer. Bailey let herself in past the bar, then looked around for a door leading to the basement. But there were only walls, no doors.

Bucket noticed her confusion and pointed at her feet. She looked down, wondering what the hell her shoes had to do with it, until she realized she was standing on top of a genuine, bona fide trapdoor.

"Holy shit," she muttered as she knelt and pulled it open. "What the hell kind of place is this?"

"A magical one!" Bucket called to her.

A flight of metal stairs led directly to an office, whose door was wide open. She stepped onto the staircase and shut the trapdoor over her head. "Hello!" she yelled. She realized the music from above wasn't filtering past the floor, and so she lowered her voice and tried again. "Hello?"

The reply sailed up to her: "Yeah." It wasn't exactly an invitation, but she had the feeling it was the closest she'd get.

The office was cramped. There were no filing cabinets, just a small old desk with a computer, whose keyboard curiously had no letters. Next to the desk, a large dog with salt-and-pepper fur lay curled on the floor asleep. It was a giant schnauzer, its ears uncropped and its beard as resplendent as any wise man's. But the dog and the computer drew her attention for only a moment.

Vincent Long was old—maybe as old as Garrett—but the similarities ended there. Long was a solid brick of muscles and tattoos. Unlike Bucket, whose arms were covered in flowing sleeves, his looked as if they'd been collected piecemeal over decades, turning his arms into a collage. His light gray hair was cropped Marine close, and he wore jeans, combat boots, and a plain black T-shirt. Bailey got the distinct impression that his closet at home was filled with nothing but more of the same.

She winced preemptively when she stuck out her hand and introduced herself, imagining his grip could crush her bones into a fine powder. But to her surprise, his handshake was gentle, though calloused.

"Bailey Chen," she said. "And you must be—"

"Yeah," Vincent said, and he sat down. "So you're the latest thing Garrett's dumped in my lap."

Something was off about the way he looked at her.

"We're old friends," she said. "I mean, Zane, his nephew, is technically my old friend—" She felt a squeeze of guilt, since technically she and Zane hadn't spoken since their ill-fated patrol. "But, um, I've known Garrett forever."

"Hope not," Vincent said darkly. With an unconvincing lightness, he added: "I've known them longer than you, and I don't like the idea of being older than *forever*, is all. What experience you got, Bailey Chen?"

Bailey tried not to wilt. One of the biggest pains in the ass about searching for employment was its horrible catch-22: you needed experience to get a job, but to get experience you needed a job. Browsing job sites, she'd silently flipped off every scumbag corporate HR rep who thought having a half decade of relevant experience was the definition of *entry level*. But she never expected to run into similar problems trying to work in a *bar*.

"I barbacked at the Nightshade Lounge for two weeks," she said. "And I also—"

"Kicked the shit out of a tremens, then kicked the shit out of its shit," said Vincent. "Pretty cool stuff. But I'm gonna be straight with you, kiddo. Right now you're pretty much useless."

"Hey," she said, then shut her mouth. She didn't really have a good rebuttal. At least not one that was fact based and nonprofane.

"Nothing against you personally," he said. "You're what, twenty-one?"

"Twenty-two." She couldn't stop staring at his face. He wouldn't even look her in the eye.

"Same difference. Everyone's useless at your age," he said. "Hell, my boyfriend's eight years older than you, and he's still useless. And you know what? The world out there didn't help Gavin with that, and it's not gonna help you. Everyone agrees you need training and experience and all that. But they also all agree that *giving it to you* is not their problem."

Entry-level job, two years' experience required. "Yeah. But if you're my"— Bailey still had trouble saying the word with a straight face—"*master* now, doesn't that make it *your* problem?"

Vincent grunted. "Yeah," he said. "Emphasis on *problem*. I've got a business to run, and it's not like you're gonna be a big draw for my clientele."

She felt a stab of indignation. "Well, if you didn't *want* an apprentice, why'd you ask for one?"

His chuckle was hollow and mirthless. "You think I asked for you? No, this is old Garrett up to his tricks, the tiny rat bastard."

So she'd been inflicted on someone as a punishment. It felt like a slap to the face. But Bailey shook it off.

"Then get back at him." She still thought of Garrett as Zane's goofy uncle, not someone to be bested. But if she was being honest, she was the one who wanted to get back at the Whelans. Show off. Prove herself. "Make me the best bartender in town. Put me out on the streets, and I'll kick ass. You'll see. I promise."

Her words rang out in the small space, and Bailey slowly realized the situation: his indirect stare; the letterless keyboard; the dog.

She gasped.

Vincent grinned. "Now's the part where you realize I'm blind and you feel like an asshole."

Why the hell hadn't Bucket or Zane mentioned this to her? "Vincent, I'm sorry," she said, mortified. "I had no idea—"

His grin spread. "Bet you're pretty embarrassed right now."

She nodded—nodded!—and then flushed, not that he could see that either.

"Um, yes," she said clearly. "Yes, I am."

"Well, trust me," he said, "you'll be twice as embarrassed when you see that a guy with two bum eyes is still ten times the bartender you are. They told me you've put in a night on patrol with the little Whelan. Kid was out of line, taking you with him. You ain't ready."

"I'll never be ready if I don't get to see a master at work." She kicked herself again for her poor word choice. Who knew English had so many sight-based idioms?

Vincent appeared not to care. "It's not about watching a master work," he said. "It's about rebuilding you from the ground up. You're right that you need a good grip on your foundation, but killing tremens isn't our foundation."

"It isn't?" Bailey said. "I thought that's why this whole crazy . . . society existed."

"Yeah, and Halloween's just an innocent, fun-filled night where we all pass out gumdrops to kids in bedsheets." Vincent shook his head with a chuckle and Bailey shivered, remembering Mona's words: *It's not just a holiday for children.*

"But I won't scare you with that just yet." He rose to his feet. "I got a bigger point to make." When the dog saw Vincent stand, it followed suit, ears pricked and tail wagging. "All right, Poppy. Nice girl. She's a friend."

Determined to be friends, Bailey smiled down at the dog. "Poppy, as in the flower?" she said, a "my dad is a florist" anecdote at the ready.

"Actually it's short for Populist Uprising to Overthrow Our Systemic Oppressors," said Vincent. "Good guess, though. Bring us up top, Poppy."

The dog barked twice in assent. Tail still wagging, she wedged her way past Bailey and out the office door. Vincent followed right behind her, and Bailey behind him.

"You were a business kid, right?" Vincent started down the narrow hallway, each footfall ringing dully. In front of him, Poppy kept looking over her shoulder, making sure her master wasn't too far behind.

Bailey hastened to keep up. "Yeah. But don't hold my capitalist upbringing against me."

"We all make mistakes," he said. "Hell, I was an army kid. Business school and the army. Two terrible places for someone to go when they're eighteen, and not much in common except for one important thing."

She got the sense he was enjoying making her ask the inevitable question. "What?"

"Service," he said. "What's your shiny new job title, kiddo?"

"Bartender?"

"That's right." Vincent had reached the top step. He knocked against the underside of the trapdoor, then turned to face her. "You'll get your first smoke break. But before I put you up against monsters, I have to make sure you can handle something even more difficult and impossible to please."

Bailey caught on. "Horny, drunk gentlemen?"

Vincent grinned approvingly. "No to the third thing, yes to the first thing. As for the second, that'll be up to you."

He shoved the trapdoor, and it swung open. Poppy stepped out first. Vincent motioned for Bailey to follow, then disappeared topside. Bailey took her time, hoisting herself up to face a sea of dudes dancing, dudes drinking, and dudes kissing. The wolves to which she was about to be thrown.

Vincent pointed to Bucket, who was working through a line of beer orders. "Kill the music," he called. The Canadian saluted and then hit a button on the jukebox remote. The music died abruptly, amid groans and shouts.

Vincent stepped forward, putting up his hands. "Everyone, shut up!" he called. "I'm Vincent Long, the owner."

"We know who you are, Vince!" an older customer called back.

"Yeah," said a younger one. "Put the fucking music back on!"

"Tell me what to do in my bar again, and the only music you'll hear is me using your head as a drum," Vincent said. That alone was enough to shut everyone up. He continued: "I've got two announcements to make, so listen up. First off, this is your new bartender, Bailey." He gently prodded her forward into view. "Everyone say hi to Bailey."

To her great surprise, the entire bar chorused like schoolchildren: "Hi, Bailey."

"Now Bailey's brand new here at Long & Strong," Vincent said. "So we're gonna welcome her. In honor of our newest family member, for the next three hours all cocktails are half off! *But,*" he said, shouting over the rumbling cheers, "only if *she* makes it for you. Bucket: music on. Drink up, gents."

Bailey glanced back at Vincent, desperation etched on her face. "But—"

Vincent grinned.

"Best way to hit the ground is running, kiddo," he said. "Welcome to the life."

Bailey turned back just in time to see the wave of customers descend upon her counter, orders on their lips and dollars in their hands.

The Negroni
A cocktail to fortify the flesh

1. *Fill an old fashioned glass with ice.*
2. *Mix an ounce apiece of gin, sweet vermouth, and Campari. Stir well.*
3. *Garnish with an orange twist, and serve.*

The negroni was commissioned by Count Camillo Negroni in the summer of 1919. Italy had lately been ravaged by a mutated strain of tremens whose bladelike forearms could slice a man in two. The count turned to the nearest, most consistent source of enlightenment: his local barman. After three weeks of painstaking research, the bartender, whose name has regrettably been lost to time, debuted a new gin cocktail that rendered its drinker all but unbreakable.

Flush with his servant's success, Count Negroni bullied his way into the next convention of the Organisation Européenne des Échansons et Sommeliers—the Continental equivalent of the Cupbearers Court—held that year in Belgrade. There he demanded an exorbitant fee of the OEES in exchange for his recipe. When officials balked, he demonstrated the drink's strength on the convention floor when his skin turned aside all attempts to pierce it. But he also demonstrated its inability to protect against internal damage when he provoked the convention's host, a local bartender named Damjan Zupan, into beating him over the head with a fire poker. Zupan's poker is today on display in his family's bar and still carries the contours of Count Negroni's unbreakable skull.

SWEET VERMOUTH.

Not to be confused with dry vermouth—and because dry vermouth is far from sweet, such confusion would theoretically be difficult to manage in the first place. Where the use of dry vermouth traces back to France, sweet vermouth is an Italian innovation. Its deep red color prompted the Florentine barkeep Vittorio Serrano to market it as *il sangue imbottigliato*, "bottled blood." But Serrano proved a far better bartender than he did a capitalist. His sanguine nomenclature put off the wider drinking public while disappointing the few customers whose interest his sales pitch had piqued.

CAMPARI.

A bitter liqueur of Italian origin, Campari first rose to prominence as an ingredient in the Americano, an early precursor to the modern negroni. The cocktail in question was equal parts Campari and sweet vermouth, with a splash of soda water added for texture. Despite its close relation to one of bartending's best defensive drinks, the Americano is best known as a thirst quencher, though it may induce blindness if thrown into the eyes of an obnoxious bargoer.

CHAPTER EIGHT

"You've got forty seconds to make me a perfect negroni, or you're giving me fifty push-ups."

Bailey had taken many courses and studied under many instructors, but she'd never had a rougher classroom than Long & Strong. The place was a rainbow-spangled rat hole, but it did a brisk business, and on top of the grind of mixing-drinks-making-change-running-tabs, the mixology challenges that Vincent threw down were grueling for her and a delight for him. But not nearly as much of a delight as the perfect negroni she set down in front of him with three seconds to spare.

Vincent had yanked her down to his office for a midshift pop quiz. Now he picked up the crimson-glowing cocktail and breathed in its vapors.

"Think I can smell the magic on this one," he said. "You know what a negroni does?"

"'A cocktail to fortify the flesh,'" she recited. Gin was the transformative liquor, and the negroni made the drinker's skin unbreakable.

"Good memory, kiddo, though it wouldn't kill you to put things in your own words once in a while," he said. "So we're gonna have ourselves a wager." He took a decent gulp. "You want to get out on patrol, right? Have yourself a smoke break?"

The thought of finally testing out her new knowledge was

almost irresistible. Every night there'd been a never-ending press of men demanding drinks that Bailey barely knew how to make: shooters, twisters, Jack and Cokes—or Jack and *Diet* Coke, and God help you if you forgot—with no magical value but plenty of popularity. It was a good thing the staff pooled tips; her inexperienced service left plenty to be desired, and it wasn't like she could fall back on flirting to score a few extra singles. She practically limped to the end of her shifts, and not once had she gotten anywhere near patrol duty.

"Yes," she said, trying but failing to hide the eagerness in her voice.

"Then here are the terms," Vincent said, and he gulped a bit more of the negroni. "By the time I finish this, I should have unbreakable skin. If I do, you hit the streets tonight."

"Unsupervised?"

He chuckled. "You're not in business school anymore. Quit acting like greed's a virtue. No, you'll shadow young Bucket." He drank again, closing his eyes to relish the flavors. "If I've got unbreakable skin, that is."

"And if you don't . . . " Bailey tried not to groan. "How many push-ups?" Physical exertion was Vincent's favorite punitive measure ("a bartender's gotta be in shape, kiddo"), and though she was still a far cry from strong, under his tutelage she could drop and give him thirty without stopping.

"Not push-ups. You'll have to do something a whole lot worse." Vincent polished off the drink, placed the empty glass on the desk, and calmly laid his hand next to it.

"Which is . . . what?"

"Take an old man to the hospital."

And then with blink-and-you'll-miss-it speed, Vincent slammed a paring knife into his outstretched palm.

Bailey yelped.

But the blade bent, and in what seemed like slow motion shattered, spraying metal across the room. The force had indented Vincent's skin, but the knife point hadn't made a mark.

And he was *howling* with laughter.

"*Are you crazy?*" Bailey sputtered.

That only made him laugh harder. He had to squeeze out words between gasps.

"Wish I could . . . see your face . . . *love* doing that . . . "

"Vincent, that wasn't funny!" Bailey said, still rattled. When she saw the knife shards strewn across the desk, and his intact hand next to them, she couldn't help but grin. She'd done it. "It wasn't *that* funny," she added.

"You're on deck, kiddo," Vincent said. "Soon as Bucket's back and he's had another drink, you're hitting the streets."

For the next twenty minutes Bailey was antsy. She wished the customers could've honored the occasion by taking it easy on her, but obviously she couldn't tell them why she was smiling so wide; and even if she had, they wouldn't have cared. Experience on both sides of the counter taught her that you don't go to a bar to hear about what a great day the bartender is having.

When the time came, Vincent lumbered out of his office with Poppy plodding along in front of him. "You two are up," he said. "I'll take over here. Supplies are laid out downstairs. And kiddo," he added, pointing to Bailey, "don't forget your keys. That one keeps losing his, and I'm not buying another goddamn set."

Bailey eyed all the beer taps, liquor bottles, glasses, and garnishes, not to mention the customers clamoring for them in varying combinations. She'd never seen Vincent tend bar, and she couldn't imagine how he did it with only a dog to back him up.

Bucket, on the other hand, didn't seem even slightly fazed. "Come on, B-Chen—"

"Call me that again and die."

"—Bailey. Let's go be good guys."

As they clanked down the stairs, Bailey glanced back at the open trapdoor. "Will he be all right up there by himself?"

"Vincent?" Bucket said. "Yeah, don't let the blind thing fool you. He's like some kind of Zen master, except with booze. Just worry about you. You know what you're doing?" They stepped into the office, and he shut the door behind them.

"I—I think so." She'd been confident, even eager, right up until he'd asked her that question. Now she felt her poise evaporating. She stared down at the small forest of bottles and wondered which one she could trust to save her life in the face of skinless death.

Bucket stepped up next to her and patted her shoulder reassuringly. "I know you're scared," he said. "But you can't let fear freeze you up. People need us, whether they know it or not, so you've—"

With quick, decisive motions, Bailey started yanking out bottles of rye, bitters, and water, and then a short thick-bottomed glass to put everything in. She turned to Bucket. "Where do you keep the sugar?"

The two of them stepped out a few minutes later. It'd been raining all day, and though the skies were dry, the rainfall had smothered whatever heat the summer had left behind. Bailey shivered, wishing she had more than a hoodie and an old fashioned to keep her warm. Looking not even slightly bothered by the chill, Bucket bobbed along next to her. He'd drunk a mai tai that he'd practically built inside its glass.

"So what does a mai tai do?" she asked to fill the silence. From skimming the *The Devil's Water Dictionary*, she knew that rum drinks produced elemental effects, but she couldn't remember the specifics for mai tais.

He grinned. "Let's hope I won't have to show off. But if I do, well, you're in for fireworks."

"So it's fire?"

"I didn't say that."

"But it's fire."

"I didn't say that."

"You didn't need to. It's fire."

He sighed. "You done?"

She nodded. But to herself, she repeated: *fire*.

Boystown was unusually tame. They headed south on Halsted, past locked-up leather shops and about a billion frozen-yogurt places and a dog boutique called I Ruff My Pup. The occasional stragglers weaved around the corners and ducked past them, giggling. No one was running in terror or screaming for help. Bailey stifled a yawn. A drink's effects lasted about as long as it took the drinker's system to metabolize it, which gave her roughly an hour to work. Slightly less; pushing it too close and she ran the risk of losing power midfight. Theoretically it'd be good to have a quiet night, but Bailey just wanted to get her encounter over with.

"Hey," Bucket said, interrupting her thoughts, "I gotta ask you something. It's kind of been on my mind since you started working here."

"Um, shoot," Bailey said, wondering what he wanted to ask. Bucket had been Zane's friend first—if Bucket was even Bailey's friend at all. He'd been unfailingly polite and cheerful since they'd become coworkers, but maybe that was just Canadian niceness. How did adults figure this stuff out?

"Ladies' night," he said seriously. "Vincent should totally do one, eh? Probably counts as discrimination if he doesn't, right?"

Bailey laughed so hard she snorted. "I'm sorry, what?"

"Yeah, dude," Bucket said. "Think about it. You get more tips, and I get to show these American girls my rugged Canadian charm."

They'd hung a right past the Chicago Diner onto Roscoe, and Bailey shook her head while following Bucket's lead onto a single-block street lined with apartment buildings.

"Sorry again, but I'm so not following," she said. "We work at a gay bar."

"Yeah. The mesh tank tops tipped me off."

"But you want to pick up girls?"

Bucket laughed. "Duh. Why wouldn't I? . . . Wait, you think I'm gay?"

"Um, yes," Bailey said. "You're a man who works in a gay bar, so yes, I thought that was a reasonable assumption."

It was Bucket's turn to look confused. "So Zane didn't tell you? Or Vincent?" When Bailey shook her head, he sighed. "Right, okay, let's set it straight. Follow me on this one because it could get complicated: I'm transgender. Oh, and there's a tremens behind us."

"What—seriously?" Bailey wheeled around, but the street was deserted. Relatively well lit, even. Bucket kept walking.

"Yeah, I've known since I was a kid," he said cheerfully. "There were some rough times, but I started transitioning a few years back and I've never been happier—"

"No, about the tremens," Bailey said, trying to catch a reflection in one of the parked cars' back windshields. "But congratulations on your transition," she added hastily. She could hear something skittering over dead leaves in the alleyway behind them. "Um, not to be rude, but why aren't you more worried?"

"Well, the statistics in the trans community are sobering, but I've had really supportive friends—"

"Still talking about the tremens," she hissed. "Why the hell are you so calm?"

He beamed. "Because you're going to save me."

"Save you?"

He nodded solemnly. "Vincent told me it was an important step in your personal journey as a bartender to feel responsibility for another life, and the safeguarding thereof." After a moment, he added: "Duh."

"Shit." Of course. She was an idiot to have expected a straightforward lesson from Vincent. "But you have to help me."

"No, I don't," said Bucket. "I'm just a wee powerless civilian."

Bailey thrust out a hand and sensed a kind of telekinetic phantom hand mirroring her own. Her brain pressed on Bucket's torso, sending him staggering back a few steps, to a safe spot behind an SUV flagrantly disobeying a prominent NO PARKING sign. Her skin prickled and she turned to face whatever was shivering behind the alleyway trash can.

The trash can trembled.

Holy shit. Holyshitholyshit.

"Hey!"

Bailey had mentally grabbed Bucket by his shirt collar and flung him farther away. The tremens, small and stocky and six legged, scuttled out and immediately lashed one of its thick, muscly limbs at her. Panicked, she backhanded the air, her old fashioned-induced telekinesis swatting the tendril like a tennis ball.

Okay. Think. Trip it? Doing so would tip it right onto Bucket, who had left the SUV's safe zone and was leaning against a metal fence with irritating calmness.

"You got this, Bailey!"

Focus, she thought. Zane had telekinetically thrown around a heavy manhole cover like a Frisbee. So maybe she could—

The tremens scuttled away from the trash can. She had to get it away from Bucket. Imitating what Zane had done, she pointed her finger like a gun, willing her mind to attack as she "fired."

Kick. Hard.

Sure enough, the tremens rippled as an unseen force hammered it; it fell forward, front tendrils flailing.

Bailey sprang back, yanking herself ten feet down the sidewalk. She had just long enough to look in awe at her impossibly long jump before the tremens shook off the impact and wobbled upright.

"Eye on the puck, Bailey!"

Bucket's voice snapped her back into the moment. They were in the middle of an ordinary street. No manhole cover close by. No convenient piece of debris. Nothing sharp or heavy or on fire enough to kill the damn thing.

But its attention was wavering. She could feel it, and mentally she tugged hard at its limbs, once, twice, three times, feeling her brain recoil each time.

Okay, you ugly demon beast. Follow the leader.

She turned and started running, focusing her psychic energy on the space between her shoulder blades, willing her legs ever faster with the superfocus of her brain waves. But the tremens could leap, and in a heartbeat it was beside her.

Now.

Bailey stopped pushing herself and yanked her body laterally off the street. The tremens lashed out to seize her, but its tendril only managed to graze her forearm. She had banked hard enough to slam into a brick facade, but the brief tentacle contact sent a chill racing to her skull.

No. She wrested back control of her head space. She couldn't waver. Not when she was so close. Feeling the mental fatigue, she shoved the tremens toward the NO PARKING sign, the force of the collision bending the aluminum pole like a flower stem.

Perfect. She had only one chance. Swinging her arm through the air, she forced the broken section of the post to yank itself from beneath the tremens. The sign dangled downward like the blade of a guillotine.

Her brain burning, Bailey slammed the post onto the neck of the tremens. The impact jarred her as the beast's neck gave way beneath the sign's thin edge. She expected a loud squeal, but nope: just the clang of the broken signpost and faint patter as the black matter that had once been a demon sprinkled onto the sidewalk.

Bucket, eyes wide and hands clapping slowly, appeared at her shoulder. He seemed genuinely awed.

"Holy shit, Bailey," he said. And then, after another moment of staring at the stinking, sputtering puddle: "Seriously. *Holy shit.*"

Bailey looked at the sign. It was beyond repair, covered in whatever substance dead tremens turned into—dark and sticky as oil, with that same unnatural sheen.

"Should we . . . " Her voice trailed off.

"Don't worry about the sign. We should go." Bucket glanced up at the apartment windows, some of which were glowing with sleepy yellow light. "You were pretty noisy—awesome but noisy—and I bet someone's about to call the Royal Chicago Mounted Police."

"Right." Bailey couldn't help feeling a little let down: all that hard work, and the only one who'd ever know was Bucket. She gave her handiwork a final glance before Bucket pulled her away.

"I knew you were gonna be okay," he told her as they hurried off. "But you took that thing down like a goddamn pro."

"Yeah. Thanks. Needed the therapy." Despite the pounding in her head and the pulse of adrenaline in her veins, she managed a smile. "Just wish I could . . . share it or something, you know?"

"No, I get it. But that's why you have us, your fellow bartenders," he said, leading her back to Roscoe. "We're always around if you need to vent or brag or—"

Just as they rounded the corner, Bailey ran right into Zane Whelan.

He wore a brown striped suit and sneakers, his tie loosely done. Mona was with him. She yelped and jumped back.

"Shit," Bailey said. "Sorry. I thought you—"

Zane raised a hand. "No tremens here. Just your friendly neighborhood Alechemists."

Bailey swallowed. "Right. What're you guys, uh, doing here?"

She realized too late that the question probably sounded rude.

"Bucket told us what was happening tonight," Mona said, her arms folded across her chest.

"Yeah," said Zane. "We didn't want to miss your *bar* mitzvah." He glanced around for approval but no one laughed. "Oh, come on," he grumbled. "That was hilarious."

"I thought it was very funny," said Mona in a tone utterly bereft of amusement.

Bailey wasn't so easily distracted. "Aren't you on duty tonight?"

Zane straightened his tie. "I basically run the Nightshade now. I decide when I'm on duty. And if Garrett's got a problem with that, he can come back and mind the place for himself." Before Bailey could ask where the attitude was coming from, Zane shook it off. He was positively giddy in the way that only demonic carnage seemed to make him. "Enough about that, though. Using a sign as a battle-ax? Awesome."

Mona shot Bailey an odd look.

"Resourcefulness, Bailey." Zane tapped the side of his nose. "That's how you last in this business."

"Not dying also helps," Mona said.

Bucket and Zane laughed, but Bailey did not. Something about Mona's eyes told her it hadn't been a joke.

Zane's excitement subsided, and he reached into his coat pocket. "Hey, guess what? I got you—well, I found something, and I—I thought of you." He shoved a slim plastic something into Bailey's hands.

"A CD?" It took Bailey a second to recognize what it was. The cover depicted four brooding men in black: long and lopsided haircuts, makeup tears running down their cheeks, a stylized logo that read "4DL" superimposed beneath them.

"For Dear Life?" Bailey cracked a grin. "Zane, I think we've both way outgrown—"

"Look inside."

She flipped open the case and her eyes widened.

"Holy shit." The familiar face of the disc winked up at her, but it featured something her old copy had not: four signatures in black marker. "How did you—"

"They came through town while you were out," Zane said, as if her four years in Philly had been a long trip to the store for milk. "I got backstage passes. I, uh, brought Mona."

Mona nodded. "It was loud."

"Anyway, that's yours, and don't try to give it back to me." Zane lowered his voice. "It's a gift."

As it happened, Bailey had been about to protest. This was too much. She and Zane had listened to a lot of music in high school, but For Dear Life's discography was the true sound track to their teenage years. And even though most music fans their age had moved on from "no one understands me" angst punk to experimental acoustical lo-fi indie whatever, Bailey still carried her torch; 4DL's single "Dark November" was in regular rotation on her playlists. In fact, she'd acquired an unfortunate reputation in college as "that girl who always puts on 'Plastic Eyes' at parties." Apparently Zane felt the same way. About the band, anyway.

"It's not, you know, all filtered up or whatever," Zane said. "But—"

"Thanks," Bailey said. "Thank you, Zane."

Zane grinned. "That's only part one. Part two will have to wait till tomorrow. It's a surprise."

"Oh. Um . . . " Not really sure what to make of that comment, Bailey instinctively reached for her purse to stow the album. But her purse wasn't dangling from her shoulder; she'd left it at the bar, where she and Bucket were technically still on duty. "Actually, we should probably get going."

"No problem," said Zane. "Mona and I will walk back with you guys. We'll drink up until closing, and then we can hit Nero's and celebrate properly." He nudged Mona. "What do you think, baby?"

Baby. The word thudded off Mona like a bird off a window. Bailey resisted the urge to make a face.

Mona just turned to him, almost smiled, and said, "I can't think of a socially acceptable way to disagree."

On the way back, Bucket regaled them with a dramatic re-telling of Bailey's fight, one in which he played all the characters himself and changed the story's emphasis as he saw fit.

"So then Bailey is all 'Monster, you interrupted a super inter-esting chat I was having with my good buddy Bucket about gender and personal identity, so I'm gonna fuck you up,' " he said, pitching up his voice into a passable imitation of her own. "And I'm standing there like, 'Oh, shit, this tremens won't even know what hit it.' You know"—he added in an aside—"because telekinesis is invisible and tremens are dumb."

Bailey laughed. "Skip to the good part," she said. Her walk had a bit of a strut, and why not? After tonight she'd earned it.

"Which good part?" said Bucket.

"Oh, you know," she said, pretending to modestly examine her fingernails, "the part where a tremens thinks it can just show up out of nowhere—"

"Tremens!" Bucket yelled.

"Exactly," Bailey said.

"No, I'm serious!" Bucket's eyes were wide, his voice hoarse. "Tremens!"

He pointed up at a busted-out streetlight just as the demon launched itself toward them.

"Shit!" Bailey jumped back, witless and terrified and com-pletely forgetting she was supposed to run *toward* these things now. "Zane! Mona—"

But like her, they had both jumped out of the way. Bucket, on the other hand, jumped forward. He spread his hands and blasted twin columns of pale blue flame, as if his arms were jet engines. The sudden heat ignited the air with a small *snap*, then a giant *crack!*, and finally a brilliant explosion that sent the tremens flying, its hide scorched.

"*Holy shit!*" Bucket said, sliding into a wide defensive stance. His hands were wreathed in tongues of fire, which had cooled from blue to orange. "Did you guys see that?"

"Hard not to," Mona said drily.

"Yeah," Bailey said. She wanted to smirk about how she'd guessed right about Bucket's fiery fists, but she was too rattled to say anything but "Fire."

"We're not armed," Zane said. "You guys have to handle this one."

The streetlight sputtered back to life, bathing them all in an orangish glow. The hairs on the back of Bailey's neck pricked again as she heard skittering behind her. She turned and felt the last of her cockiness drain away.

"Not one," she said, her voice soft with fear.

A second tremens lurked on the edge of the illuminated circle, its steps tracing an elliptical path around them. Down the sidewalk the first tremens had risen, and the pair of beasts moved in concert at opposite edges of the light. One was what she'd come to think of as the basic tremens: almost wolf shaped except that it rippled and oozed like a jellyfish. The other was completely different: a writhing ball of tentacles that scuttled sideways like a crab. Out of the blackness between its tendrils, angry yellow eyes glared thirstily at its prey.

Zane's mouth flapped before any noise came out. "Two tremens at once," he said. "That's not possible."

"Or convenient," Mona said.

Bailey tried to take refuge in logic. "Let's worry about the probability later and kill them now," she said. "Bucket, you take that one. This one here's mine. Each of us can go one-on—"

Suddenly from down Roscoe Street a third tremens stalked into sight. From behind a mailbox emerged a fourth. Then a fifth from underneath a car. And a sixth. And a seventh. Bailey and Bucket were pacing in a circle to keep Zane and Mona behind them, and Bailey had lost track of how many there were.

As one, the demons bared their teeth and then surged in to feed.

The Mai Tai
An infusion of infernal nature

1. *In an ice-filled shaker, mix one and a half ounces of white rum, half an ounce of curaçao, a teaspoon of orgeat syrup, and a teaspoon of lime juice.*

2. *Shake vigorously until well mixed.*

3. *Strain into an iced highball glass.*

4. *Float half an ounce of dark rum on top of the drink. The result should be multilayered and multicolored.*

5. *Garnish with a wedge of pineapple, and serve.*

Like many other rum drinks, the mai tai (in Tahitian *maita'i*, "good") is one whose usage has grown with the increasing availability of fresh ingredients. Once a colorful curiosity available only in certain areas of the world, it has since risen in stature to become perhaps the most popular rum cocktail used in the field.

Three reasons account for this popularity, all of which are rooted in the drink's side effects. First, its pyrokinetic qualities afford the user greater levels of visibility at night, when the lion's share of patrolling takes place. Second, the power lends bartenders a key combat advantage, as tremens possess the same primal fear of fire as do their mundane animal counterparts.

The final reason for the mai tai's prevalence was eloquently summed up at the 1970 National Symposium of the Cupbearers Court by the Chicago bartender Robert Whelan: "Fire is cool."

Dark Rum.

Unlike its white counterpart, dark rum is aged in charred oak barrels. In addition to the difference in color, rum processed in this fashion imparts a stronger flavor and is more conducive to being consumed neat. In fact, dark rum actively resists being mixed with other ingredients, an expression of the spirit's elemental nature. The mai tai illustrates this same principle because when it is properly made, the dark rum is meant to float on top of the other ingredients rather than mingle with them.

Orgeat Syrup.

After the two rums, orgeat is the most essential ingredient in the mai tai. While serviceable substitutes exist for curaçao, garnish, and fresh lime juice (see *GIMLET*), not even the weakest pyromancy has been achieved via a mai tai not made with orgeat syrup. The substance, an emulsion of rose water, sugar, and almond oil, is not particularly fiery in nature or manufacture, but as leading mixology experts are universally quick to point out, the same is true of everything else in the mai tai, save perhaps the glass it's served in.

CHAPTER NINE

"Move!" Bailey shouted, shoving a wall of force at the tremens behind them. It wasn't enough to freeze them in their tracks, but if her brain pushed hard, she could hold them back. "Bucket!"

"On it!" yelled Bucket. He threw out a wedge of fire, and the tremens scattered. The four bartenders rushed into the gap and darted up the side street to the stump of the severed NO PARKING sign.

"*Holy shit holy shit holy shit holy—*"

"Not helping, Zane!" Bailey snapped. She lashed her hand like a whip, psychically grabbing the leg of one tremens midstride, and yanked it to the side, sending it tripping into the one next to it. But the beasts slowed for only a moment. The rest of the pack had streamed up the street and was circling the Alechemists like border collies herding sheep.

"It's no good!" Bucket said. "We're surrounded!"

"What do we do?" said Zane. He sounded afraid and Bailey didn't like it. Zane wasn't supposed to get rattled. Zane was supposed to know what to do.

"We stop being surrounded," said Mona, as if it were that easy. They couldn't make it back to Roscoe Street, and they couldn't head north either. The only open space was behind them.

"The alley!" Bailey yelled. The apartment buildings would act as shields if they could slide between them in time. Again she pushed with her brain force, which stalled the wall of tremens for another precious few moments, and then she practically dived into the narrow darkness. Zane and Mona rushed after her, and Bucket followed last, blasting fire to keep the tremens at bay. As soon as he stepped past the Dumpster at the alley's edge, Bailey mentally seized the huge trash bin. Even empty, it was far heavier than anything she'd tried to move, and she felt the psychic strain deep in her brain. Still, she managed to heave the makeshift barricade into the middle of the alley, sealing them off.

Bucket immediately leapt to the lip of the Dumpster and shot a steady stream of fire. His mohawk flopped to the side, succumbing to his own sweat and the heat of the flames.

"What do we do now?" Bailey said. "They'll just try to get around us."

"We would be surrounded again," said Mona, "which would be bad."

"They're working together," Zane said. "Which is fucked because it's supposed to be impossible. We're never going to make it back to Long & Strong on foot. And you two must be getting close to your one-hour limit."

"Really digging the optimism, guys!" said Bucket, blasting another a fire bolt. The alley ended in a four-foot fence overlooking a vacant lot that smelled like ripe garbage; the corridor was so narrow that Bailey could either jab Mona in the ribs or stand clear of Bucket's flame blasts. She chose to risk getting singed.

"We can't stay here," Bailey said. "As soon as we run out of juice, we're sitting ducks."

"Again, not encouraging!" Bucket swept hair out of his eyes.

Distracted by Zane and Mona, who were engaged in a hurried conference, Bailey ignored him.

"Black Cat Inn is closest," Mona said. "Type a telephone message to Anna. Or Lucky Lounge. Or the Diversey Dive—"

"I can't." Zane held up a blank screen. "The tremens' energy must've fried the hardware or something. My phone's toast."

"Okay! Okay." Bailey closed her eyes and willed her brain to work. "We need defense, but we also need to get out of here."

"We need a miracle," Bucket said.

"We need a howitzer," Zane said.

"Not artillery, Zane," Bailey said. "We need a tank!"

And that was when she realized they already had one.

Bailey patted the Dumpster they were leaning against, and its double lids flew open. "Everyone get in. I'll use telekinesis to pull and steer. Bucket, you push us with your fire blasts and keep them off our tail. Zane, Mona, keep your heads down until we can get back to the bar. And hopefully—"

A shape surged over the low wall behind them.

"Tremens!"

Before Bailey could react, Zane threw himself toward the creature, which slammed his bony frame right into Bailey's. They both hit the Dumpster with a loud *clunk*, and for a moment Bailey saw stars. As her vision slid into focus, she watched as the tremens reared up, its eyes glistening with greed. She reached out psychically, seized its tentacle, and jammed it straight into its eye.

The creature's mouth tore open in a silent scream and the tremens fell back.

"Get off, Zane!"

But he was slack against her. When she rolled his body aside, blood trickled through his thick hair.

"Mona!" Bailey scrambled to her feet, but Mona was nowhere to be seen.

"Up here," Mona called back. She had already vaulted into the Dumpster. "Get him in."

Bailey hefted the unconscious Zane with her, stumbling despite the extra beef of her psychic muscle.

"Keep his head up," she said, her voice cracking. "He's bleeding.

Bucket!"

"These are new boots," said Bucket, grimacing, but he vaulted over the edge and into the trash. Bailey was right behind him. With eyes closed, she tensed her brow and willed the wheels to spin; despite its immense weight, the Dumpster pivoted.

"Okay, Bucket," she said. "Mush!"

Spin. Spin. Still concentrating on the wheels, Bailey opened her eyes just enough to see Bucket spit another fiery explosion from his palm.

She was ready. At that instant, she directed a spike of telekinetic energy at Bucket's back, which propped him upright against his own recoil. With nowhere else to go, the energy burst out behind them and sent the Dumpster rocketing into the street, a single wheel rattling like an old grocery cart.

At once Bailey refocused, turning the Dumpster's front wheels while holding the back ones steady. Catching on, Bucket called up another explosion. Once again she braced him at detonation, and just like that they were zipping along the asphalt toward Roscoe Street, the loping pack of tremens farther and farther behind.

"Bailey, this shit is crazy!" Bucket whooped over the rushing wind. "Also, you're so my new favorite person!"

"Just keep them away!" Bailey shouted back. She spared a glance down at Zane. He was half buried in trash, his suit and shirt covered in stains. Mona held him with surprising tenderness, shielding him from the bumps and impacts.

"Fire in the hole!" Bucket yelled. And again Bailey's mind shoved him, causing another burst of speed and ungodly amounts of noise. In less than an hour the street would be crawling with cops, and they had to be safely out of sight by then. There'd be no explaining the situation to normal authorities or, worse, her parents. But telekinesis was draining her fast, leaving behind a bone-deep exhaustion.

She glanced down again at Zane. His phone was still loosely in his grasp, its screen completely scrambled by the ambient magic in the air. Her phone would be the same way. They couldn't call for help. Instead, they were going to lure a bunch of hungry tremens straight to a bar full of customers ripe for harvest.

We can't escape, Bailey thought. *Not if it means putting people in danger.*

"Mona!" she yelled. "Only magic can hurt tremens, right?"

"Yes," said Mona.

"And if I'm using my mental powers on this Dumpster—"

Mona seemed to understand. Despite their dire situation, her faint smile returned. "Then yes, for the moment, this is a magic Dumpster."

Bailey glanced back. The tremens had fallen into a loose formation, flowing over Roscoe Street like a skinless, scuttling flood. And because the Dumpster's momentum was flagging, the demons were gaining on them. Bailey did a quick calculation, then gave up and hoped her guesstimate was close enough. "Bucket, get over here!"

He did a double take. "What?" he said. "Why would I—"

"We're making artillery," she said. "Going nuclear."

Bucket understood and grinned madly. "Okay, seriously, my new favorite person." He scrambled into position next to her. She could feel the temperature rising as he superheated the pocket of air surrounding his palm.

"Make it count," Bailey said. "We need to be faster than they are." Even as she spoke, she could feel him drawing in more heat. A small orb of fire was suspended a few inches from his hand, white hot like a tiny star.

"Now?" Bucket said.

Bailey turned. The pack of tremens was less than twenty yards away and closing fast. "Now!"

Her word was lost in the *snap-crack* of the explosion, and she had to squeeze her eyes shut against the searing heat. Though she threw all her psychic weight behind Bucket's slight frame, the force was enough to send them both nearly toppling. They all lurched as the Dumpster pushed through its own inertia and shot back at the beasts like a giant, smelly bullet.

Two demons at the rear peeled off, but the other five weren't so lucky. The improvised tank cut a swath through them, wreathing the area in smoke and scattering bodies with wet *thud*s and a stench acrid enough to make the Dumpster smell pine fresh by comparison. Bailey felt the wheels waver on the asphalt, which was now slick with the black ooze that dead tremens left behind.

"Awesome," Bucket said, exhaling. "Look, they're fleeing! Flee, you pitiful demon things!"

"No," Bailey said. She'd already turned a Dumpster into a tank-slash-bulldozer in the pursuit of public safety; she wasn't about to leave behind any loose ends. "We can't let them get away."

She nudged Bucket, and as he hurled a fire bolt at one of the creatures, Bailey scanned the trash for a worthy projectile to hurl at the other. Nothing was small or hard or sharp enough; all of it was old and squishy and vaguely resembled food. *Think, Bailey, think.* What else could she—

Her hand fell on the lump inside her pants pocket: keys. The ones Vincent had insisted she take.

Perfect.

She pulled the chain out of her pocket and held it up for Bucket to see. "Got one more explosion in you?"

"That's what she sai—er, yes," Bucket said, seeing her scowl.

Bailey hurled the keys into the air, using her telekinesis to strengthen her arm. When its flight path started faltering, the keys righted themselves and zoomed after the retreating tremens. As they flew, Bucket superheated the thread of air behind them until at last a bubble rippled and exploded.

Bailey felt her brain lurch with the explosion's force, but she kept her grip on the key chain. She didn't know if being propelled by magical fire was enough to give it the mojo it needed, so she was leaving nothing to chance. She felt the rush of the keys zooming through the air like bullets and the sickening impact as their jagged edges buried themselves in the beast's flank.

"Nice!" Bucket went in for a high-five, but Bailey didn't take it. Not yet. The explosion cleared, but there was no smoke, no ooze. She'd hurt it but hadn't managed a kill shot. She swore and braced herself against the edge of the Dumpster, ready to haul herself out and take the fight to the tremens even though she'd formed only half an idea what to do next.

But someone beat her to it.

Mona flitted past like a shadow, jumping from the speeding Dumpster and hitting the ground in a somersault. She came up in a crouch, then took off sprinting.

"Mona!" Bailey yelled, yanking herself out of the trash with the help of a psychic boost. She slowed her fall with a telekinetic cushion and hit the ground running. "Mona!"

But Mona was headed for the wounded tremens. Its leg gave out, and the wounds inflicted by the keys were starting to ooze. Bailey might not have killed it, but she'd robbed it of its speed.

Mona threw herself into a dropkick and planted her feet on the beast's injured leg. It arched its back in pain but didn't cry out. Yellow eyes brimmed with rage as it whipped a tendril at Mona. But she'd already sprung up and nimbly danced out of the way. She kept herself behind the beast, forcing it to pivot on its wounded side and presenting one big target to Bailey. Her psychic fingers dug into the tremens's three wounds, and when she wrenched her hand, the keys were yanked into the air. The tremens shook violently, whipping at the air but hitting nothing. Without hesitating, Bailey drove the keys through the back of its head. A final cloud of sulfurous smoke erupted, and then she and Mona stood on the street, reeking of trash and Hell itself.

"Well fought," Mona said, wiping her hands on her pants.

Before Bailey could answer, Bucket hobbled up, carrying Zane. "We're getting the fuck out of here. Now."

CHAPTER TEN

It wasn't until she heard Vincent's voice through the bar door that Bailey felt safe.

"Quit fucking banging! Jesus. I gave you keys for a reason." The door to Long & Strong creaked open and Bailey's boss emerged. His nose wrinkled. "What the hell happened to your patrol? And that smell—"

"We'll tell you inside," Bailey said. "We've got Zane Whelan. He's hurt."

Vincent scowled but moved aside. As they shuffled in, Mona hung back. "I'm going on a coffee run," she said and then disappeared.

Bailey couldn't believe Mona could think of a caffeine fix at a time like this, but she was too exhausted to protest. Vincent settled into a booth at the back of the room, but by the time they bandaged Zane, rinsed off the tremens stink, and explained what had happened, he was up again, pacing the length of the bar. Poppy dutifully trotted alongside, but he didn't need her guidance.

"This is bad," Vincent said.

"With all due respect, boss," said Bailey, "no shit."

At some point Mona had reappeared, bearing a cardboard carrier balancing five coffees. She brought the first to Zane and helped lift it to his lips.

"Worse than you know," said Vincent. "Group events are some *serious* shit."

"Group events?" Bucket shook his head so hard his piercings rattled. "But the energy fields or whatever—"

"Horseshit," Vincent said. "Those suckers will group if they're strong enough. I've seen it happen. Meaning, that was so long ago I really could see."

The Alechemists fell silent.

"The summer I was back from fighting in the jungle," Vincent continued, "I got my first job as a bartender and signed up for a whole new fight. Just a little bit after I started, we got tremens popping up by the delirium—that's what you call a group of them. At one point we topped out with a delirium nearly thirty strong wreaking havoc up and down Diversey. It took sixteen bartenders to beat them down, and then we worked overtime to make the citizens forget. Blamed it all on some antiwar protest or something."

"And then what?" Bailey said. Bucket offered her the last cup of coffee, but she shook it off.

"Trust me," he said. "You need this."

In the corner Zane was already sitting straighter, blinking behind his gauze, and Mona was carefully, almost tenderly, dabbing blood from his eyebrow. Bailey took the coffee and slurped it so fast she burned her mouth.

"We asked the Court for more resources," Vincent said. "We were pretty sure the next time was gonna be fucking Armageddon."

"And what happened?" Bailey said.

"Nothing." Vincent practically spat out the word. "The Court told us it couldn't verify our reports—that's why you always get a witness statement before you black them out, kiddo—and it needed to weigh its options."

"But what about the next time a delirium showed up?" said Bucket.

"That's the fucking thing," said Vincent. "They didn't. After that one, it went right back to solo events. Overnight. The Court patted us on the back for scaring the monsters away, and that was that." He hesitated for a moment before continuing. "A couple months later, after I'd lost my eyes, the Court got in touch again. Wanted to set me up with my own shop. Said I'd shown I was ready."

"You make that sound like a bad thing," Bailey said as Poppy jingled past her.

"I was in rehab," Vincent said. "I was busy learning how to live without my goddamned eyes. But you know who else got the same offer as blind boy Vincent? Everyone who survived the Battle of Diversey. Got their own bars and were soon too wrapped up in running a shop to worry about when the next delirium would show up. But that wasn't right. I could see it wasn't right, and I'm blind."

"Why?" said Mona. Bailey jumped a little; Mona had been so quiet.

"Bad batch of gin," he said. "Thought everyone knew that."

"No," said Mona. "Why did you notice?"

"I was fresh out of the jungle," he said. "I was done taking things at face value. Done with governments. Done ignoring my gut. But when I went around and talked to everyone, everyone who survived that night, no one wanted to talk back. Never wanted to mention it again. Someone shut them up."

Bailey's eyes narrowed. "The Court?"

"They never said so," said Vincent, "and I got too wrapped up in this place to push the issue. Last time I tried to bring it up at a Tribunal meeting was back in eighty-two, but the topic got spiked by their newest Tribune. My old battle partner. Got the sweetest deal of us all post-Diversey." He scowled so hard it was almost a smile. "Last time I ever trusted Garrett Whelan."

The room went uncomfortably still.

"Enough with the history lesson," Vincent said. "This shit'll get sorted out later. Right now you're alive, and that's what matters."

"Thanks."

It was Zane who had spoken.

"I can't believe—" He swallowed. "There were so many of them."

"I wish I could've seen it," Vincent said, and Bailey almost believed him. "You know what you kids need after a night like this?"

"A cleanup crew," Bailey said, thinking of the oozy puddles of tremens goop still pocking the street. "And maybe the police and—"

"No," Vincent said. "You need a cab ride home. I'm paying."

———————————

Bailey awoke on Zane's couch with her coat draped like a blanket over her body. Bucket, snoring on the floor, was curled around the coffee table. The door to Zane's room was closed, but she assumed he was in there.

She stretched and caught sight of her own arm, still crusted with dried garbage. *Gross.* Bailey groaned and jumped up, but Bucket didn't stir. She rubbed her head, then padded over to the kitchen and set about making coffee. Maybe it was rude to rummage through the cabinets, but her overpowering need for caffeine won out over politeness. Besides, they would all thank her when they woke up to a fresh pot.

Once the coffee started brewing, she walked over to the makeshift bar and sat on a stool. She must've dozed off because after what seemed like a minute, someone was prodding a cup of black coffee under her nose. Through blurry vision, Bailey took note of dark, slender fingers wrapped around a mug. Mona. She moaned and pushed herself upright. "Thanks," she said.

Mona nodded. "It will help you feel less dead."

Was Mona ever *not* drinking coffee? Bailey frowned. "You know caffeine will stunt your growth, right?"

Mona grunted.

"I take it we've got you to thank for this?" Holding his own mug, Zane popped up over Mona's shoulder. He was wearing an old drama club T-shirt and ratty sweatpants, and his unruly hair poked out between bandages. Much more like the old Zane.

"Yeah," Bailey said. "I had to be good for something."

Mona was wearing pajamas, too. Peach silk. *She must keep a set here,* Bailey thought. Her heart wriggled inside her chest.

Zane was grinning. "You're good for more than just coffee," he said. "Mona was telling me about last night. Using a Dumpster as a getaway car *and* a projectile? I knew you could be resourceful, Bailey, but damn."

"You should've seen me the time I tried to steal a birdbath."

"What?"

"Nothing," Bailey said with a shrug. "I just get good ideas when I'm drinking, I guess."

"Yeah, well, still." Zane smiled. "Thank you for saving my bony ass."

"And mine," added Mona.

"Yours is *not* bony," Zane said, kissing her cheek. Bailey grimaced into her coffee.

"Hey!" Bucket stuck his head out of the kitchen. His unmohawked hair had swooped over one side of his face, and he wore a bright blue apron that read "#1 Grillmaster."

"Hey!" Bailey said a little too brightly. "Hey, everyone, it's Bucket! Let's all talk to him!"

"Um, yeah," Bucket said, looking to where Zane and Mona were making dumb faces at each other. "Break it up, lovebirds. These pancakes aren't going to eat themselves."

Pancakes. Bailey could've wept. "Make them be here," she said, pointing at her mouth.

Bucket beamed. "You can get them yourself, American scum," he said cheerfully.

"Come on," said Zane, pulling away from Mona. "I splurged on all the best supplies. Pure maple syrup, so *some people* won't bitch every time they come for breakfast."

Bucket stuck out his pierced tongue.

"Bacon for me." Zane said. "Pop-Tarts for also me, and pancakes for . . . other people." He looked for a long moment at Bailey.

Bucket, oblivious, swept a hand into the kitchen. "Well, who's hungry?"

Apparently all of them were. Together the Alechemists chowed through a box's worth of pancake mix, plus two pounds of bacon, three packs of strawberry Pop-Tarts, and half a tube of burned pop-and-bake cinnamon rolls.

"Did you forget to grease the pan?" Bailey hiccupped. Zane had mixed up a round of nonmagical bloody marys, and it was a little difficult to keep her dexterity as she chipped a blackened hunk of roll with a butter knife. The room was galley style, with barely enough space for two, but somehow the four of them crammed in.

Bucket and Zane, wearing one oven mitt apiece, stared down at the tray. Zane swallowed. "Um."

"Using a Bundt pan was also inadvisable," said Mona with a bored glance at Bucket. She sat on the windowsill, smoking.

Bailey finally freed a chunk and popped it in her mouth. "Tastes okay, though." She chewed thoughtfully. "Who cares if it's weird shaped?"

"That's what she—"

"*Bucket.*"

Bailey ate and drank and laughed until her stomach hurt. She was still hung over and stiff from sleeping on the couch, but for the first time in a while, she felt happy. Really happy. Normal, even.

At long last they threw all the dishes into some soapy water and flopped into the living room.

"So," Zane said.

Bucket belched.

"*So,*" Zane said again, "now that we're all up and fed, we've got stuff to talk about."

Bucket, full of food or alcohol, or both, had flung himself onto the couch, so Bailey dropped onto a cushion on the floor. When they were seated, Zane thudded his mug against the coffee table, much like his uncle had done with the shot glass at the Tribunal. "This is an emergency meeting of the Alechemists," he said, not un-pompously, "to discuss what the fuck we saw last night. Everyone's present, and I've got Bucket's proxy vote."

From the couch, a sleeping Bucket grunted in assent. *Maybe he's Sleepy Ernie's long-lost son*, Bailey thought.

"Tremens are, by nature, solitary hunters." Zane said. "For them to be appearing in numbers, let alone working together so closely, means something's up."

"Like what?" Bailey said. "Like what Vincent saw?"

Mona and Zane exchanged a glance.

Bailey frowned. "What?"

"Vincent has credibility issues," Zane said. "You heard how he found a way to drag my uncle's name into it."

Bailey swirled the milk in her fifth cup of coffee. "And?"

"And . . . here's the thing," said Zane. "Vincent hates Garrett. Always has. The two of them were coming up as bartenders around the same time, and they used to patrol the North Side together. Vincent's always had his whole rebel complex. The second Garrett became authority, Vincent got too cool to team up."

"So you're saying Vincent thinks he's a sellout?" That didn't make sense. In the few weeks she'd been his employee, she'd known Vincent to be sly, blunt, and coarse enough to sand floorboards. But she'd never had reason to think of him as jealous or petty.

Zane shrugged. "Garrett's a Tribunal on the Chicago chapter of the Cupbearers Court and the longest serving in the Court's entire history. He's made this town what it is. Vincent's still stuck in the same hole the Court gave him as a handout a quarter century ago. He's bitter."

Bailey pursed her lips. "He's a good bartender. And a damn good teacher."

Zane fell silent.

Mona regarded Bailey coolly. "We should bring this to the Court," she said. "Vincent may have credibility problems, but you don't, Zane. Your uncle will listen to you."

Bailey shook her head. "Zane doesn't have proof," she said. "He was down in the garbage while I—*we* were killing them. Will they even listen to the rest of us? Maybe we should just go investigate. Get some data."

It was weird. Bailey was ordinarily all for hierarchy and structure and had no problem running to authority when things got sticky. As a kid she'd been called tattletale almost as often as she'd been called know-it-all. But something about handing this off to the grown-ups felt wrong. *She* wanted to be the grown-up for once.

Mona gazed at her as if they were playing chess and Bailey had just made a particularly interesting move.

Zane tapped a finger on his chin. "You're both right," he said thoughtfully. "Mona, we do have to bring this to the Court, and I'm probably the best guy to do it. Bailey, you're right that we should be handling this ourselves. Which is why we're going to. And we're going to do it with the best tool a bartender can have." His eyes gleamed with manic energy. "The Long Island iced tea."

Mona and Bailey shared a glance. Neither had expected the conversation to take this turn.

"Zane—" Bailey started.

But he sprang to his feet and dashed barefoot to the makeshift bar. "Last night I said I had a surprise for you guys. It's something that came in the mail yesterday." He rummaged through the bottles under the counter. "The Court manufactures all the optimized liquor we use for magic, but obviously it's never worked for mixing the Long Island. Privately distilled small-batch stuff has more unstable magical frequencies, but that kind of chaos is exactly what makes this cocktail work. And since I don't have a distillery in my back pocket, I've been collecting top-shelf 'shine from the best makers in the world. Yesterday I finally got my hands on the angels' share." He stood up, holding a tiny burlap sack. He pulled out a tiny brown bottle like a sword from its sheath. "I got it from a collector in Hong Kong."

"What is it?" Bailey said as a look of recognition crossed Mona's face.

"This," Zane announced triumphantly, "is aged rum from a batch commissioned by Hortense LaRue. And it's going to be the key ingredient in the first successful Long Island iced tea in centuries."

Bailey gaped. Mona's jaw tensed. On the couch Bucket snored softly.

"We've spent so long talking about the good we could do with a working Long Island iced tea." Zane set the bottle gently on the bar. "About how we'd need something for the day the court wasn't enough. If we have more nights like last night, then that day's already here. Chicago needs this. It needs us."

"I've got your back, bud." Bucket had snapped awake to a seated position.

"You didn't hear what he said," said Mona, unfazed by his sudden entrance into the conversation.

"No, but it sounded like he was doing one of his big inspirational speeches," said Bucket with a languorous yawn. "I'm in. Also, is there more coffee?"

Zane turned to Mona. "What about you, baby?"

Mona, utterly unbabylike, eyed the bottle. "Home distilling is a dangerous game, Zane," she said. "Vincent tried to make his own gin for a Long Island. It didn't end well."

"Vincent is no Hortense LaRue," said Zane. "If he'd kept his eyes on what was in his glass instead of on what my uncle had, they'd still work. He could've—look, we can't afford to wait, Mona. I was useless last night. Never again."

Bailey thought briefly of Vincent: his blank eyes, his letterless keyboard, Poppy curled in her bed. "Wait," she said. "If that's how Vincent lost his sight, then maybe Mona's right. That rum is crazy old. Maybe there's a reason no one drank it."

"Bailey," Zane said, "it's *me* we're talking about here. This is my life's work. You've seen that I know what I'm doing. I'm just asking you to trust me one more time."

Bailey wished she could've just taken him at face value. But right now she didn't know how the hell to feel about Zane Whelan. Not even when he was in his sweatpants.

"I don't think you should," Mona said, folding her arms. "No, you shouldn't. Full stop."

But whatever Bailey did feel, she wanted it to be more than what Mona felt. "Let's do it," she said quickly and then tried not to worry about what she'd gotten herself into. "Let's mix ourselves a proper Long Island."

Zane's face broke out into the crazy, contagious grin that made Bailey smile, made her feel proud and a little special. "That's what I like to hear," he said. "I'll start measuring ingredients. Mona, there's a special glass I keep in the top cabinet. Bailey, I've got some lemons in the fridge. Grab one, slice it, and shave off a few twists. There's no way we're making a Long Island without a garnish. And Bucket—"

Bucket sat up, eyes filled with hope.

Zane stopped. "Actually, I'm so used to having only three people, there's kind of not anything for you to do. Uh, you can handle the music."

Gravely the Canadian drew his phone from the pocket of his biker jacket and held it aloft like a battle standard. "This is why God put me on this earth."

Zane pulled out a collection of tiny old bottles. Each shape was radically different: one was round as a teakettle; one so thin it looked as if it barely held a needle, let alone a dram of vodka; one curved into a loop and stopped with a cork. Apparently he'd been collecting them for a while. Carefully, as if they contained nitroglycerin, he poured the contents into special brass jiggers.

Mona retrieved the glass: a highball, plain in design but with a particular curvature to the sides. She washed it so clean that it looked invisible in her hands.

Bailey found a cutting board and laid waste to two lemons, giving Zane every kind of option for slice size and shape, as well as peels for garnish.

With a few flicks of his thumb, Bucket filled the apartment with appropriately ominous punk rock. Over machine-gun drums and a tight spiky guitar, a singer wailed about digging up the bones of his lost love. Satisfied with the atmosphere, Bucket picked up a towel and polished the bar, lifting each bottle Zane had set down.

Bailey took a plate and spent a moment arranging her peels and slices. It probably didn't matter, but it made the task feel more like a proper arcane ritual. She figured that if she was investing in magic, she might as well go for broke. Admitting it to herself untangled a knot of unease. They were going to do it, goddammit, and she was going to help them. She wasn't a tech millionaire at twenty-two, but she'd be part of the dev team responsible for a historic and delicious mystical breakthrough. Only she probably couldn't put that on a résumé.

The three Alechemists brought together their collective effort. On the space Bucket had prepared, Mona placed the glass filled with ice cubes. She didn't have Zane's or Bucket's fervor or Bailey's nervous excitement, but she moved with the same decisiveness she'd had last night, when she'd taken on the last tremens by herself.

Wait, holy shit, that happened, Bailey thought. But before she could explore the memory in greater depth, Zane nodded for her to approach. She placed the plate of garnishes next to the glass, then out of instinct gave the bar a reverential nod before stepping back. She could've laughed. She was a barback again. It didn't matter. Maybe it was their group enthusiasm, or maybe just Bucket's choice in music, but she felt something palpably electric.

When Zane saw that everything was in order, he nodded. In turn he reached for each jigger and poured the contents into the glass. The ice cracked and shifted. Eyes blazing, he intoned:

"Vodka, from potato stilled
Gin, from juniper bush milled
Rum, from cold, dark cask of steel
Tequila, from—"

"Does the chant do anything?" Bailey whispered to Bucket. She'd never needed to chant over a cocktail.

"No," said Bucket. "But pretty cool, though, eh?"

Zane layered in the triple sec, the lemon juice, and a sweetener called gomme syrup. The mixture was still transparent, albeit a little yellow from the lemon juice. Apparently it was going well because triumph was written all over Zane's face as he threw in the last liquid ingredient, a splash of cola, which stained the glass a soft brown. He caught Bailey's eye, and they shared giddy grins that said, *Holy shit, we're doing this.*

He inserted an old-timey straw: straight and white, with a thin red stripe spiraling like a candy cane. He stirred seven times counterclockwise, then once clockwise, before releasing it. The liquid swept the straw around the glass rim before it came to a rest. Then, with a nod of thanks to Bailey, Zane selected a long twist of lemon peel and carefully slid it into the glass.

No one breathed as they waited for the telltale glow.

All four of them jerked forward as a light sparked inside the liquid. It died, but less than a second later another light popped in and out. And then a third, as if the drink harbored a cigarette lighter refusing to catch.

The Long Island iced tea lit up for a seventh time, then guttered again. This time there was no spark.

Zane's hands fell to his sides. "No," he breathed.

Bailey's heart broke. All the artifices of manliness had fallen away, and he looked more than ever like the boy who'd been her friend. She wanted to throw her arms around him, even if it was awkward, just so he wouldn't be standing there alone and crestfallen. "Zane …"

He seemed not to have heard her. "I was so close." The goth punk music, so fitting a moment ago, now seemed to mock his sadness.

"Yes," said Mona, stepping forward. "Closer than anyone has ever come since the last time someone succeeded." For once Bailey could read her: Mona hadn't expected it to work, but she hadn't expected it to be nearly as successful as it was. She looked, for the first time, rattled.

"I was so close!" Zane pounded a fist on the table. The drink shook but didn't spill.

Bailey nudged Bucket. He spread his arms helplessly—*And what should I say, exactly?*—so Bailey took a deep breath and gave it a shot.

"It's okay. I mean, it's not *okay*," she said, putting up her hands defensively. "But you still have your eyes. You still have your mind. If you got this close, the next time will be closer. The next time will be *it*."

"What next time?" Zane said. "I had a single shot of LaRue's private stock. That's a chance I'll never get again, and I fucking blew it." He really was like a teenager again—enraged and sullen at the same time—and she was the grown-up, sensible but with no idea how to end the exchange nicely.

"You found some once, you can do it again," she said. She'd thought it sounded good, but Bucket gave her a tiny but violent shake of the head. She decided to take his advice and change tack. "Besides," she said, "the important thing isn't the Long Island iced tea. Bartending is about protecting Chicago from deliriums or whatever else is happening. It's about service."

"Bailey, you don't know the first thing about bartending," Zane said. "You've been doing this for, like, a month, and for once I actually know more about something than you do. So no offense, but shut up."

The words hit her like a slap.

Zane's face fell. "Wait, I—"

"No," Bailey said, her voice as calm and unwavering as she could make it.

"I didn't—I'm just—you have no idea how frustrating—" He paced, glancing from Bailey to the drink on the table while Bucket and Mona stood silent on either side.

"No," Bailey said again, "you're right. I don't know what I'm talking about. I'll shut up."

"Bailey." Zane's voice was practically pleading. "Don't—"

"She *doesn't* know what she's talking about," Mona said, arms folded and eyes cold. "I've been doing this a long, long time. Longer than any of you and certainly longer than *her*."

That was ridiculous. Granted, Bailey had no idea how old Mona was—it was hard to guess when you didn't have a four-year academic paradigm to fall back on—but she didn't look that much older.

"Don't talk about me that way," Bailey snapped. "I'm right here."

Bucket stepped back as far as he could. Zane stared blankly at the floor—with Mona's hand on his shoulder.

"Well, then," Mona said coolly, "maybe you shouldn't be."

Two minutes later Bailey hit the sidewalk and stomped toward home. She was unshowered, stringy haired, wearing smeared make-up and clothes covered in garbage. Everyone she passed, even the dogs out for a walk, gave her wide berth.

Something buzzed in her purse. Bailey swore and dug around for her phone without breaking stride. She heard it clattering but of course couldn't find the damn thing. If it was her parents, she wouldn't answer. If it was Zane, she would answer and unload invective so blistering it would set his ears on fire.

But when she finally unearthed the phone, the screen said JESS.

"Bailey Chen!" a cheerful and familiar voice crackled. "What it is, girl?"

"Um, fine," Bailey said, scrambling to flip on her brain's small-talk switch. "Fine. It is . . . just . . . fine."

"Right on," said Jess. "So I know this is *super* late, and out of the blue, and on a weekend and stuff, but I just wanted to know: what're you up to this Monday?"

"You mean for, um ..." Bailey struggled to remember what normal people did to socialize. "Drinks?"

"No, dummy. To come in for your sit-down."

"My what?"

"Your interview! At Divinyl!"

Bailey looked back over her shoulder at the distant apartment building. It wasn't a bar, and it wasn't Zane. But it was symbolic enough.

She cradled the phone on her shoulder and flipped off that symbol with both hands.

"As it happens," Bailey said, "I'm free all day. When should I come in?"

CHAPTER ELEVEN

Divinyl's offices were in the beating heart that was Chicago's famous Loop, a district named for the aboveground train lines that encircled the block inside Lake, Van Buren, Wabash, and Wells. Bailey rode in on Ravenswood's own train, the Brown Line, which she'd always thought of as her line. Whenever she'd wanted to venture outside the neighborhood, the Brown Line was always her first step. She'd never ridden it like this, though. Back in the day, she and her friends had been just another group of loud kids swinging on poles, jumping from seat to seat, and generally annoying the commuters. Today *she* was the commuter.

Bailey wore a blue pantsuit, matching heels, and her hair in a tight bun. She looked, in other words, sharp as hell. Total corporate villainess. Inside her purse she was toting twenty fresh copies of her résumé, ready to pass them out like candy the second she got through the front doors. She was a Spartan girded for battle. She was ready.

Get used to this commute, she told herself, glancing around the quiet train car. *Play your cards right, and you'll live to see the day you get bored of it.*

She'd given herself enough time to find the building without rushing, and security was helpful in pointing the way.

"Oh, yeah," said the desk attendant, "I've been up there. Cool office." She eyed Bailey's outfit. "You with the IRS or something?"

"What?" Bailey frowned. "No, why?"

The woman shrugged. "No reason. Go on ahead to the elevators. Eighteenth floor."

Well, that was . . . whatever. Bailey put the exchange out of her mind and tried to focus. This was her life now. This was what she was born to do. Not cutting lime wedges or salting margarita rims. *Business.* Spreadsheets, accounts payable, profit margins, spreadsheets . . .

Okay, so she wasn't even sure what her role at Divinyl would be. But she was showing up, and that was, according to a poster from the UPenn career office, half the battle. (The poster had also featured, for reasons Bailey never quite divined, an eagle winging its way across a rainbow.)

Right off the elevator she got a good vibe. Instead of the austere white or beige or eggshell paint in most offices, Divinyl's lobby walls were covered with, well, covers. Album art spanning six decades of pop culture had been jigsawed into a giant mosaic, connected by stylized vines, chains, and wires. At the center of each wall, like a red island in the swirl, was one of the four stars of Chicago's flag.

"Isn't it just the coolest?" A young woman sidled up. "They commissioned Logik—you know, the graffiti artist?—to do the lobby. We think it's a good way to let people know what we're about. If they're into it, we'll be into them. And if they're not, at least it's close to the elevator, right? And also," she added, finally taking a breath, "hi!"

Like Zane, Jess had changed since high school, but not nearly as much. She still had the same honey-blond hair—cut into an aggressively angular bob—and the same Easter-egg-colored wardrobe. Only two things stuck out to Bailey. The first was that in the four-year interim, Jess had adopted a pair of retro glasses that gave her a mischievous, catlike air. The second was that despite working for a firm powerful enough to change the way people listened to music, she wasn't dressed like a corporate player. She rocked a bright pink T-shirt with Divinyl's logo splashed across the chest, plus a skirt and sneakers. No wonder the security guard thought Bailey was there to audit them. Next to Jess's casual-casual ensemble, Bailey's sensible, graduation present pantsuit felt like full-plate armor.

Ignoring the hand Bailey had stuck out, Jess dove in for a hug. Bailey cringed but reciprocated. She much preferred to reserve hugging for the people who really mattered, but in the last few years society had decided that brief embraces were the best way to greet everyone everywhere.

A dude would never have to hug his interviewer, Bailey thought and then immediately chastised herself. *Get over yourself. You need something from her. And you kind of liked her once, right?*

Right.

Just try not to look so awkward.

"It is *so* good to see you again," Jess said, stepping back.

"You, too!" Bailey said through a forced smile. In school Jess had been, effectively, Bailey's competition, although the feeling had never been mutual. Bailey got better grades thanks to an endless supply of Post-its, flash cards, and instant coffee, but somehow Jess breezily kept up in every class with a fraction of the effort. She'd ended up at Northwestern—not Ivy League, like Bailey, but still pretty damn good. And now Jess—the one who'd never pulled an all-nighter, who'd slept through a semester's worth of English lectures and still got extra credit for writing a rap song based on *Julius Caesar*—was the one with the job.

"And I love your outfit!" Jess looked Bailey up and down. "You look like such a grown-up. Like you're running for election or something."

"Thanks," Bailey said.

"I'd vote for you." Jess winked. "Let's head back to my office, huh?"

They rounded the corner and emerged into the kind of space that Bailey imagined an overzealous tour guide might introduce as "where the magic happens."

"And *this*"—Jess gestured grandly—"is where the magic happens."

"Oh," Bailey said politely. "Um, I can tell."

The space was gigantic, with thirty-foot ceilings, windowed walls, and impossibly huge square footage. Instead of a cubicle labyrinth, it held every kind of workstation imaginable. Some employees sat at desks—in chairs or balanced on exercise balls. Some had settled on the floor, typing away at laptops as overstuffed beanbag chairs swallowed them inch by inch. There was even one guy off to the side who was coding while pedaling away on a stationary bike.

"We're big into personalized workspaces here," said Jess. "Once we hire someone on, we have them put in a request for what they need to be comfortable. As long as it won't kill the work flow, management will sign off on it."

Bailey realized she was grinning—not her precise, professional grin, but the toothy, goofy one a kid got when she walked into an ice cream shop. "What if I want a cubicle?" she said.

Jess chuckled. "A rebel, huh? We're not big on following the rules, but maybe we can make an exception. Hey, Kyle, come over here."

A slouchy guy in a knit cap walked over and gave Bailey a once-over; she stood as straight as she could without wobbling in her heels.

"This is Bailey," Jess said. "She's going in for Alexis's old gig."

"Alexis left?"

"She went full-time doula."

"Oh. Right on, right on." Kyle nodded rhythmically, like he was listening to a song no one but he could hear.

"I love Divinyl," Bailey said quickly. "I listen to—er, with it all the time."

"Right on," Kyle said again.

Bailey cocked her head. "Are you an engineer?"

Kyle laughed. "Nah. Tastemaker, brah."

"Ah," Bailey said. Was that a job title?

"You know," he continued, head still bobbing, "spreading the word, making the waves."

"Right," Bailey said. "Cool."

"That's what we do out of the Chicago office," said Jess. "Dev stuff is mostly out in Esseff."

"Oh. Is that in the suburbs?"

Jess and Kyle exchanged a look.

"SF," Kyle said. "Like, San Francisco."

"Of course." Bailey flushed. Stupid, stupid. She should've known better; her parents were from *Esseff*. But she was determined to bounce back. "What's your favorite part about working here, Kyle?"

"Probably . . ." Kyle considered. Whatever it was—the product, the teamwork, the management style—Bailey readied herself to nod eagerly.

"Spicy lunch club," he said finally.

"Oh, I *love*—" Bailey faltered. "What?"

"A bunch of us order lunch and see who can get the spiciest thing. This one time, Emily? She got a ghost pepper burrito and spent the afternoon crying under her desk."

"Fuck you, Kyle," called someone a few desks away. Kyle shrugged.

"Oh. That sounds great!" Bailey said, trying not to sound too forced. "Um, lunch is my favorite part of the day, too."

It was, actually, but she still felt weird saying so during what was technically a job interview.

Kyle stifled a laugh. "Cool to meet you, Hayley. Want a T-shirt?"

Something soft and gray smacked her in the face before she could answer.

"It's Bailey."

"Yeah. Those shirts are dope," Jess said. "They make them from that really soft Mexican cotton, you know? Here, check out the kitchen."

Bailey balled up the shirt and stuffed it into her purse while following Jess around another corner. In her limited professional experience, an office "kitchen" was rarely more than a fridge, coffeemaker, and microwave with a permanent garlic smell. But the cavernous fishbowl room to their right had an espresso machine, two stainless-steel refrigerators, and a six-burner oven/stove that someone was currently using to bake a pan of mac and cheese.

"Bowie says—wait, do you know Bowie?" Jess wrinkled her forehead. "Bowen Sorensen, I mean."

Bailey nodded eagerly.

"Sorensen's the VC"—venture capitalist, Bailey was already speaking the slang (she resisted giving herself a high-five)—"with an eighty percent stake in the company. He revitalized the flagging beeper industry in the late nineties with his idea to sell them to chain restaurants for table reservations and then broke into the app market with Fontdue, which allows users to render their outgoing correspondence in customized fonts. Since then he's taken both calculated risks and leaps of faith on investments and built a miniature empire in the telecommunications and mobile software business."

Jess's eyes widened. "Whoa. Someone did her homework."

Bailey grinned. She'd made flash cards.

"Fab," Jess said. "Anyway, he says happy employees are productive employees. If happiness means being able to cook yourself shrimp scampi for lunch, he's all for it. Sometimes when we have to stay late, he'll get a guy to come by and do a whole hibachi thing." She mimed chopping meat on a grill and tossing it in the air.

"Does Mr. Sorensen work out of the Chicago office?" Bailey asked.

Jess blinked. "Yeah, sometimes. Right now he's in Belgrade. Or Belarus. Which one has that offshore tax exclusion thing?"

Bailey barely had time to shrug.

"Anyway, he'll be back soon. He wants to build a movie theater here that shows nothing but kaiju cinema." She did a little fake Godzilla stomp, then frowned. "Assuming that whole women's arena-football thing doesn't fall through. Hang on." She whipped out a phone, furiously thumbed out a message, then stuffed it back in her pocket with a smile. "Sorry about that."

"It's okay," Bailey said. The sooner they could slip into the routine of questions and answers, the sooner she'd feel at ease. "I don't need the hard sell. You can just go ahead and start, uh, interviewing me—"

"Interview. Right." Jess laughed huskily. "Cute. Want to step into my office?"

"What is it, a pillow fort?" said Bailey.

Jess laughed. "Oh, man," she said. "You're gonna fit right in."

The rest of the journey to Jess's office became an informal tour. There was the game room, where techs went to unwind because company policy mandated they spend time away from their desks to avoid burnout. And there was the records station, which allowed employees to transfer digital music onto vinyl discs, a casual undoing of two decades' worth of technological progress.

The farther they went, the more impressed Bailey grew. In her most recent workplaces the sole amenities were the huge collection of booze she wasn't allowed to drink and a bathroom that may or may not have breathable air, depending on the night. "I'm surprised you don't have a place for live music," she said as they rounded yet another corner.

"Ooh!" Again Jess's phone appeared like mag—well, not like

magic, but very quickly. A moment later she put it away and beamed. "I just texted management. Someone will start looking into it tomorrow. Here we are."

Bailey didn't know what incited more jealousy: how nicely put together Jess's office was or the fact that she had an actual office. Apparently Jess had gotten very into upcycling; almost everything in the room was made from used wooden pallets painted in pastel colors. Bailey secretly loved clicking through DIY projects online, but Jess actually Did Them Herself.

As they took seats on opposite sides of a seafoam-colored desk, Bailey tried to hand over a résumé, but Jess waved it off. "I've got it here," she said, holding up a tablet. *Of course.* This was the future, after all. Self-consciously Bailey undid one jacket button in a last-ditch attempt to casual it up.

Jess set aside the tablet without reading it. "So what've you been up to, girl? I heard you kicked ass at Penn. What brought you back? Did you get tired of eating cheesesteaks and running up all those library steps so you could punch the Liberty Bell?"

Bailey didn't know whether to answer or correct Jess's wild misconceptions about Philadelphia. "Well, they're museum steps," she said.

"Right," said Jess. "I guess it makes more sense to have the Liberty Bell at a museum than a library."

"Actually—"

"And what've you been up to?" Jess plowed on. "I know it took me forever to get back to you—once again, so sorry about that—but what's been going on in Bailey world? Just being cool, doing Bailey things?"

"Oh, you know—" *Killing monsters. Secretly protecting the city. Madly crushing on Zane Whelan of all people. Getting magic lessons from the hulking blind anarchist who runs a gay bar.* "—stuff."

"Cool, cool, cool," Jess said. "So, let me walk you through the major details of this job first, and then we can get to your questions, okay?"

The job was nothing groundbreaking. If hired, she'd start out doing administrative work in the firm's finance department: scheduling, copies, logistics, research.

"Oh, and spreadsheets. Can you make a spreadsheet?"

Nailed it. "Absolutely."

"Excellent." Jess beamed. "It was so, so, *so* nice to catch up, Bailey. Really. Hey, wow, did you realize your name almost rhymes with *really*?"

"Nope," Bailey said. *Because it doesn't?* Then again, this was the girl who'd rhymed "Ides of March" with "That's way harsh."

Jess grabbed her buzzing phone off the desk. She read the message and then looked at Bailey. "Good news," she said.

Bailey's heart swelled. They were going to hire her on the spot. This was a tech start-up after all; things moved fast. Maybe amid all the reconstituted driftwood and bare Edison bulbs, there was a CCTV camera beaming her top-notch interview to the Powers That Be. Maybe Bailey was about to be officially done with bars and bartending forever.

"You can come with us to the bar!" Jess said.

"Thank you s—what?" Bailey frowned.

"Brian's canceling on our wristband deal, so we've got a spot open," Jess explained. "You're totally in, right?"

Wristband deals were the only way around the quirky Illinois drinking law that prohibited happy hours: drink prices couldn't go down (nor could their potency go up) based on time of purchase. But if a big enough group bought special wristbands in advance, they could get discounted drinks for a few hours because it was part of a "private promotion," rather than an all comers' happy hour.

"Oh," Bailey said. "I mean, um, totally!"

That was how Bailey, Jess, and thirteen other Divinyl staff

members ended up packing into McNee's, a pub in the South Loop that was exactly what Bailey would have expected from a joint with an Irish name: dark wood everything, shamrocks posted up all over the place, and absolutely no traces of genuine Irish culture. There were huge banners of bikini-clad women, smiling and holding up cans of light beer against the backdrop of the Rocky Mountains. *That's not very smart,* Bailey thought, *drinking something cold while near naked in a frozen wasteland.* Then she remembered the target audience was probably unconcerned with being very smart.

Each group member wore a bright orange wristband, tagged like an animal to be tracked. "Look," Jess said, holding up hers. "Orange. Your favorite color, right?"

"Uh, yes." Bailey couldn't believe Jess remembered; she'd never embraced the hue with quite the same extravagance as Jess had loved pink.

"What'll it be, everyone?" The waitress appeared at their table, and Bailey realized it'd been months since she'd ordered in a bar like a normal person.

"Lager," said one of the Divinyl guys.

"Yeah, lager."

"Lager."

"Lager for me," said Jess with a nod. "Bailey?"

"Uh, I'll take a chimayó," Bailey said. The waitress dutifully wrote down the order, but the Divinyl guys looked at her as if she'd just ordered a glass of human blood.

"Is that one of those girlie cocktails?" one said. "I bet it's pink."

"Actually, it's an apple-based tequila cocktail," Bailey shot back. *Which lets you astrally project your consciousness, if you make it right.* "And I happen to be quite fond of it, so there."

"Ooh, on second thought, I'll take one of those, too," said Jess.

After ten minutes of shop talk, office gossip, and Bailey politely sipping at her ice water, the waitress returned with their drinks.

Bailey perked up and said "Thank you" when she got her glass, but the Divinyl guys were silent except for grunts and a shared annoyed but knowing look. The waitress started to head off, but one of the guys—Kyle, from before—threw a hand into the air and snapped his fingers.

Mortified, Bailey gripped her drink. She heard Vincent's voice in her head: *If a guy snapped his fingers at me, I'd snap his fingers off.*

"Hey," she said to Kyle, "can you not do that, please? She's got a lot of tables to get to. She'll be here soon."

Clear across the floor, the waitress saw him, adopted what anyone in the service industry would recognize as a gunpoint smile, and headed back over.

"What?" Kyle said. "I'm doing her a favor. If she doesn't serve us fast, she's not getting tipped."

Not tipping. Unfathomable. Monstrous. "You can't just *not tip,*" Bailey said, sipping at the surface of her chimayó. "She needs that money."

"Then she can earn it," said a scruffy-looking guy sitting to Kyle's left. Bailey recognized him as the one who'd been working on the stationary bike. "He just snapped at her. It's not that big a deal. Also, who are you again?"

"Bailey's an old friend," Jess said, "and we were looking very seriously at adding her to the team. I think it's great she's so, uh, service oriented?" She flashed Bailey a warning look: *I get it, and I'm sorry these guys are assholes,* it said, *but don't push this any further.* At least that was how Bailey read it.

The waitress reappeared. "Sorry," she said, rictus smile still in place. "We're just a little busy right now. What can I do for you guys?"

"We're just dying of thirst over here," said the only other girl in their party. "Can we get some more water?"

"And a round of Jägerbombs!" added Kyle, whose light-light-beer was already almost empty. Their companions whooped approval.

Bailey did not. When the waitress left, she got up. "I'm just going to . . . the bathroom."

"Oh, cool," said Jess, standing, too. "I'll come with you."

"Oh, um, great." *Great.*

As they pushed through the crowd, Jess said, "Don't let them get to you, okay? Boys are dumb. Except the cute ones. I mean, they're still dumb, but it's not as bad because they're cute."

"Sure." Bailey shook her head, distracted. How did people think this behavior was okay? No, that was an easy one: they were dumb, like Jess said. But Bailey had done a lot of dumb things in her life. How many times had she been careless when talking to Zane? Or her dad, a shopkeeper? How many times had she mindlessly complained about the service at a restaurant when her overworked waiter was within earshot?

She stopped beside a giant neon shamrock with the slogan "Erin Go Braless" tastefully spelled beneath. "Actually," she said, "I think I'm going to head to the bar for a sec and grab a shot. I'll, uh, check on how our drinks are coming. See you at the table?"

"Sure!" Jess said, brightening. "Order me another of those tequila things you're having. I'm so into apples right now."

Bailey nodded and then threaded her way through the thick crowd of off-duty professionals, one of the few situations in life where her small size was useful. (The rest of the time it was just a parade of high shelves designed to mock her or hilarious people using her as an armrest and thinking they were the first person ever to do so.) She burst through a forest of blazer-coated shoulders and elbows to seize a scrap of barside real estate. Leaning up, she looked left and saw only a barback hurrying away with a stack of dirty glasses. She looked right and saw someone familiar standing two feet in front of her.

"Hello, Bailey," Mona said.

The Chimayó

A libation to extend consciousness's reach

1. *Pour one and a half ounces of tequila into an iced highball glass.*

2. *Add one ounce of apple cider and a quarter ounce apiece of lemon juice and crème de cassis.*

3. *Stir once, garnish with an apple slice, and serve.*

Much like the martini, the chimayó produces passive effects that render it unpopular for fieldwork. Indeed, astral projection does not immediately lend itself to the eradication of tremens and the protection of human life. Nonetheless, separating one's consciousness from the body has dozens of practical applications, which will doubtlessly be added to subsequent editions of this book when someone thinks of them.

The chimayó is named for Chimayó, New Mexico, the small apple-growing town in which it first was mixed. Though pre-Blackout documents suggest the existence of a cocktail with similar effects, the modern chimayó wasn't perfected and codified until the 1960s. It came about in a similar manner to many other great mixological breakthroughs: by taking whatever was at hand and mixing it with booze until the results were palatable.

TEQUILA.

FIG. 47—Tequila was named a *Pueblo Mágico* ("Magical Town")
by the Mexican federal government.

The national liquor of Mexico, this agave-derived distillate
(named for the city of Tequila, whose name comes from the
Nahuatl word for "place of tribute") is by nature a projective
force, and its presence in cocktails encourages like effects.
Although the world knows this from a mostly vomitative perspective, savvy bartenders appreciate the edge that a properly made tequila drink may grant in an otherwise impossible
situation.

Tequila comes with a high historical pedigree; its distillation has been patronized by the Spanish throne since the
seventeenth century. But its clout and power come with a degree of volatility. As such, its popularity tends to vacillate relative to the mood of regional Cupbearers Courts. Conservative
Courts frown upon the spirit because of the havoc it's been
known to cause, whereas more experimental-minded Courts
encourage its use for precisely the same reason.

CRÈME DE CASSIS.

A black currant liqueur native to France. While liquors go through some manner of aging process, liqueurs are usually bottled and sold soon after being mixed. This relative youth renders them less potent, making them unfit as a base ingredient for a cocktail, which of course has not discouraged bartenders from trying. Vivienne Vandenberg, a celebrated Dutch bartender from the early twentieth century, fed her famous coffee addiction by attempting to reinvent many standard cocktails using coffee liqueur. In her time she successfully invented other major cocktails (see *WHITE RUSSIAN*), but ultimately she met her end attempting to take on a tremens when armed with a cocktail that, upon postmortem inspection, was found to be merely a glass of pure coffee liqueur.

FIG. 48—*Ribes nigrum.*

CHAPTER TWELVE

Bailey stifled a squawk and nearly tripped over a nearby stool. "Mona," she said, "I thought you worked in Humboldt Park."

Mona shrugged. "I work where I'm needed. Do *you* need me, Bailey?"

"No," Bailey said but then corrected herself as Mona started to turn away. "I mean, yes. I'd like a shot of bourbon, please." Determined to make up for her companions' karmic debt, she kept her manners impeccable.

Mona poured a shot and slid it over. "When you're done, join me outside for a smoke break."

Bailey nearly dropped her shot. "What?" she said, casting a glance at a nearby window. It was still light outside, if only barely. There would be no tremens activity as long as the sun was up. "Now?"

"Not now. In a few seconds, when you finish your shot. And not *that* kind of smoke break." Mona pulled a pack of cigarettes from her pocket. "See you outside."

The well whiskey still burned in Bailey's mouth a minute later when she and Mona stepped into the back alley. It was classic Chicago: Dumpsters lining the brick walls, asphalt that always seemed to have puddles even though it hadn't recently rained, and black iron fire escapes that had likely seen more use as make-out spots for rebellious teenagers.

They rounded the corner of the alley and leaned against the wall of McNee's. Mona tapped out a cigarette.

"Uh, I know it's a cliché," Bailey said as Mona sparked her lighter and leaned into the flame, "but those things will kill you."

"No, they won't." Mona took her first drag and exhaled blue-gray smoke.

"Okay, then complications caused by a malignant tumor growing in your lungs will kill you."

"No, they won't," Mona repeated. She sounded matter-of-fact, as if she had simply decided not to get cancer. "You're probably wondering why I left behind a rush to talk to you."

"Um," Bailey said, "yup."

Mona exhaled more smoke, then cocked her head. "You're dressed very nicely today."

"Uh, thank you?" Bailey said. She cast around for an excuse. "My friend invited me because she needed a fifteenth for the wristband deal. She told me it was a work thing, so I dressed up to fit in. I didn't realize her job was so . . . casual."

Nice work, me. Bailey wished she could high-five herself. Not only was the lie perfectly plausible, but every word was technically true.

"So that's why I'm here," Bailey said, unable to quit while she was ahead. "I guess you wanted to, uh, talk about that but—"

"I want to talk about Saturday morning." Mona flicked ash to the damp ground. "About Zane, and you, and what you said about the Nightshade."

"Oh."

Bailey would've been floored if not for the icky floor. Mona was talking about the Fight. It was one of the most important events, if not *the* most, of Bailey's and Zane's friendship. It was in fact the reason Bailey and Zane were *just* friends, and sometimes barely friends at that. How on earth had he never mentioned it to his girlfriend?

"I've asked him," Mona said, as if she could read Bailey's mind. "He wouldn't elaborate."

"So you're asking me?"

"I'll like your answer more."

Bailey bit her lip. She wasn't proud of that moment in her life at all, and especially now she hated revisiting it. But Bailey had definitely wronged Mona when she'd kissed Zane, so she owed her the truth. Or some of the truth. Mona didn't need to know the real reason Bailey had been bounced to Long & Strong, but a frank account of the Fight would balance the scales.

Right?

"So," Bailey said, "Zane and I have been friends basically since we were born. We grew up together and played together and taught each other about music and stuff."

"The loud band," Mona said impassively.

"For Dear Life is one of the best third-wave pop punk—okay, anyway." Bailey cleared her throat. "Point being, I guess I always kind of wondered, you know, why he never seemed to go after any girls. I mean, I figured out early on he wasn't gay." She shuddered, recalling the one time she'd accidentally uncovered the search history on his laptop. "And yeah, a lot of the girls at our school kind of sucked, but not all of them did. So I didn't get it."

Mona nodded. "Because you were missing the obvious answer."

Bailey's mouth twisted as if she'd just tasted something bitter. "Luke Perez's graduation party. It was Zane and me and a lot of cheap beer we couldn't really handle, and we, you know—" She didn't really know how to phrase it tactfully for the ears of the guy's girlfriend.

"Fucked," Mona said helpfully.

Bailey blushed. She knew that she, a feminist woman of the twenty-first century, probably shouldn't be so precious about blunt mentions of sexuality, but still, ugh. "Um, yes," she said after a moment. "And after—" She hesitated. This was the part of the story that was impossible to spin in her favor. "Zane said he'd been waiting all his life for me to notice him and told me he'd be working in the Nightshade, and the money he got would help him fly out to Philly to visit me a couple times a year. He had it all worked out."

"But?" said Mona.

"I told him—" A sick feeling rose in the back of Bailey's throat as she remembered what came next. "I told him the bar was trashy. I told him I was going away and there wasn't any point. Basically I told him he wasn't good enough for me. And until a month and a half ago that was the last time I talked to my best friend."

For a long moment Mona merely stood there, leaning against the wall and smoking her cigarette.

"I'm a totally different person now," Bailey said hastily. "I realize how stupid and elitist and mean that was, and I know I didn't have any fucking clue what I was talking about. If I could take it all back, I would. I totally would. And I'd kick my own ass, too, just to make the lesson stick."

"And you didn't—" Mona stopped short. "That's all he told you about the bar? That he was working to save money? Nothing else?"

"I . . . yeah."

Mona stomped out her cigarette. "I like you, Chen. And I like the truth. So I'm giving you a gift in kind."

"You—what?" Bailey clamped her mouth shut and shook her head. "I mean, um, I like you, too?" It was kind of true, in the sense that she was too creeped out and/or terrified of Mona to dream of saying otherwise. "What are you going to give me?"

"The truth," Mona said simply. "The truth is that you were right to stay away from the Whelan bars. Don't go back. Not even if—"

Someone screamed.

Mona instantly headed back into the alley. Bailey whipped around and followed her. They saw the waitress standing frozen, holding a bag of garbage, cornered between the wall and the Dumpster by something squat and fleshy and evil.

"Tremens," Mona said.

"What?" Bailey gaped. Impossible. It was still daytime and the sunlight stretched up to the bar's back door, shining on the creature's ugly exposed muscle skin.

Mona leapt forward and kicked the tremens in its side.

"Angie, get inside!" she yelled. "Chen! Get in there and mix me something."

The waitress screamed again, dropped the garbage, and bolted for the door.

"But this can't—" Bailey started to say. Again Mona kicked it, but the thing made an ugly snarling sound and latched on to her boot. She shook it off, hard enough to slam it against the Dumpster.

"Now! Anything! Please!"

It was the *please* that did it. Mona could kick ass—probably could bruise up that tremens pretty well—but if she was going to kill it, she needed magic. And Bailey could help her.

Inside, Bailey pushed through the crowd, ignoring the *hey*s and *what the hell*s, just shoving blindly until she got to the bar. Angie was hovering at the end, looking terrified, and Bailey took the opportunity to wedge her way behind to the bottles and glasses.

"It's for Mona," she said shortly, and started pulling together the first recipe that came to mind: Vodka. Orange juice. Ice. The one thing she knew she could make without even trying. As soon as the glasses started to glow, Bailey downed her screwdriver in a single gulp, then jerked open the lift-up bar and booked it for the back entrance. When she flung open the door, she didn't see Mona.

"Mona!"

She was flat on the ground, pinned by two tentacles, her face twisted in pain as a sickening mouth opened above her. Bailey reacted before she realized what she was doing.

"Get off her!"

With her superpowered arm, she pitched the second screwdriver as hard as she could at the tremens's head. The glass glanced off its stubby face and smashed on the asphalt in a shower of citrus and ice—not enough to kill it but enough to distract it.

"Do it!" Mona yelled, pushing it off. "Now!"

"Do what?"

"*Something!*" Mona had wrestled the tremens onto the shards and was grinding it down as hard as she could. "Just do it now!"

"Okay! Um, okay!"

Panic clutched Bailey's chest—*whatdoIdowhatdoIdo*—and then she got an idea.

"Move!"

A two-foot running start was all she needed. Bailey booked it for the middle of the alley, superstrong legs propelling her with impossible force, just as Mona released the tremens from her half nelson. As soon as she did, Bailey jumped.

With a vicious *crunch,* Bailey landed on the beast, heels first. Her shoes—her sensible, expensive, no-nonsense business-lady shoes—gouged it right between the eyes. Liquid gushed.

"Are you okay?" Bailey took a squelching step out of what used to be the tremens and what used to be her shoes.

"I'm fine." Panting, Mona pushed herself up. "I don't get hurt. But you . . ." She stared. "Not bad for a *tite pichouette.*"

"A what?" It sounded French.

Mona shook her head. "You need to get out of here, Chen."

"Get out?" Bailey stared back at the puddle hissing around her ruined high heels. "But that was a *tremens.* In the *daylight.* The waitress saw it. This is serious. We have to tell Za—"

"You're not telling Zane," said Mona, "or Vincent. You'll go home and leave the rest to me."

"No way."

"I'm no fool, Chen," said Mona. "I know why you're here. Those people you were with—they were all wearing T-shirts with the same logo. That company that does the applicatives for your music phones."

"Well—" Bailey frowned. "Yeah."

"So tell anyone about what happened in this alley, and I'll ensure that the Court knows why you were here to witness it."

Bailey balked. "I just saved your life, you ungrateful—"

"*Chen.*" Unmoved, Mona stared her down. "I know you don't care for me. But you have to trust me."

And with that she opened the door, zipped past Bailey, and disappeared into the crowd.

Mint leaves, sugar, lime juice. Concentrating on details always helped.

Bang.

The door to Long & Strong flew open and Bailey jumped, but it was just Bucket returning from patrol, red cheeked from the night air but seemingly unharmed. She had spent her preshift Saturday drinking coffee and staying as alert as possible; now that she was up next for patrol, she was making herself a mojito—her ex-coworker Trina's favorite, which would give her the power to manipulate ambient water to her will—and her hands were shaking. From caffeine or from fear, she couldn't quite tell.

"Phew." Bucket staggered to the bar and mimed wiping sweat from his brow.

Bailey rolled her eyes, acting more relaxed than she felt. "You're fine."

Bucket perked up instantly. "Damn right I am. I found three tremens and made them into dead- . . . mens?" He grimaced. "Oof. Even Zane would not have gone for that one."

Bailey smirked. "You underestimate him."

"Probably. You ready for your turn?"

"Almost." Bailey dropped a mint sprig into the white mixture, but it wasn't glowing. "Dammit," she said under her breath.

"Everything okay?"

Bailey looked up. "Why? What happened?"

"Well, you put salt in your mojito, for one."

"Shit." Bailey dumped out the liquid and started over.

"Hey, it's okay. Happens to everyone. Also, like, crazy shit's been going on lately." Bucket grabbed a fresh lime, split it with a knife, and without even being asked, squeezed out a fresh measure of juice.

"Thanks," Bailey said. This time her mojito glowed.

Bucket shrugged. "Just looking out for a friend."

Friend. Bucket was maybe the first friend she'd made since returning to Chicago. "Actually," she said, "Bucket? I need to tell you something."

"Sure." Bucket scooped a loose strand into his mohawk, but it refused to stay put. "What's up?"

Bailey fiddled with a paper coaster. She'd been true to her word and hadn't breathed a word to Zane, but Bucket was different. Bucket was, after all, her friend.

"I saw one in the daytime," she blurted out.

His eyes widened. "What? Where? How?"

"With my eyes," Bailey said. "In the Loop the other day. I killed it but—"

"Yeah." His complexion turned arctic pale.

"You . . . believe me?"

"Uh, duh," Bucket said. "I mean, one, you were onto the delirium before anyone else even noticed, eh? And B, you've always got my back, so I trust you." He grinned weakly and Bailey felt better, demonic upsurge notwithstanding.

"Do you think it's got something to do with Halloween?" he added.

"I was thinking that, yeah," she said, poking her cocktail with a straw. "But that's still not for a week. It comes but once a year, right?"

"Right. Well. I guess we've just gotta keep doing the job, eh?" Bucket tried and failed again to smooth his hair to its full height. "You ready to take over? I'm gonna go make myself pretty before I start tending."

Bailey said "sure," but he wouldn't leave until she tagged him in, like they were wrestlers. When she finally slapped him five, he struck a dynamic pose, then practically skipped toward the bathroom.

She'd almost got the mojito to her lips when Vincent appeared at her side. "He made you do the wrestler thing, huh, kiddo?" he said.

Bailey put down her drink. "Yeah."

"And you saw a tremens pre-twilight."

She froze, remembering Mona's warning. *Ah,* a little voice in her head said. *But you didn't tell him. He told you.*

"I—yeah," she said. "I know I sound crazy but—"

Vincent interrupted with a wave of the hand. "You know what you sound like, kiddo?"

"What?"

"Someone who asks the right questions." Despite his blindness, Vincent had no problem navigating the back of the bar to fill the meager stream of orders. Granted, it was a slow night, but Bailey had seen sighted bartenders unable to keep up with demand. Hell, not too long ago she'd been one of them. "Been rolling it over in my head a bit. All this shit with the delirium. Got a theory, if you'll let me bend your ear."

"Should we wait for Bucket to come back?" she said.

Vincent shook his head. "Bucket's a good worker, but he's too tight with the Whelans for my liking."

Bailey nodded, then blushed as she realized her mistake. But Vincent was already smirking.

"You tried to nod, huh? And now you're blushing?"

"Okay, *how* could you know I'm blushing?"

"I didn't," said Vincent, "but that mental picture was funnier. So here's what I'm thinking. The way I figure, you gotta go at this scientifically. If the control is the way things have always been, then that means the variables are the tremens, the environment, and us. The tremens have remained constant, and so have we, at least as far as I can tell. That means the one variable in this experiment is the environment."

She cocked her head. On the floor, Poppy did the same thing.

"What, you're surprised I know the scientific method?" Vincent slid a freshly poured beer down the counter to a regular. "Just 'cause I'm a blind donkey working a bar doesn't mean I don't remember high school science, kiddo." He nodded down to his dog. "And thanks for the vote of confidence there, Poppy. Really feeling the love."

In response, Poppy stood on her hind legs, leaned against him, and energetically licked his hand.

Bailey weighed his words. "So what do you think caused the change, boss?"

"Told you I wasn't sure."

"Then hypothesize."

"You won't think it's some crackpot theory?"

She put a firm hand on his shoulder. "I would never."

"Okay." Vincent rubbed his jaw. "Those suckers want arcane energy, and they can't mix drinks with those stumpy legs of theirs, which makes sauced-up human souls—or animus, whatever you want to call 'em—the best source. But what if we *weren't* the best anymore?"

A patron flashed a hand from the end of the bar and Vincent grunted in response, scooping ice into a shaker.

"There's something I didn't tell you the other night. You know why I got blind?"

"Yes," she said without thinking. She regretted being so quick to answer, but he didn't seem fazed. "Home-distilled gin. It's more powerful but less stable than—"

"Not *how,*" Vincent said. "Why. Why I was distilling in the first place."

The answer slid into Bailey's mind, and it was so overwhelming and obvious that she barely dared say it louder than a whisper.

"Speak up, kiddo," he said. "Unless I'm going deaf now, too."

She cleared her throat. "The Long Island iced tea."

"Bingo." He rattled the cocktail shaker a few times. "I never got close enough to making the full thing, to be sure. But I got close enough to know that shit is *powerful.* And if I hadn't been too young and too dumb to fuck it up . . . " He poured the drink and slid the glass down the bar. "Let's just say that if you're old and too smart for your own good, and you've got the family name to keep this town under your thumb . . . " He shrugged his huge shoulders.

She stared. Zane wasn't old and he wasn't that smart. And he definitely didn't have infinite resources; otherwise he wouldn't have flipped out after using up Hortense LaRue's rum.

But maybe Zane wasn't the only Whelan with his eyes on the prize.

"Garrett," Bailey said. "Garrett's trying to make a Long Island iced tea."

"Yeah, His Royal Tininess Garrett." His expression turned ugly. "Guess when you're staring death in the face, you start to lose your grip on your principles a bit. Good thing I can't stare, huh, kiddo?"

He chuckled.

Her mind was two steps ahead. "And you think the tremens are attracted to the energy in a Long Island iced tea."

"It ain't no mojito, that's for sure," Vincent said, nodding at the glowing drink in Bailey's hand.

"How did you—"

Vincent tapped the side of his nose. "What, you think I just *guess* what's in all these bottles?"

"So you think the closer he gets, the more tremens appear." Bailey frowned. "But Garrett can't be distilling it himself. Where would he even find the space? Or the money?"

"I think a lot of things, kiddo," Vincent said. "But I *know* that whoever gets their hands on that power will also be the only one able to stop a full-blown delirium."

She shivered.

"All right," he said. "That's enough conspiracy theories for now. Drink your mojito before it gets warm, and go kick some eldritch ass."

Bailey did as she was told.

The Mojito

A concoction to assert dominance over elements aquatic

1. *Drop six mint leaves, a lump of sugar, and the juice of one lime into a Collins glass.*

2. *Muddle until the leaves are bruised and the sugar has dissolved.*

3. *Add two ounces of white rum and a splash of soda water.*

4. *Fill the glass with ice, garnish with a mint sprig and a slice of lime, and serve.*

The mojito is the signature drink of Cuba. The island's extensive coastline and large aquatic beast population give local bartenders little reason to serve anything else in the field. The preparation of a mojito is time-consuming endeavor, and its drinker requires a large source of water nearby in order to take full advantage of the aquatic affinity it grants. However, the mojito's advantages outweigh its faults: not only does it allow the drinker to control all forms of water, including ice and steam, but the mint leaves also leave a pleasant smell on one's breath.

WHITE RUM.

Fitting for its Caribbean roots, white rum is aged in steel drums. The metal barrels have an anomalous effect on their contents; though the process diminishes the rum's inherent power, it creates a product much more suitable for mixology (as opposed to dark rum, which must be coaxed into playing well with others).

The exact magical properties of steel barrels have remained a mystery since antiquity, though some bartenders have attempted research into the matter. Ángel Noriega, a bartender from Santiago de Cuba, once went so far as to have himself sealed into a barrel of white rum with an oxygen tank in the hope of observing the process. When his barrel was unsealed at the 1920 summit of the Organisation Européenne des Échansons et Sommeliers in Belgrade, the shock of finding his rum-bloated corpse was overshadowed only by the immediate appearance of a mad, gin-drunk count from Italy.

COLLINS GLASS.

Taller and thinner than the highball glass, the Collins is named after the Tom Collins, a gin-based cocktail it was first used to serve. Its eponymous inventor was a Manhattan bartender who began selling Court secrets to New York high society. In 1874, Court representatives were dispatched to apprehend him, but Collins seeded a hoax among the Manhattan public, in which people would ask friends if they'd seen Tom Collins. They would then insist that a man by that name was defaming their character just around the corner, hoping to provoke their friends into foolish action. Eventually Collins was cornered in Boston by Hortense LaRue, and the memories of him and his customers were modified by the Court. But by then the term *Collins glass* had gained too much traction, leaving it and its namesake the sole tribute to one of the Court's earliest traitors.

CHAPTER THIRTEEN

Bailey knew she had to level with Zane. But after she'd slept off the exhaustion of liquor and demon slaying and conversations with Mona, Bucket, and Vincent, she woke up not at the crack of noon, full of purpose and vigor, but at some actual morning hour to the sight of her mom perched on her bed like a cat eager to be fed.

Bailey jerked upright. "What'd I do?" she said, her voice thick with sleep.

Her mom practically sparkled with joy. "Landed a follow-up interview at Divinyl, I hope."

Bailey felt as if the mattress had been yanked out from under her. She blinked stupidly. "What time is it?"

She groped for her phone, which was missing from its usual place on her pillow; her mother continued blithely. "Well, I still see Jess's mom from time to time, and I *may* have done a little reconnaissance." She smiled and Bailey felt a flash of annoyance.

"*Mom.*"

"What?" Her mother looked contrite. "Hollie said Jess thinks you'd be a perfect fit at Divinyl."

"Mom! I don't need a copilot right now."

"And"—her mother's voice dropped to a conspiratorial murmur—"she told me they weren't bringing in anyone else for the first round. I just wanted you to be prepared. I know how much you hate surprises."

Bailey was only half listening, too absorbed in rooting around for her phone amid the mess of her bedclothes.

"Looking for this?" Her mom held out Bailey's phone. A voicemail was already waiting, time-stamped 4:38.

Bailey snatched the phone.

Her mom peered over her shoulder and smiled triumphantly. "You put that on speaker right now, Bailey," she said. "This could be the most important phone call you ever get."

Not unless Jess knows how to stop a demonic onslaught, Bailey thought. But she desperately wanted to be left alone, and pushing play seemed the fastest way to get there.

"Hiiii," slurred Jess's familiar voice. "I apologize for the late hour. I just got home. My town car driver's phone died, and he was like, 'Just give me directions to your place,' and I was like, 'How do you not know how to get around? Chicago's on a grid, duh.' And he was all, 'I'm new in town 'cause my wife left me and'—okay, anyway, I made it alive and I wanted to call you. Oh, and this message is for Bailey. What it is, B-Chen?"

"Ugh, that goddamn nickname," Bailey muttered.

"Language," said her mom, pointing to the phone.

"—were super impressed by your interview, and we definitely think there's a place for you at Divinyl, and those apple cocktail things were *so* good." Jess hiccupped. "So, yeah, let me know when you get this so I can set up a final face-to-face for you and the higher-ups. Give me a call at, uh, this number! 'K, bye!"

Bailey's mom flashed an enormous grin. "Can you believe it?"

"No," Bailey said truthfully. Maybe Divinyl thought she'd been a perfect fit, but the feeling wasn't mutual. Not if people like finger-snapping Kyle and his spicy-lunch-club cronies were going to be her coworkers. Even the T-shirt they'd forced on her was the wrong size.

"You left a great impression on them. I knew you would." Her mom patted Bailey's knee.

"Yeah," Bailey said, trying to feel excited.

With eyes sharp enough to notice a financial irregularity at fifty paces, her mom saw her hesitation. "What is it, sweetie?"

Now there was a hell of a question. "It's just . . . ." Bailey paused to consider her words. She hated lying to her parents, and that was all she'd been doing lately. "I'm just settling into a groove at work. I'm meeting people. I'm starting to enjoy my job. I can actually see it taking me somewhere."

What she didn't add was that the bartending world's shadow government would be none too happy about her moonlighting; that she, Zane, and the other Alechemists had barely escaped death at the hands of an extra-weird supernatural phenomenon that wasn't playing by the rules of the magic world, and that she couldn't feel safe until she'd gotten to the bottom of the top-down conspiracy she suspected was making deliriums descend on Chicago.

"Bailey," her mom said.

"I'm really good at it, Mom. And it's important work."

"Important?" Her mother's eyes fluttered closed. "Bailey, I'm not hearing what I just heard."

Bailey frowned. "The tautology of that sentence—"

"You've worked so hard. Middle school, high school, college. Over half your life. When all the other kids were huffing spray paint and necking in the backseat of their parents' cars, you invested in your future."

Bailey was fairly certain hers was a generation removed from paint huffing (not to mention the term *necking*), but she didn't dare interrupt.

"Your dad and I have been patient since you've been back," her mom said. "And with all the frustrations you've faced, after how hard you've worked to avoid them, I can understand wanting to stay down."

Her resolution to let her mom talk flew straight out the window. "I'm not staying—"

"You are, Bailey. And you're capable of so much more."

Bailey was silent. She couldn't disagree. Not without telling the truth.

"Someone's trying to give you a chance," her mom said quietly. "Right now." She closed the distance between them and laid a gentle arm around Bailey's shoulders, which were drowned in an oversize Penn T-shirt. "Your dad and I worked hard, too. You did all the heavy lifting, but we still did everything we could to give you stable environment to grow up in. We made sure you never wanted for anything. We tried to keep you happy so you could focus on what mattered. Remember when you brought home that C-plus?"

"Ugh, yes." A mistake that Bailey never dared repeat. "I spent the entire walk home mentally writing out my last will and testament."

Her mom smiled. "Do you remember *why* your dad and I were upset, though?"

Bailey sifted through her memories of that evening; it was mostly a blur. Her mom had thrown around the word *unacceptable* at varying decibel levels. Her dad had mostly let his wife take the lead, instead hitting the other parental power button: muted disappointment.

"Because you knew I could do better," Bailey finally said.

Her mom nodded. "We want you working in a nice, safe office, with people who have things in common with you. We don't want you coming in drunk at five in the morning, wearing ripped clothes and smelling like garbage. There's nothing wrong with working in a bar, or a shop, or a store. Those jobs are really important, and people need to do them. But you can do more. And you *want* to do more, remember?"

"I *am* doing more," Bailey said. She couldn't help it. "I'm doing a lot more than you know, okay?"

"What you are *doing*," her mom said, perfectly calm, "is setting up a follow-up interview."

She held out the phone, but Bailey didn't take it.

"You're setting up that interview," her mom repeated, "or you're looking for a new place to live."

Bailey gaped at her. "Are you giving me an ultimatum?"

"I like to think of it as a push in the right direction," her mom said. "The day you interview could be the day that changes your life. Now call."

———————

Twenty minutes later Bailey had a problem. Well, she had a few problems, but one of her problems was new, immediate, and more terrifying than a tremens: she had an interview in two hours, she wasn't prepared, and she was fiercely hung over.

"Dammit."

Bailey dropped her phone, rolled over in bed, and landed right on *The Devil's Water Dictionary* stashed under her pillow, college style, for late-night cramming.

If only there was some kind of "ace your interview" cocktail, she thought miserably. *Or at least "don't completely fuck your interview up so you'll still have a place to live."* She fanned through the pages, half to procrastinate about picking out an outfit and half with a niggling spark of curiosity.

Bailey Chen had never cheated in her life. Not even after that C+, or when her valedictorian competition with Jess heated up to nuclear levels (at least in Bailey's head), or when she'd arrived at a midterm and realized she'd studied for the wrong class. Cheating wasn't right. It wasn't fair.

But nothing about life right now was fair. Maybe cheating would even things out.

As if by magic, her book fell open to a perfect solution.

————————

When the cab arrived, Bailey threw herself into the backseat and choked down a fistful of breath mints to hide the smell of bourbon on her breath. The flavor mixed unpleasantly with the cocktail's citrusy aftertaste, but it was worth it. Unless Divinyl was even more casual than she thought, management wasn't about to hire a new admin assistant who reeked of whiskey.

"Washington and Clark, please," she said to the cabdriver. "Fast as you can."

As she settled back on the smoke-scented leather, the familiar warmth of a cocktail crept into her system, but nothing else. A flame of worry sparked. Had she mixed it wrong?

Within three minutes she knew the answer.

A gold rush was made from bourbon, honey, and lemon juice; the result was telepathy. She'd know exactly what answers her interviewers were looking for the moment they asked a question. It wasn't a "nail your interview" cocktail, but it was pretty damn close.

But the telepathy didn't happen gradually. It was more like a light switch flicking on inside her skull. And it was *on*.

Thoughts hit her in snatches, like a radio tuner roving for a signal. With every passing car, new bursts of information assaulted her, all in different voices. She caught words and phrases, but also images, noises, songs in people's heads, even phantom smells, some alluring, others decidedly not.

Bailey clamped her hands over her ears, regretting her decision. She'd never heard another voice inside her head, but now her mind was a public venue, and tickets had sold out almost instantly.

The driver noticed her discomfort in the rearview mirror. "You okay, miss?" he said. "I bring you home?" She shook her head. She had to see this through.

The feeling only intensified farther downtown, where she absorbed the idle thoughts of commuters, tourists, and residents. By the time the cab pulled up to the curb, she felt as if a rowdy mosh pit was balanced atop her scalp.

Jess was waiting for her in the lobby. "Bailey," she said, practically bouncing over, "so great to see you." As Jess leaned in for a hug, thoughts wafted off her like perfume: fond memories of the avocado omelet she'd had for breakfast (which Bailey could taste on her own tongue). Flickering images of the other interviewees, though Bailey detected fewer traces of excitement for them. Not quite excitement. Something else, though she couldn't peg what it was.

Then they hugged, and Bailey saw an instant mental image: she and Jess passionately making out.

"So I'll just take you back to . . ." Jess's voice trailed off as they broke apart. "Um, Bailey? Are you blushing?"

She was. But to be fair, it was a perfectly natural reaction after learning that a former schoolgirl nemesis was harboring a huge crush on her.

"Bailey?"

"I'm fine," she said shakily, and a bit too quickly. "I just panicked about, um, leaving the stove on."

Jess stared at her.

Bailey's face burned like a fictitious stove. "But I didn't."

"Well, that's a relief," Jess said. Feeling more waves of attraction, Bailey seized on the memory of the avocado omelet. Whatever other thoughts Jess had, Bailey stashed them behind the shield of breakfast foods. "So how about we head back to Bowie's office then?"

As they walked, Bailey battled a war of feelings. On the one hand was guilt. Telepathy was more invasive than she'd ever dreamed. Just being in the same room together opened all of Jess's deepest secrets, which were none of Bailey's business. On the other hand, guilt and flattery weren't mutually exclusive.

Bailey was so busy combing her own memory for retroactive clues about Jess that it didn't occur to her until they were almost at their destination to say, "Wait, did you say Bowie? As in Bowen Sorensen?"

"The Third," Jess said airily. "Yeah, he's gonna be your interviewer today."

Bailey bit back a gasp. "Don't you think you could've mentioned that?"

"Oh, don't be nervous!" Jess squeezed her shoulder. "It's not that big a deal."

Bailey begged to differ. Admiring the beeper mogul cum tech billionaire from afar was altogether different from getting grilled by him in person. "Does he normally interview people for entry-level positions or—"

"When he's in the office, totally," said Jess. "You're actually super lucky. He'll *love* you."

Bailey nodded. Her eyes were still on the bullpen, where workers sat, lay, biked, and posed in downward dog while hammering out lines of code and content. The clacking keyboards were music to her ears. All that typing for one purpose: to create, well, a digital construct meant to be laid over a preexisting audio file. It wasn't quite the same as building a mai tai from scratch. And it wasn't as if she'd ever see a customer's satisfaction. But she'd also be a lot less likely to die on the job. An app was still *something*, wasn't it?

Maybe.

And I'd get to work in private. It didn't hit her until just then, how for the past few months she'd been working on display in front of a constant rotation of strangers. Here she'd enjoy relative anonymity. She'd be able to go to bars and not worry about inventory or check times or empty tip jars. She'd just walk in, sit down, order an old fashioned, and enjoy herself.

Bailey noticed they'd reached Sorensen's office. It looked as if a genuine stone archway had been grafted to the wall. The sides were engraved with Egyptian hieroglyphics, and the door was heavy and wooden and overlaid in gold. Bailey stared.

"This is his office?"

"Yup," Jess said.

"Is he embalmed?"

Jess laughed, and one of her thoughts darted into Bailey's mind: *Was she always this fun?*

Yes, Bailey thought with indignation. *I'm tons of fun now. In fact I'm a little bit buzzed as we speak.*

"He's expecting you," Jess said. "Come on."

The door scraped against the carpet, revealing an office lavishly decorated in the style of ancient Egypt. The carpet was burnt orange, plush enough that Bailey's heels sank into it, and it was adorned with images of hieroglyphs, stylized eyes, and animal-headed people in profile. The desk looked to be carved from white granite. More Egyptian imagery was embossed into the front of it, and a sphinx-shaped paperweight held documents on top.

Bowen Sorensen III sat sandwiched between the desk and a spectacular view of downtown Chicago. He looked healthy and vital, and not in that fake country-club way rich people sometimes looked. His dark hair was like a Korean pop star's—messy and long but carefully styled—and his groomed goatee made him resemble his own evil twin. He wore a dress shirt that probably had one too many buttons undone, but he was young enough to get away with it. When he looked her up and down, it was intense. Serious. He didn't proffer a hand to shake.

Normally Bailey would've been intimidated, but her telepathy told her Sorensen just liked messing with people who didn't know him well.

"Hi, Mr. Sor—Bowie," Bailey said. And because the whiskey

seemed to think it was a good idea, she kept on talking. "So are we going to chat, or are you going to weigh my heart on a scale like Anubis?"

Sorensen's grave facade cracked into a smile, and he clapped his hands. "Oh, I *like* you!" He nodded over her shoulder to Jess. "We're good here."

Bailey felt Jess's pang of disappointment, and Jess's thoughts betrayed exactly where her eyes lingered in the seconds before she left. Bailey tried not to blush.

She and Sorensen sat down at the same time and he laughed, deep, from his gut. "Can you *believe* that?" he said, gesturing at the space between them. "That's crazy."

She blinked. "What?"

"You know. You sat down, I sat down . . . at the same time. What're the odds, right?"

Bailey prodded at his thought stream, thinking this was some kind of strange game he played to keep interviewees off balance. But to her surprise, he appeared to be engaged in no underlying cognitive activity. As far as she could tell, he was really saying whatever popped into his head.

She glanced at a pyramid-shaped clock on his desk. The cab ride had taken nearly twenty minutes, and another seven or so minutes had passed on her trip from the ground-floor lobby to his office. That gave her approximately thirty-three minutes before the gold rush wore off, which meant that she couldn't go in for too much small talk. "Is that something I need to know to work in admin around here?"

Once again she felt the telepathic glow of his approval. "All that and more," he said. "At least I think." He spun in his chair, scanning the office, before stopping exactly where he'd started. "This is my music filter company, right?"

Bailey chuckled, until her telepathy clued her in that he wasn't joking. She composed herself quickly. "Um, yes."

"Right on," said Sorensen. "Then why don't you and I talk about that for a bit?" He searched around the surface of his desk. "Most people are all about digital résumés these days, but I'm a sucker for the feeling of papyrus in my hand. You didn't happen to bring a—"

Before he could finish his sentence, Bailey was sliding a copy across his desk. And as a cherry on top, she smiled. Nicely.

As Sorensen read her résumé, Bailey read his thoughts. She'd already gotten the impression he was eccentric, and apparently one of his eccentricities was that he operated on surface level and surface level only. His subconscious practically handed her answers. When he asked questions, he rarely had a specific idea in mind; more often than not, he just wanted her response to strike a certain mood or tone, and all Bailey had to do was act accordingly.

"So one last question," Sorensen said after a long round of largely perfunctory quizzing about her internships and goals.

"Anything," Bailey said.

"Do you want a beer?"

"Um." It was 10:30 a.m. Day drinking would mean losing her grip on the gold rush, but she'd already felt him mentally scratch a checkmark next to her name, so at the very least she'd succeeded enough to placate her mother. Why the hell not? "Sure."

"Excellent." Sorensen extracted two bottles from a drawer that apparently doubled as a minifridge and then patted his chest pockets, frowning.

"Here." Bailey handed over her UPenn bottle opener. Figured it would be *that* part of her education that proved useful in an interview.

"Wonderful." Sorensen bowed his thanks and popped open the beers. Bailey took hers with a smile, threw back a healthy glug, and almost coughed. It was darker than she'd expected, and much stronger, too.

"You like it?"

Bailey nodded, smiling even as her eyes watered.

Sorensen brightened. "It's my own microbrew. Russian imperial stout, about twelve percent ABV . . . or maybe it was fourteen percent. Are people still drinking beer a lot? Like, it's still cool?"

"I'm more of a cocktail person myself," Bailey said politely, "but—"

"Yes!" Sorensen jumped to his feet. "See, I knew it." He pointed out his window to a huge black facade. "Next Sorensen venture's gonna be a little cocktail place right up there, in the Willis Tower."

Bailey stopped herself from wincing. That name was something no true Chicagoan would ever call the Sears Tower. Her mental broadcast of Sorensen's thoughts came in a bit slower after half a beer, but still, when she racked his brain, she discovered he genuinely had no idea that the landmark had recently—sacrilegiously—been renamed. In fact she wasn't even sure he knew where he was. Then she remembered that she should speak.

"Oh?" she said, sipping the beer. "Really?"

"And," Sorensen said proudly, "it'll be a distillery, too. Not of everything, of course; just gin, vodka, rum, tequila, and . . . what's the one that tastes like oranges?"

"Triple sec?"

"That's the one!" Sorensen said. "My business partner—he's the one with all the booze knowledge—he says it's better to start small. But *I* thought up the name," he added proudly. "Apex. It'll take up the top three floors—"

Dimly Bailey could read his mental image: a stylized logo that made the *A* look like the tower—the *Sears* Tower, thankyouverymuch—in silhouette. Along with it was an image of his partner, a small, energetic old man with an impressive mustache.

"You're working with Garrett Whelan?" Bailey burst out.

Sorensen paused, his hands spread in a dramatic representation of Apex's facilities. "How'd you—"

"I, uh, read about it in the *Trib*," Bailey said. It was a stupid lie—who even read newspapers anymore?—but Sorensen didn't seem to notice. If anything, he was delighted.

"Gary—I call him Gary, although I don't think he likes it—he's a *great* guy," he said. "With the way he talks, though, I'm not gonna play Scrabble with him anytime soon. How do you know him?"

"He's, um, an old family friend," Bailey said, her heart sinking.

Garrett can't be distilling it himself. Where would he even find the space? Or the money?

Sorensen. He was the money, Apex was the space, and with every sip Bailey was losing her ability to investigate telepathically.

She plunged back into his brain. He was picturing busy bartenders behind counters, fending off customers who reached for drinks like a horde of brain-hungry zombies. And there was Sorensen, dressed as a pharaoh, mingling freely beneath gigantic steel vats—

The image wavered. *Shit.*

"Is the beer not good?" Suddenly concerned, Sorensen leaned over the desk.. "Would you prefer an IPA? Or a lager? I could have Jess come in and make you a cocktail: martini, old fashioned—"

"No," Bailey said, hastily gulping her beer. "It's great. Tell me more about Apex."

"Right on. Except, well, there isn't that much more to tell," Sorensen said. "We're not officially open for business yet. Oh! But you should definitely come to our grand opening. You don't have other plans on Halloween, right? I mean, I know there're a lot of cool parties going on but—"

Halloween. Bailey resisted the urge to shiver.

"Um, yeah," she said. "That'd be great."

"Radical." Sorensen gave her the hang-loose gesture. "I'll have

Jess get you an invite."

She saw him imagining the party—people in costumes from glass wall to glass wall, drinking until it was November—but her bottle was down to the last few mouthfuls, and the picture was faint.

"Anyway," Sorensen said, "enough about me. Did I forget to ask you anything?"

Plenty, Bailey thought.

"Um, no," she said, then smiled. "I think you covered it."

"Well, I really liked meeting you, Bailey," he said, rising. She rose, too, and they shook hands. "You'll hear from us soon, all right? And please do come to the party!"

Bailey was out the pyramid door in two seconds.

"Bailey!" Jess popped out of nowhere. "How'd it—"

"Move!" Bailey yelled, practically pushing her to the side. "I mean, um, sorry! Let's just be friends, okay?"

Once downstairs and out of the elevator Bailey dug out her phone and stared at its empty black screen. The number she dialed would determine the course of everything that happened next. Her mom was right: the day she interviewed *was* going to change her life.

She made the decision and dialed. After three rings, a voice growled, "What is it, kiddo?"

"Vincent—wait, how'd you know it was me?"

"Got a special phone. It tips me off in case I'm about to get a call I don't want. This one of those?"

"Probably." She bit her lip. The worst-case scenario flashed through her head: he would hang up, abandoning her for breaking bartending law. She would have to face this crisis alone, and do it before someone managed to slip her a shot of oblivinum.

But it wasn't just about her; it was about all of Chicago. So she explained everything: the forbidden interview; the cocktail she used outside her official duties; the telepathic information that fitted together all the terrible pieces.

"What am I going to do, boss?" she said. Her chin trembled, and when she touched her cheeks, she found they were wet. She scrubbed at her eyes, mascara streaking her hand. Even if Vincent disbarred her and forced her to knock back oblivinum, there was no use crying.

"You're gonna get up here," he said. "And when you do, I'll tell you what's next."

The Gold Rush
A beverage to bridge the abyss between minds

1. *In a shaker with ice, mix two ounces of bourbon, one ounce of honey syrup, and three-quarters of an ounce of lemon juice.*

2. *Shake well.*

3. *Strain results over a single large piece of ice in an old fashioned glass, and serve.*

The power of telepathy has been known to bartending since at least 1872 in the form of the whiskey sour. The Wisconsin bartender Zedediah "Lucky" Gurnisson took credit for the cocktail's invention. Though initially good publicity, the claim backfired when another bartender fixed himself a whiskey sour and used telepathy to determine that Gurnisson was lying—both about inventing the drink and about people calling him Lucky.

Variations of the whiskey sour evolved into what is now known as the gold rush as early as the 1950s, although its initial applications were less than aboveboard: in particular, the Philadelphia bartender Chester Lyndon set out to refine the unreliable whiskey sour after mistakenly believing that it was necessary to root out communist spies among his regular customers. (Lyndon was later forcibly disbarred.) The editors of this book advise that the gold rush is best deployed in sparsely populated areas, where the psychic feedback is more manageable.

Lemon Juice.

Fig. 62 — *Citrus limon.*

Unlike orange juice, which is still magically functional even after extra levels of processing, lemon juice must be squeezed fresh. (Commercially available lemon-shaped squeeze bottles are rightfully regarded as a joke.) It has been effectively combined with all five of mixology's base liquors, rendering it perhaps the most vital nonalcoholic mixing ingredient besides ice. Lemon juice is frequently used with a sweetener to counteract both its acidic flavor and its chaotic effect on a drinker's animus. Some point to this necessary harmony of sour and sweet as symbolic of the need for balance in the practice of the craft; more literal minds will realize that lemon juice simply tastes awful straight up.

Honey Syrup.

The substitution of honey syrup for sugar was Lyndon's true breakthrough. In the interests of keeping his ingredients "all-American," he chose honey harvested from bees he kept in his backyard, using only rainwater to boil it into syrup. The result was improved telepathic clarity and control, which he misattributed to his own patriotic fervor. When a bartender in Greece duplicated his success using local ingredients, Lyndon denounced the result as nothing more than a fluke, a label he affixed to every non-American gold rush until his death in obscurity some years later.

FIG. 63 — *A beehive.*

CHAPTER FOURTEEN

The impromptu courtroom erupted in shouts of outrage at Bailey's accusation. Oleg Kozlovsky had to bang his shot glass five times before the audience calmed down. "Apologies, Ms. Chen," he said, stooping forward to lean on the bar. "Repeat, please, what you've said."

At his side stood Ida Worth, the South Side Tribune, and Garrett Whelan, who knew perfectly well what Bailey had just said. With volcanic eyes he stared down at her, as if he were trying to boil her from the inside out.

But Bailey wasn't backing down. Warmth coursed through her, and she used it to shield herself from his withering gaze. It was almost fun, she thought, standing in open defiance against him. Maybe she imagined it, but even now her fingertips felt electric.

"I said, 'On the charges of conspiracy, conduct unbecoming, and extralegal distillation, I accuse Garrett Whelan.' Unless we stop him—"

More shouts of outrage.

"Silence!" roared Kozlovsky. Again he slammed the shot glass.

The bar—a Greektown joint operated by Kozlovsky—was filled with a few staff who had sat down to watch the proceedings but then jumped out of their chairs in protest. A young woman bartender taking minutes on a yellow legal pad paused long enough to give Bailey a withering stare. And of course Bucket, Mona, and

Zane were there. She'd expected them to come, and to be angry, so she wasn't surprised by their looks of utter disgust. Vincent's hand tightened reassuringly on Bailey's shoulder as Poppy stepped forward and raised her hackles.

"It would appear I was errant when I remanded young Bailey into your custody for the furtherance of her education, Vincent." Garrett's gaze passed through Bailey and landed on the hulking man behind her. "Certainly, I underestimated the magnitude of your persuasiveness. Scarcely a month under your tutelage, and already she appears to have wholly adopted your vendetta-driven credo."

"It's not about vendettas," Bailey said. "It's about safety. It's—"

"Absolutely about vendettas," Zane interrupted. Bailey swallowed a lump in her throat. "You may not know, Bailey, but there was a time when Vincent was in here every other week accusing my uncle of something shady."

"Unnecessary commentary," Worth shot back. "But not inaccurate. Ms. Chen, do you want to tell us why this charge is any less of a snipe hunt than all the other crank calls Vincent has made over the years? What exactly is the immediate danger?"

Bailey breathed deeply and swallowed. Just yesterday she'd carried on a pleasant casual conversation with one of the greatest tech success stories of the recession age. Now she was in danger of becoming tongue-tied in front of this pack of oddball bartenders.

"Go for it, kiddo." Again Vincent squeezed her shoulder. "Just tell 'em what you told me."

Bailey felt a surge of gratitude that he was standing next to her. "Garrett Whelan is, through illicit means, attempting to manufacture a Long Island iced tea. And once he's succeeded, he intends to use it for personal gain."

She heard a chair scrape behind her and turned to see Zane standing, with Mona tugging at his forearm to sit him back down. Bailey flashed him the most sincerely apologetic look she could, but she got only a steely glare in return.

"Eyes forward," Vincent said.

"Yes, Ms. Chen," said Kozlovsky. "Explanations are for our ears first."

If Zane was pissed off now, he'd be downright livid when she was done.

"Two weeks ago I, Zane Whelan, and, er"—it occurred to Bailey that she didn't know either Mona's or Bucket's last names or even if Bucket was his real first name—"Bucket and Mona were attacked by a delirium of tremens. We barely managed to escape. When I relayed this information to Vincent, which as his apprentice I was required to do, he told me it had happened before. He theorized that the tremens were attracted to something bearing a more potent magical signature than that projected by people— specifically, the Long Island iced tea. According to him, the last time a delirium had shown up was while he and Garrett had been trying to complete their own formulas."

She had more to say—lots more—but Kozlovsky raised a finger. Both he and Worth turned to Garrett, who shrugged and said: "I was callow then, and bearing the simultaneous burdens of a surfeit of ambition and a dearth of common sense. Moreover, the world we lived in wasn't the one we inhabit today. I would add, however, that neither Mr. Long nor Ms. Chen has offered any proof to correlate heavy tremens activity with the appearance of our noble craft's panacea."

Can't you just use normal words? Bailey thought. *You sound like you swallowed an SAT prep book.*

"Look." She yanked a folder out of her bag and opened it to reveal a color-coded graph. "Vincent and I conducted an informal poll of bartenders in the Chicagoland area. Across the board they reported higher levels of tremens activity in the past year." She tapped the oldest coordinate on the graph's timeline, which dated back to

November of the previous year. "And do you know what's special about twelve months ago?"

"Halloween?" Kozlovsky's thick brows knitted. "More tremens. Is usual."

But Garrett knew where Bailey was going. He smiled ruefully. "Eleven months ago I broke ground on my newest enterprise, Apex."

More muttering throughout the bar. Bailey thought she could hear Zane sizzling with anger through the white noise.

"No," Bailey said. "You broke ground earlier than that. A year ago was when you began distilling and aging." She flipped to the next page and held up her dossier for all to see. It showed the article from the *Chicago Tribune*. "Apex's financier, Bowen Sorensen—"

"—the Third," Garrett interjected.

"—was interviewed by the *Trib*, and he mentioned his intent to distill and distribute his own liquor. So I decided to sit down with him on a fact-finding mission."

"Who sent you on this mission?" Worth said.

"I did," said Vincent. "She said she had an in with the guy, so I told her to look into it."

Kozlovsky frowned. "You are running hotels?"

"Not an *inn*," Bailey said. "A connection. Someone I went to high school with works for him and—"

"Who?" Zane interrupted. He was no longer standing but had settled for slouching moodily in his seat.

"That's your second outburst," Worth said.

"Sorry, Ida," Zane said. The woman was at least twice his age and far higher on the food chain, but apparently being a Whelan gave you an in—*not a hotel*, Bailey thought with irritation—with the powers that be. "Bailey and I went to high school together. Anyone she names, I'd know."

Bailey and Zane locked eyes for a long moment. "Jess Storm," she said, daring him to interrupt her again. Then she turned and continued: "During my interview with Sorenson I was able to glean that they were manufacturing vodka, gin, tequila, and rum, as well as triple sec, in industrial vats. No other liqueurs, and no whiskey. Just the ingredients necessary for a Long Island iced tea. And since one of the Long Island's alleged effects is supernatural longevity—"

"Fuck that," Vincent said. "Try immortality. And that's exactly what a guy might want if he's set to be mothballed in the next year."

When Vincent spoke, no murmurs arose, only gasps followed by crushing silence. Finally Garrett stirred, shooting his longtime rival an ugly look.

"I'm almost as old as you, Garrett," Vincent said. "After everything I've done in life, you think I like the idea of walking away from it all? I figure even a guy like you's gotta feel the pinch when his ass is against the wall."

Bailey laid a hand on his tattooed forearm to let him know she could handle it from there. "Each attempt at mixing the Long Island creates powerful shock waves. The more he tries, the more the tremens start coming."

"Which Thumbelina over here knew, of course," Vincent said.

"Garrett's going to rile up the demons enough to justify wartime powers from the Court," Bailey said. "Once he's secured an effective dictatorship, he'll make himself untouchable via the Long Island. Unless we do something to stop him, he'll rule Chicago forever."

"That's one hell of an accusation," Worth said.

But Bailey wasn't even looking at Ida Worth. She was looking at Garrett, who was whispering in Russian into Kozlovsky's ear. Whatever he said Kozlovsky seemed to like, and he turned back to Bailey.

"Where did you get this idea about wartime powers?" he asked.

"From me," Vincent said, stepping forward protectively.

"I was asking Ms. Chen," said Kozlovsky. "Where?"

"From Vincent," Bailey said. "But it still—"

"Are you aware of the history between Garrett and Vincent?"

"This ain't about me, Oleg," Vincent said. "It's about the—"

Kozlovsky pounded his shot glass on the counter. "No more interruptions. Ms. Chen, you have proof of your accusations?"

"Well, no," Bailey said. "But I believe that if the Court investigates, they'll find—"

"Ms. Chen," said Garrett, "Bailey. Kindly describe the distilling equipment Mr. Sorensen showed you."

"Um." She didn't know much about the technical specs of distilling equipment or even what that had to do with anything. "They're big. Made of steel."

Garrett nodded. "I see. And how did you know they were made of steel? How did you know specifically which liquors they were manufacturing?"

"Sorry?"

"The machinery used in Apex's distillery is indeed made of steel," Garrett said. "But as we all know, the standard material is copper. To my knowledge—and I know quite a lot—you've never visited Apex. Nor was the equipment pictured or described in the news article you've submitted for our scrutiny."

Shit, Bailey thought. Apparently someone *did* still read newspapers. "Sorensen showed me," she said, which was sort of true.

"How?"

"On his phone," she said. "He'd taken pictures during a visit to the construction site."

"I see." Garrett pulled out his own phone, which seemed surprisingly advanced for a man of his age; she supposed that being partners with a tech kingpin had its benefits. "And would it surprise you to know that shortly after your departure from his office, my esteemed partner sent me a communiqué informing me of your conversation? And that just now I sent him one in return, asking if at any point he had shared pictures with you. Do you know what he said, Bailey?"

"Um . . ."

"That your assertion was categorically untrue," Garrett said. "Which leaves unresolved the matter of how you obtained information you should not have."

"I can explain," Bailey said.

"Really?" Garrett raised an eyebrow. "Because it seems to me that you came by this information as if by *magic.*"

He knows. The words sent a chill through her. *Fuck, fuck, fuck.* She'd just have to hope the Tribunes would hear her out.

"Ms. Chen, have you ever ingested the concoction known as a gold rush?"

Before Bailey could answer, Vincent said, "Yeah. She has. I watched her do it."

Bailey wheeled on him. "Boss—"

"Kiddo, I'm not letting you take the fall for something I put you up to," he said. "You want the truth? Yeah. This was always about me and the runty little bastard."

That wasn't the truth at all. But Vincent wouldn't let her stop him.

"A guy knows when he's lost the game, and I got outplayed. You wanna take down the king, there's no need to drag the pawn with him. It's not Bailey's fault."

Bailey felt a stab of guilt. She'd broken the rules, but Vincent was taking the fall.

"Using a cocktail on a civilian is forbidden." Garrett couldn't hide the triumphant gleam in his eye. "And so is utilizing said cocktail outside the parameters of work. Both offenses have been admitted to, and both carry the penalty of erasure and . . . *disbarment.*"

No. Bailey's stomach gave a sickening roll. *Not oblivinum.*

Vincent nodded. "Yeah. Figured you'd give me the clean slate."

Bailey clenched her fist; the tingling electrified her fingertips. This was it, her do-or-die moment. And she sure as hell wasn't going to die.

"Boss," she said in a low voice, "get ready."

Before Vincent could ask why, Bailey threw up a hand and, with an ozone-scented crack, shot a blinding blue-white lightning tendril from her palm. The feeling was like sticking her finger in a socket but in reverse, and she stumbled from the recoil.

"Kiddo!"

The bottles behind the bar exploded in a shower of glass and liquid, and the air filled with smoke. No one could see, but one person knew how to move without sight.

"Come on!" Bailey said, placing her small hand in Vincent's calloused one. "Get us out of here!"

Vincent pulled Bailey and Poppy through the confusion of blasted chair legs and jagged bottle fragments and out to the street.

"Trust no one, huh?" Vincent shouted over the din.

"You taught me well!"

"Well, school's out!" he said. "You're in the real world now!"

Planter's Punch
A libation of lightning

1. *In a shaker filled with ice, combine two ounces of dark rum, one and a half ounces apiece of pineapple juice and orange juice, half an ounce of lime juice, and one teaspoon apiece of grenadine and simple syrup.*

2. *Shake well; then strain into an iced highball glass.*

3. *Add three dashes of Angostura bitters.*

4. *Serve garnished with a maraschino cherry and an orange slice.*

Planter's punch, so named for the Planters Inn in Charleston, South Carolina, is alike in procedure (if not in makeup) to the mai tai. But where the former comes from Western appropriation of Polynesian culture, the latter is rooted in Western appropriation of Jamaican culture, which is a different matter entirely.

Though some version of planter's punch is believed to have existed in the Caribbean during the pre-Blackout era, the modern iteration suddenly and inexplicably emerged in Charleston in the mid-nineteenth century. When local bartenders arrived to contain the situation, they were greeted by a lightning-singed disaster area, an unfortunate side effect of the hotel's policy to make its signature punch by the bowlful.

GRENADINE.

A sweet and tart syrup made from pomegranate juice, grenadine is known for its distinctive red color. A curious problem unique to modern-day America is that the industrialization of grenadine has led to a product made entirely of artificial ingredients. The average bottle of commercial grenadine, though similar to the genuine article in taste and appearance, is dangerous because of its utter lack of magical utility. Bartenders are encouraged to buy grenadine in international markets, where the original recipe is still in wide use, or to make it themselves.

PINEAPPLE JUICE.

Despite its close association with the Pacific islands, the pineapple is in fact native to South America. Caribbean natives were using it for culinary purposes centuries before Europeans arrived and spread it throughout the globe. The fruit's flavor is strong and distinct, making it an ideal partner for dark rum; the similarly aggressive nature of the two substances creates a feedback loop, which the New Orleans barmaid Dorothy Deschamps once compared to a shouting match in a glass.

CHAPTER FIFTEEN

The double doors to the street were bolted shut, but Bailey was ready. Fists up, she sent another snap of lightning barreling outward, shattering the glass.

She hurled another bolt and struck a heavy industrial light. Even with adrenaline and electricity coursing through every limb, she knew a successful escape meant stalling their pursuers. The light wobbled and smashed into bits that skittered across the floor, a minefield for anyone trying to catch them. All they had to do was get to the doors and—

"Boss!"

A burly barback threw a hook straight for Vincent's face. Vincent jerked out of the way, giving Bailey just enough time to grab the man's fuzzy forearm. With a sharp blast, she expelled all her energy. The barback lit up with blue electricity before crumpling unconscious to the ground, the smell of singed hair filling the air.

"Door!" Bailey shouted. Without thinking, Vincent ducked and rolled through the opening and out into the night.

The sky was the deep purple of fresh nightfall and Greektown was starting to bustle. Valets were taking car keys in front of the squat, wide restaurant buildings that sat below boxy high-rises. To the east loomed the Sears Tower, its black facade dotted with yellow windows and its twin antennas glowing like burning magnesium.

Bailey grabbed Vincent and ran toward the parking lot, secluded on one side by trees and on the others by tall boxy buildings. If shit was going down, they needed to keep a low profile. Plus, there was no way to slip out of sight if they stayed in the open.

"Gavin's waiting with the car at the park on Adams!" Vincent yelled. "Northwest corner!"

"How did you—"

"You're not the only one who's paranoid, kiddo." He darted between parked cars, Poppy's leash in one hand and Bailey's hand in the other. "He'll get us to the Loop, and I'll arm up with some booze—"

They were halfway across the lot and no one had come after them yet. It didn't feel right. Bailey looked over her shoulder just in time. "Boss, duck!"

Ever the unquestioning soldier, Vincent stooped just as a jet of orange flame blasted over their heads. Bailey smelled her own singed hair. Another of Kozlovsky's staffers was on their tail, and more were pouring out onto the street, no doubt having been served hastily prepared drinks. She couldn't believe they'd managed to mix them so quickly. "We're outnumbered," she said. "They'll catch us."

"Like hell!" he said. "Shoot!"

Bailey squeezed her eyes shut as another burst of lightning cracked from her fingertips. The weedy Russian in pursuit threw himself out of its path, but not for long; he soon sped up as he drew more fire around his hands.

"Let her go, Vincent!" someone yelled behind them. Bailey didn't need to turn around. She recognized the voice and felt a sinking in her gut. It was Zane, and that meant they weren't just fighting off random strangers; they were up against the Alechemists.

Vincent skidded to a stop.

"Here. Go." He released Bailey, slipped Poppy's leash into her hand, and turned to run blindly toward their pursuers.

"*What the fuck are you doing?*" Bailey's voice burned in her throat even as she realized she knew the answer: buying her time.

Poppy didn't hesitate. Yanking on the leash, she dragged Bailey toward the bus stop. When Bailey didn't follow, Poppy turned, barked, and yanked again more insistently. Still Bailey wouldn't go.

When she was twelve, Bailey had stumbled upon her dad's collection of movies about a blind samurai who wandered into a town that needed him to fend off a small army. She'd loved them, but Zane never bought it. "That was great and all," he'd told her, "but no way could a blind guy kick that much butt." When she tried to argue that his hearing was enhanced because of the absence of his sight, Zane waved it off. "No one can hear *that* well," he'd said.

But Vincent could.

He moved like a tiger: forceful, precise. Kozlovsky's flame-throwing bartender jumped out from behind a parked delivery truck, but Vincent dodged the projectile and then slammed a palm into the guy's chest, knocking him over with nothing but sheer might. With a *crack,* the bartender bent at the ankle, caught in a storm drain, and Vincent surged toward the Alechemists.

Bailey hurled another lightning bolt, aiming for the ground at the Alechemists' feet. Bucket was ready, and with the stomp of his boot he summoned a purple bubble-shaped shield of light that absorbed Bailey's attack amid a crash of sparks. Then, as quickly as it had come, the purple bubble evaporated, and Mona and Zane vaulted forward.

Mona darted in first, moving astonishingly fast.

"No!" Bailey sprinted forward, with Poppy in tow, and shot a bolt in front of her. Not only did Mona dodge it, but her body stretched and distended itself out of harm's way. She wasn't moving like liquid; she *was* liquid. Vincent, who'd been relying on hearing a solid target, couldn't pin her down. He swung but missed, the momentum throwing him completely off balance. Before he could correct himself, Zane landed a blow that sent Vincent flying.

A screwdriver, Bailey thought. There was no other way Zane's matchstick frame could put out that kind of power. Bailey was seeing something truly new in Zane. And it was ugly.

As Vincent jumped to his feet, Bailey felt a sharp pain below her ankle. Poppy had nipped her heel. The dog had one instinct—obey—and she strained every fiber of her leash in an effort to carry out Vincent's order: get Bailey out of the parking-lot battleground.

But unlike the dog, Bailey refused to obey. "Poppy," she said sharply, "go save Dad."

The dog seemed to understand. She barely gave Bailey a look before barreling toward her master.

Vincent sprang back not a split second before Zane kicked his leg like an ax. His super strength cracked the concrete, but Vincent was unhurt.

"Playing for keeps, huh?" Vincent said, his head whipping toward the sound.

"You're done!" Zane shouted. "You're losing your mind!" He lunged for Vincent, but a growling Poppy jumped up and wrenched her jaws around his outstretched arm. The sudden addition of seventy pounds of dog was enough to throw Zane off course. He ceased his attack, trying to dislodge Poppy. "Ah! Fucking dog!"

"*You leave her alone!*" Vincent yelled. "Poppy! Down!"

Obedient as ever, Poppy released Zane, and Bailey took her cue. She flung her fist forward, surging with electricity, but Bucket jumped into her path; instead of hitting Zane, her lightning slammed into the purple force field that erupted in its path. Mona bounded over the top of the shield bubble, her form rippling like a summertime mirage, and aimed her booted feet at Vincent's chest. The kick sent him staggering backward.

"Three of us and one of you!" said Zane. "Give it up, old man!"

Vincent growled and rolled to his feet as Mona landed hard beside his head. She pulled back her fist, but instead of ramming forward, her arm warped into an arc. Bailey understood: Mona couldn't surpass Vincent's hitting power, but she could use momentum and her liquid form to turn her arm into a whip.

"Boss! Duck!" Vincent tensed in surprise but bent down. As the whiplike punch swept over his head, he dived forward, grabbed Mona by the waist, and pivoted her body. "Go, kiddo!"

Mona's elongated arm struck Bucket with a slosh. No sooner did Bailey see the splash than she fired a jolt of electricity straight into her rival. The blue-white energy trail shot through both Mona and Bucket, knocking them to the ground; for a single terrifying moment Bailey thought she'd killed them. But they were alive, just flattened and shivering from shock.

Bailey leveled a defiant glare at Zane. "He's not alone."

Vincent straightened, breathing hard as Poppy took her place beside Bailey, teeth bared. "You lose, Junior. Let us walk."

Zane glowered past Vincent at Bailey. She'd never seen his face so full of contempt. "So that's it, huh?" he shouted to her in a ragged voice. "You really believe all this crazy shit? You're going to just ignore what the Court says is truth?"

"You don't need to do the whole monologue thing," Vincent said.

"Zane," Bailey said, trying to steady her voice even as her body quaked with the effort to contain a lightning storm. "We're going now, and you're not going to stop us. Think about what I said. Or if you don't want to think about me—I get it, you're mad—think about Chicago. Think about keeping the city safe. And when you realize—"

"*I was your best friend!*"

"And I'm still yours!" Bailey could see Vincent's hands tense, but she held him back. "Zane, you have to listen to me—"

"No monologuing for you either, kiddo," Vincent said. "His ears ain't open."

Bailey lowered her arms, a zap traveling up her spine. "Okay. Let's go."

"What makes you think I'll let you do that?" Zane said, stepping forward. Again Poppy bared her teeth.

"It's us against you, Zane," Bailey said. "Well, us and Poppy. And I know you won't hurt a dog."

"Call her off." Zane said. "This is between you and me, Bailey."

"Fat chance," said Vincent. "The easiest fight to lose is a fair one. You might think you're a hot-shit bartender, little Whelan, but I know what this girl can do. She's saved your ass before. I guarantee she won't hesitate to kick a dent in it this time, either. And she'll have help."

Bailey's first instinct was to protest, but she stopped. Vincent was right. She was ready. She'd worked hard. And she would kick ass, even though it terrified her to think that she could take down her best friend. She steeled herself for the worst.

Zane's narrow shoulders slumped and Bailey's heart soared. He'd listen—and they'd stop Garrett and fight off the tremens. Together.

"All right," Zane said. "I—"

Suddenly a wet *crack* split the air, followed by an inhuman yelp. Poppy collapsed, dead at Vincent's feet.

Bailey's hands flew to her mouth. She screamed, but only for a moment. Zane yelped and darted back, his fury instantly replaced by horror.

Vincent roared. "Poppy? *Poppy! You son of a—*" But his hands slapped to his sides, as if he had suddenly turned into a marionette. His boot heels forcibly clicked together. And then he stood tall at attention. His square jaw trembled as it tried to resist the force clamping his mouth shut.

Garrett Whelan stepped into view, one hand outstretched. "I believe this matter has been sufficiently argued in a public forum." He gestured, and two shot glasses levitated into view, each full of a glowing purple liquid. "You've become an agent of destruction too great for the Court to allow. It will take all night to properly modify the recollections of every civilian your antics have entertained."

"Uncle Garrett," Zane said, breathless, "you killed that dog. She—"

"Was being held at your throat like the tip of a rapier," Garrett said calmly. "You're my family, Zane. I would do it again, every time." He stalked forward deliberately, preceded by the floating shot glass. As he swept his arm upward, Vincent's chin jerkily copied the movement. When Garrett spread his fingers, Vincent's mouth opened. The oblivinum drifted closer until it hovered just above his lips.

And then, to Bailey's surprise, Garrett's demeanor softened. "My deepest apologies that it ever came to this," he said quietly. "You were a paragon, Vincent. Even in your deepest doldrums, you perched at a height few could reach—even me. But I fear that with a higher height comes a greater fall. *Bibo ergo sum,* old friend."

The glass tipped its contents into Vincent's mouth. Bailey saw his Adam's apple bob as he swallowed. Then he pitched forward onto the concrete, lying prone next to the body of his canine best friend.

The flame-throwing bartender and his coworker lumbered up, and between them they were able to lift Vincent's huge form and drag him back to Kozlovsky's bar. Garrett watched for a moment before turning his attention to Bailey. "And then there's the matter of you, Ms. Chen."

The second shot glass floated forward, but long fingers intercepted it.

"Let me do this," Zane said. "She's my friend." He looked at her with dead eyes. "*Was.*"

"No." Garrett nodded sharply. "Absolutely n—"

"Uncle Garrett," Zane said, "you were right. I need to learn to obey authority."

Garrett considered his nephew. "And I can entrust that your sense of duty won't be outweighed by other . . . obligations?"

Zane nodded.

"Then I deem the matter yours to resolve. You know what you must do." He turned and trailed after the two bartenders dragging Vincent.

Bailey felt the hold on her release as Garrett walked away, and she almost collapsed. Her breaths came shallow and hard, as if she'd just swum across Lake Michigan. She had to remind herself that Vincent wasn't dead. Not really. But he'd been fed oblivinum, so he might as well be. The next time he heard her voice, she'd be a stranger to him.

And Zane—the man who'd been her best friend—had let it happen.

Zane set down the shot glass, tore off his coat, and laid it over Poppy's body. Then he knelt to check on Mona and Bucket. "You've gone off the deep fucking end now, Bailey."

"Did you know?" she said. "Did you know what Garrett was up to?"

"Did I know that my uncle was building a bar and a distillery?" he said, his voice rising. "Yeah. You bet your ass I did. Who do you think he hired to manage it? In fact, you just tasered Apex's entire senior staff, so good on you. You want a punch card for that?"

"I was trying to help," Bailey said. "We were trying to save everyone."

Zane jabbed a finger at the bodies of the other Alechemists. "*Does this look like helping me?*"

Bailey flinched, terrified of Zane for the first time ever. He had a freshly made screwdriver in his system, and her planter's punch would be good for only another ten minutes. She could never out-run him, and besides, her will to fight was gone.

"Don't hurt me," she whispered. "Please."

Zane pulled back. Bailey wanted to think that he couldn't believe what he'd done, threatening her like that. But the truth was she didn't know what to believe. She didn't know what Zane would or wouldn't do anymore.

"If you'd stuck with us, he would've hired you, too, Bailey," he said softly. "You wanted to ride your degree to the top of the world. You could've done that if you'd just trusted me. *Literally.*" He pointed to the Sears Tower behind them.

"You always tell me to trust you, but you never think things through," she said. This was her last chance to get through to him—and dangerous or not, he needed to hear her. "You never look at what's in front of you. And because of that, I've had to save your life twice since I moved back here. I *had* to go to Vincent. I needed the Court to verify it. You never would've listened, and I couldn't leave anything to chance. Not—not when it comes to you." She'd only meant to sound concerned, but her voice cracked.

Zane didn't notice. "Vincent used you," he said. "I told you: all he ever wants is to get at Garrett, and you let him use you anyway. Even worse, you let him put you up to—to—" He shook his head in disgust. "A gold rush on a civilian? On my uncle's business partner? I'd expect that from a twisted bastard like Vincent Long, but you—"

"Oh, get over yourself," she snapped. "Vincent never told me to use a gold rush. That was all me. I'm not some wide-eyed idiot who got taken in."

Zane gave a short, mirthless laugh. "Typical Bailey Chen. Always knows best. No matter what it is, you've always got a better way, even if I've got good reasons for doing it differently. But then again, why should you care what I want? After all," he added, eyes widening with sarcastic innocence, "your way's *better*. What else could *possibly* matter?"

"This isn't about the Fight—"

"It'll always be about the Fight!" he shot back. "Four years ago you told me I'd never go anywhere as a bartender. You told me you were too good for it."

Blood rushed to her face. "I didn't say those things!"

"*You might as well have!*" he shouted, and that she couldn't deny. "How's it feel? How's it feel to see me going places while you're the one standing still?"

His words were like a cold bullet to her heart. Bailey looked down to where the shot glass sat unattended on the sidewalk, and she blinked away tears. "I won't remember in a minute anyway," she said.

"That?" He picked up the shot glass and hurled it to the ground, staining the asphalt with purple and the glitter of broken glass. "You don't deserve to forget this. It's four years later, and I'm the one who has everything. A livelihood. A life. A *purpose.* And you wanted to take it away. That's a shame I want you to live with."

The noise had awoken Bucket, who wobbled to his feet, groaning. Mona was beginning to show signs of life, too.

"Walk away, Bailey," said Zane. "It's what you do best."

Her eyes lingered on his rumpled suit jacket on the concrete and the form hidden beneath it.

"We'll handle him," Zane said. "Leave. You don't have to go home, but you can't stay here."

Bailey wanted to fight, but the energy had left her. She'd lost.

"Her," she said. "You'll handle *her.* Her name was Poppy."

And then she turned and left, finally out of things to do or say.

The Gimlet
A draft to induce ductility

1. *Fill an iced shaker with two ounces of gin and half an ounce each of lime juice and simple syrup.*

2. *Shake well and strain into a martini glass.*

3. *Garnish with a slice of lime, and serve.*

As previously mentioned, gin is relatively unpopular in the field, which is a trend the gimlet does nothing to reverse. Its effect—to liquefy the body while allowing it to move with agency—has been described as both enchanting and terrifying. Although solid boundaries cease to be an obstacle, the mental strain of constantly shifting and corralling one's mass has often proved a trial for the novice bartender.

The gimlet has not been without its supporters. Its inventor, the surgeon and erstwhile bartender Thomas Gimlette of the Royal Navy, used it to safely treat patients while under fire in the mid-eighteenth century, while Hortense LaRue famously used it to apprehend the fugitive Tom Collins by flowing in through the keyhole of an otherwise impenetrable door. But not all of the gimlet's publicity has been positive; most notoriously, the Hungarian bartender Károly Németh once consumed a gimlet and summarily committed suicide by drinking himself to death.

LIME JUICE.

Prior to the twentieth century, gimlets (and, indeed, most cocktails) were not made with fresh lime juice. Instead, bartenders were forced to make do with bottled lime cordials, the most famous of which was Rose's. A certain amount of sweetening was necessary to preserve it, leading to the slightly sugary taste that the modern version emulates through the addition of simple syrup. Post-Blackout, lime juice and cordials rose to prominence as a scurvy treatment rationed by the Navy. Soon enough, those aware of bartending's true mission found ways to tap into the magical effects of lime juice, and its use spread widely among the British Empire and neighboring territories. As in so many other matters, America remains the odd nation out, and to this day the orange and lemon are far more prevalent citruses in stateside cocktails. When asked about this tendency to avoid the tart green fruit, American bartending historians universally claim that Great Britain "knows what it did" and will not elaborate.

FIG. 77—*Citrus fraurantifolia.*

CHAPTER SIXTEEN

Bailey didn't have a lot of things. She had no job. She basically had no friends. She had absolutely no way of stopping the demonic onslaught that was about to descend on the most populous city in the Midwest.

But perhaps most significantly, she didn't have a Halloween costume.

"*Fuck!*" She raked through her closet for the umpteenth time even though she knew nothing was in there but old winter coats and a sparkly gown with a wine stain she'd had to hide under a sweatshirt when she came home from her junior prom after-party. She knew that suitable Halloween regalia meant flimsy store-bought outfits for men and varying states of themed undress for women. But among the many things Bailey lacked were the funds to buy a new costume, let alone the time to go shopping or any craft know-how whatsoever. All her old costumes had ended up in a Dumpster after the big move home, but she kept shoving hangers aside, holding out the dimmest hope that her parents had saved *something*.

Nope. Not even a stupid pair of cat ears.

She slumped onto a pile of clothes and resisted the urge to shout curses at the ceiling. Bailey knew that terrible things were about to happen. And she knew she had to do something about it because no one else would. But that was where the certainty ended.

Maybe it won't be so bad, an insidious little whisper hissed in her head. People would die at first, but Garrett would avenge them and then devote his eternal life to making sure that never happened again. And it wasn't like the man was a bad administrator; he'd been the Court's cornerstone for as long as anyone could remember. If Chicago was going to have a benevolent overlord, Garrett Whelan was the best-case scenario.

Yet no matter what the voice hissed, she always got snagged on the first bit: *people would die.*

The task ahead was so much bigger than she was, it threatened to swallow her whole. She had a good education and some youthful idealism, but what good was that in the face of a broken system and the hundreds of people who'd fight like hell to keep it broken? Normally she could've relied on Zane to help but—

She stopped herself. That wasn't right. It hadn't been right for the last four years.

And that one's on you, Bailey.

She pushed herself upright and reached for *The Devil's Water Dictionary.* Her eyes scanned martinis, manhattans, and mojitos, but no one drink seemed powerful enough. Even if she stopped Garrett and managed to fight her way through the massive delirium that would descend on the Loop, she'd still have to face down the Cupbearers Court.

For a long moment she just sat there.

Then she thought: *You done now?*

She looked around at the wardrobe she'd converted into a floor-drobe, at the book in her lap that had a hundred answers but none of the right ones. She resolved that somehow she'd get it together.

And then someone rapped on the front door.

Bailey jolted upright. Her parents, being employed adults, were at work, and for a fleeting moment she wished a grown-up were home to answer for her. But she was the grown-up now.

So Bailey took out her phone, tapped in 9-1-1 (just in case), and then answered the door as calmly as she could. "Can I help you?"

"Are you Bailey Chen?" said a pudgy, bespectacled black man. He was a few years older than she was.

The blood drained from Bailey's face. If he was a Court enforcer, she was toast. She hadn't thought to mix a cocktail first, and even if she did hit SEND, it wasn't like the police would get there in time to stop an oblivinum force-feeding.

"Who's asking?" she said carefully.

"I'm—I know Vincent," he said. "My name's Gavin."

Already calculating her options, Bailey folded her arms. If this guy tried something, she could hurl her cell phone at him and make a break for it, giving her enough time to . . . call the cops from a pay phone?

"I worked for him and I never saw you." Bailey racked her brain—where *was* the nearest pay phone? Did they even exist anymore?

"I know. Long & Strong isn't really my scene. But I'm friendly, I promise."

Bailey scowled, her thumb inching toward Send.

"I promise," he repeated. "I'm just supposed to give you this, okay? It's from him." He held out a small USB drive with a bottle opener on one end (*because of course*, Bailey thought). "I just found it this afternoon. I hope it's not too late."

Bailey hesitated. Maybe it *was* too late. She was about to launch a one-girl assault on a swanky but doomed Halloween party with no plan and even less of a costume.

"Come on, take it. It's cold, okay?"

She wanted to refuse—what if this was some kind of trap set by Garrett?—but then she saw a piece of masking tape affixed to the side. On it was a single word written in Vincent's jagged script: KIDDO.

She took it.

"Thanks," Gavin said. "You have a good night now."

"Yeah," Bailey said. "Happy Halloween."

Gavin just shook his head.

Bailey tore back to her room. In her eagerness she plugged in the drive three times before it finally synced to her laptop. A single file was waiting for her—a video labeled "Bailey."

She clicked on it and a window opened to a still image of Vincent staring sightlessly just off camera. The background wasn't his office; it was a blood-red wall with black candle sconces drilled into it. The white candles behind him were unlit, but she imagined the place would be ideal for something like a séance. She wondered: was she glimpsing Vincent's apartment?

She clicked PLAY. "Hey there, kiddo," Vincent said. The sound of his greeting instantly comforted her, and her eyes immediately teared up. "If you got this, then everything went down like it was supposed to. I'm out of the game, but you've still got your seat. I've got a lot riding on that skinny-ass mod wannabe's not blacking you out, so here's hoping that when the time came, he wasn't too much of a Whelan for his own good."

She watched, mesmerized.

"So, working on the idea that your brain's still in factory condition, here's the deal: you're on your way down here so we can head to Greektown together and stand before the Court. We're gonna make some accusations, and we're probably gonna lose. But odds are good that no matter what happens, I'm gonna end up blacked out.

"If we manage to take Garrett down before that happens, then the rest of this video doesn't matter. But if we fail, then Garrett's gonna get himself immortal. And while that's not the worst thing in the world, a lot of people will end up very mortal along the way. And I know you don't want that.

"So, listen up. First things first: there's a reason our job description is bartending first, demon slaying second. It's service, Bailey. Whether it's an old fashioned or an ass-kicking, you're serving it up. That's why I put you behind the counter for a few days before I took you out on the street. I wanted you to see who you were protecting. I wanted you to appreciate what the job means. What *your* job means."

Once again Bailey caught herself nodding to a Vincent who couldn't see her. Outside her window, the sun winked into an orange streak over the horizon.

"Now that guy Sorensen, the one whose mind you read. He's never been in my joint. From what you tell me, he'd probably never set foot in it, let alone within ten blocks. But as long as you work for me, your job is to watch his back, even if he's evil, or worse—stupid. But you didn't watch his back. You stabbed it."

Ashamed, Bailey looked down at her knees.

"So when you go out to make this right," he said, "hurt the people that need hurting, but no collateral. Don't become a murderer. And if you're gonna color outside the lines again, make sure you pick the lines that're really fucking asking for it."

He stabbed a finger at the screen and, by extension, her. "Second, and this is the important one, I need you to not come looking for me. Don't tell me what I'm leaving behind. None of that. I've been fighting this fight for decades, and even if I'm in great shape for a relic, I'm still tired. I've been shelved, and I think I'm gonna like it that way. Don't dust me off. I'll have good people to watch me.

"Now," he said, "if I know you like I think I do, you're probably already halfway to Garrett's new joint and scared shitless."

She realized she was nodding again. Vincent seemed to see her because he said: "You're probably thinking this is over your head. And honestly, you're probably right. You haven't been trained as much as I wanted to train you. You haven't been in the field that long. But you know what, kiddo? The grown-up who says they know what they're doing is a grown-up who's lying.

"Which brings me to my third and final point," he said with a familiar grin. "With me out of the picture, you're gonna need people of your own. I've been where you are, kiddo, and in a lot of ways I never really got out of that place. So that's the last bit of wisdom shrapnel I wanna lodge in your brain: don't go it alone. That was my mistake, and even though I'm a kick-ass teacher, I'm a terrible fucking role model. You're young. You've got friends, and you've got time to make more. Don't take them for granted, and don't write people off, either. Everyone you meet on your way up in life, you're gonna meet again on your way back down. I sure as hell did, and most of them weren't happy to see me."

The video was nearing its end. Bailey had barely fifteen minutes to get out the door.

"I could talk your ear off forever, but you've got shit to do, kiddo. Get on it. Camera o—" But then he stopped. "Look. Whether you do this or not: thank you for being my student and my last friend. Unless a tremens catches you with your pants down, you're gonna have yourself a good life. And thanks for—thanks for letting me be your boss."

Bailey fought every instinct to cry. Even as her vision blurred, she forced herself to keep watching.

"I'll see you in a few. Poppy!" Bailey's heart skipped a beat as she heard the familiar clacking of paws on the floor, just out of sight. "Let's go, girl," he said, leaning down to scratch his dog's ears. "We're gonna have a rough night, I'm pretty sure." He looked up, straight out of the screen. "Good luck, kiddo. You're gonna get it together, I promise. Camera off."

The image froze. Numbly Bailey shut her laptop. *Get it together.* That was supposed to be the Holy Grail, wasn't it? Zane had gotten it together. Jess had gotten it together. All her friends in Philly had gotten it together, if the filtered photo ops in their newsfeeds were to be believed.

Bailey had tried to get it together. But all the things she'd thought she'd wanted from the world—a cool apartment in a trendy but cheap neighborhood, a sizable paycheck, the occasional rich-lady treat, like a caramel latte or a gel manicure—now seemed pointless. Maybe bartending had been a messy lifestyle—literally—but at least she'd had friends. For a while, anyway.

She got up and faced her closet, and finally, on the zillionth time, she found what she was looking for. Well, not what she was looking for, but what she needed.

The dress was a little tight, but it'd serve. Paired with matching orange heels, it made her look . . . awesome. Bailey allowed herself a quick once-over in the mirror before spinning around to her wall of has-been heartthrobs.

"Oh, shut up," she said to the posters. "When was the last time you guys were in a movie, anyway?"

Getting it together could wait, Bailey thought. Right now she needed to get it right.

CHAPTER SEVENTEEN

In the big-budget movie adaptation of this adventure, Bailey thought, an oil-black town car would pull up outside the Sears Tower, where miraculously a free parking spot would be waiting. The driver would open the door and she, Bailey Chen, would step out, one high-heeled foot at a time. Her lips would be an alluring slash of red, her costume a bright dress with a matching domino mask, and her hair styled to weather both Chicago winds and possibly the end of the world.

Also, odds were good she'd be played by a white girl, because movies.

But this wasn't a movie. So there she stood in a packed Brown Line car as it jerked along into the heart of Chicago. A little sourly she wondered if any movie hero ever had to take public transit to a crime scene. *Well, you're not a hero,* she reminded herself. *You're just a girl with a bachelor's degree, her dad's train pass, and a possible death wish.*

As the El wound its way downtown, she peered out the window. Night had just fallen, but Chicago's skyscrapers were already lit up. And the biggest candle on the cake was the Sears Tower.

She'd read once that the architecture had been inspired by a pack of cigarettes: the way pulling out one caused others to tag along with it, forming little tiers. In deference to the holiday, the tower's twin antennas stood awash in an eerie orange light. It might not have been literally in the middle of the skyline, but it was the city's true centerpiece. And now, she thought, it was also a glittery gun pressed to the city's temple.

The CTA spat her out a block away, at the corner of Quincy and Wells. All around, costumed people streamed into bars and clubs to post up for the night and get good and drunk, the way a city holiday dictated they should. With a sinking feeling, Bailey noticed that the largest wave was headed to the same place she was. If the Long Island iced tea was completed that night, its magical pull would put a lot of people in the crosshairs of the tremens that came calling.

Bailey lengthened her stride. It didn't do much good since her legs were so short, but the gesture mattered, dammit.

She boarded an elevator full of revelers who were either already drunk or deliriously giddy at the thought of the drunkenness about to ensue. A one-minute tourist video kept them entertained on the ride up. It was different from the one that had played when she was a girl; she'd seen that one enough times to be able to recite it verbatim, complete with fake trivia. Performing it had been a long-running joke between her and Zane.

She frowned at her train of thought. Odds were good that before the night was over, she'd come face-to-face with Zane. She still couldn't bring herself to hate him—quite the opposite, in fact. If she hated him, she wouldn't be risking her ass to pull him out of a fire he couldn't see. No matter what, the next time she saw him, she wouldn't crumple.

As the mayor popped onscreen to thank them all for visiting the pinnacle of Chicago achievement (clearly the video had been made before the Cubs' four consecutive World Series victories), the elevator doors opened and its occupants surged out.

Despite Sorensen's bragging, Apex wasn't really on the top floor; it was on the highest floor a firm was allowed to occupy, and from the looks of the bar, it was the kind of place where people didn't so much burn money as napalm it. The floors were white marble, with veins of gold and black, and bright red lounge chairs were artfully arranged around a crystalline column in the center of the space. Wraparound dark wood shelves filled with liquor bottles were affixed to the column's sides, and in front of that stood the bar.

She could barely make out Bucket behind the counter, slinging drinks seemingly everywhere at once. He'd forgone his usual *punk rawk* look in favor of a tight black ninja costume. On the other end was Trina, who somehow managed to keep pace with the steady stream of orders while shoving up the green sleeves of her baggy Statue of Liberty costume.

Bailey turned away to scan the floor for Zane or Mona. All she heard was booming music and all she saw was a forest of people, which for someone Bailey's size meant a forest of shoulders and elbows. She bumped her way through with only a single image in her mind: Sorensen in his pharaoh getup. He was her only remaining inroad.

As she circled the floor, she kept one eye on Bucket and Trina, worried they might spot her and get her thrown out. Above the thudding music and echoey floors and air that smelled like fried hors d'oeuvres, no one paid her a second look. As far as she could tell, no one even knew who she—

"Bailey Chen!"

Bowen Sorensen (the Third) came striding over, all smiles. But he wasn't dressed like a pharaoh; he was in full Napoleonic regalia, complete with a hand tucked permanently inside his jacket. "I thought that was you!" he crowed. "Oh, I'm so glad you could make it. Can I hug you? I kind of want to hug you."

Evidently the question was rhetorical because he didn't wait for an answer before smooshing her into his waistcoat.

"It's so good to see you, Mr. Sorensen—"

"Please," he said with a wave. "Mr. Sorensen was my moms' sperm donor. Well, probably not, actually. Either way, you can call me Bowie."

"Okay, Bow——" She stopped, faced with the irresistible question: "Wait. Then how are you the third?"

"Once I succeed in creating a working time machine, traveling back to make numbers one and two happen will be my top priority."

She wanted to laugh, but Sorensen looked honest and eager as a puppy.

"Cool party, huh?" he said, beaming.

Not if a delirium gate-crashes, Bailey thought. She flashed him what she hoped was a killer smile. "Best one I've been to tonight."

She'd meant it as a joke, considering her only other appearance had been a quick wave to her parents cozied up with a bowl of candy and *Law Investigation: Homicide of the Streets*, but Sorensen's face lit up.

"Oh, that's such a relief. I was worried. Last year most of my guest list was poached by the queen of England. *That bitch!*" he added, suddenly shouting in what Bailey assumed was the direction of Buckingham Palace.

She was wasting time. She needed to figure out where Garrett was. And without a gold rush to assist her, Bailey needed to pile on the charm. Not that she had a huge stockpile to draw on, but this really was a matter of life and death.

"Um, Bowie?" Bailey threw out a hip. She was trying for seductive, but the effect was less bedroom-eyed femme fatale and more femme . . . well, whatever the French word was for *dork*. "Didn't you say you had a—what's it called?—a dis—dis—"

"Distillery," Sorensen said, clearly pleased to provide an answer that her sweet little female mind couldn't chase down on its own.

Bailey smiled wider and batted her eyelashes. "Yeah," she breathed. "Don't you want to show me where that is?"

Sorensen brightened even more, which she hadn't thought

possible. "Oh, sure," he said. "They're just upstairs. They take up the second and third floors."

"Show me," she said hastily, forgetting to be sexy. "I mean, um, can't you show me? Please?"

He doffed his bicorne hat grandly. "It'd be my honor, mademoiselle." He looked her up and down as they headed for the elevator. "Hey, what're you supposed to be anyway?"

Even though she'd anticipated the question, Bailey had a hard time making herself spit out the dumb answer she'd concocted.

"A mandarin orange?" she said with a sweep at her citrus-colored sequins.

Sorensen stared. But then he threw back his head and laughed. "Oh, I *like* you."

She couldn't help laughing, too, though less from amusement and more from mounting hysteria. Still, she thought, as the crowd parted for them, she hardly could've picked more interesting company for the apocalypse than Bowen Sorensen (the Third). He was certainly fun, if not always on purpose, and heads turned as he swept through the crowd.

"It's just up h—"

Sorensen stopped at the edge of the crowd, where to Bailey's horror, he'd scuffed the shoes of the one person she didn't want to see.

Zane had swapped his usual suit for a black tuxedo. He'd paired it with a long red-lined cape, a black top hat, and a white domino mask. He twirled a rose in his fingers like a wand.

"Ooh, I love it," Sorensen said. "What are you supposed to be? A magician?"

"I'm not a *magician*," Zane said with a flare of annoyance. "I'm Tuxedo—never mind. What're you doing here?"

"Uh, I'm kinda busy owning this place, Houdini." Sorensen gave Bailey a conspiratorial "get a load of *this* idiot" wink, but she was too flustered to respond.

"Sorry, Mr. S—Bowie," said Zane. "But I was talking to Bailey."

She couldn't be seductive. She couldn't be honest. So she'd have to go nuclear—an enthusiastic, eager combination of Bowie and Jess.

"*Zane Whelan?*" Bailey squealed with every ounce of ebullience she could fake. "What are *you* doing here? It's been *so* long!"

Now Zane was the one to shoot Sorensen a look. "You—you know exactly why I'm here, Bailey."

"Uh, why would I know that?" she bubbled. "I haven't seen you in four years! You don't even read my blog anymore," she added, sounding hurt.

"Bailey," Zane said, "you're totally lying. And you don't have a blog."

"Bowie," Bailey said, making sure to punch up his name, "does Zane work for you now?" Her eyes widened theatrically. "Oh, *right*. Of course he does. His uncle Garrett is your business partner." She smiled up at Zane. "Bowie here is going to show me the on-site distillery. Have you seen it? You should come along! If that's okay," she added with a quick glance at Sorensen.

Sorensen didn't appear to know what to make of Zane, but he nodded anyway. "Oh, uh, sure. The more the merrier?"

Zane seemed to realize this wasn't an argument he could win, and he smiled tightly. "Lead the way, Bowie."

Sorensen did just that, and as he walked over to the elevator button, Zane darted to Bailey's side. "What the hell are you doing here?" he hissed.

"Going to a party," she said airily. "Should I not be here? Because I can't remember any reason why I shouldn't be."

Zane's smile slipped. "If anyone from the Court sees you, you're going to have a lot of explaining to do."

Secretly glad for the chance to act brave, Bailey scoffed. "I can take them."

Zane goggled. "You made a cocktail."

"I didn't say that."

"But you drank something before you came here."

Bailey shrugged.

"Jesus, Bailey." Zane shook his head so hard his mask slid down his nose. She saw he'd taped it to his glasses. "Do you have any idea how dangerous it is for you to be here?"

"Nope," she said, "and neither do you. Wait." She paused. "I mean, you don't know how dangerous it is for *you* to be here. Or me, I guess. But either way we're going to see."

"See what? A bunch of distilling equipment? Because that's all that's up there. I guarantee it."

"Sure." Bailey shrugged. "If you're right and nothing's going on, then I'll just get a nice tour. And if I'm right—"

"Elevator!"

Sorensen pointed at the sliding doors with all the enthusiasm of a toddler who'd just learned a new word, and Bailey marched right to him.

The ride was short, but long on awkwardness. Sorensen was blissfully unaware.

"So you two know each other? Went to high school together, right?" he said.

"Yup," she and Zane chorused.

Sorensen grinned and tapped his temple. "I've always had a keen detective mind. Given your relative ages, it was the only explanation that made sense." His eyes lit up with a secondary realization, and he snapped his fingers. "And you two have totally done it, haven't you?"

She and Zane exchanged sidelong glances.

"I was gone—" said Bailey.

"—have a girlfriend," muttered Zane.

"Oh," said Sorensen. "That's too bad. You should try it some-time. Or maybe you shouldn't. I don't really know. I haven't banged either of you." The elevator lurched to a stop. "Here we are!"

As the doors opened wide, so did Bailey's eyes.

The space was huge. The mezzanine between the top two levels had been gutted, leaving a two-story loft with shining dark window walls. Catwalks hung from a distant ceiling, illuminated by powerful industrial lights. The steel stills in Sorensen's daydreams had been giant, but they were tiny compared to these. The machinery was industrial grade, and it was loud. The air sagged from sheer noise, a tinny churning of stills at work.

Zane looked just as thunderstruck. "Holy shit," he whispered as they stepped off the elevator. "I knew they were up here, but I—I didn't *know* know, you know?"

Bailey ran the numbers but quickly gave up. The setup was impossible. There was no way the city would've signed off on radi-cally refurbishing two floors of the most prominent building in the Chicago skyline. No way that even Sorensen's formidable fortune could've covered the entire pricetag. And there was definitely no way any of this was sustainable. Even if Apex did brisk business ev-ery hour of every day, profits would never exceed operating costs.

But, she supposed, this place was never supposed to run forever. It was all created to make just one drink.

She struggled to keep up her forced innocence. "Bowie," she said, "how did you and Garrett make this happen? It's just so, ah, breathtaking," she added quickly.

Sorensen swiveled and struck a proud pose. "Bailey, other guy—I'm going to let you in on my greatest secret because it's the answer to your question: I don't know." His expertly bleached teeth gleamed under the factory lights. "The truth is, I'm always guided by my instincts. Even if decisions don't make sense, I make them anyway. They've never steered me wrong. And the more impossibly

I dream, the more possible things become."

Once again Bailey and Zane looked at each other, as if to make sure they had heard the same thing. They had. And both agreed that Sorensen was nuts.

"Did Garrett help you . . . dream this?" Bailey said slowly.

"Yes," said a voice that was decidedly not Bowen Sorensen the Third's. "At the risk of self-aggrandizement, I would determine that my contributions were instrumental."

Garrett Whelan hadn't bothered to dress up for Halloween, but still he looked different. *Triumphant.* And as far as Bailey could see, it was because he was holding a tall glass with a lemon wheel perched on its edge, a glass containing a soft amber liquid, almost the color of black tea.

Zane swayed. "Uncle Garrett?"

"Zane. I assume Ms. Chen's presence stands testament to the failure of your fortitude. But no matter." He smiled. "I hope you find the following scrap of arcane trivia educational. What is the sole part of the distilling process that can't be hastened?"

"Aging," Zane said faintly.

"Excellent." Garrett politely clapped against the glass. "Much as with raising children, a useful result can be achieved only with patience. Fortunately, unlike you, I have experience in that domain."

"But none of the liquors in the Long Island are aged," Zane said. "Even the rum—"

"That is where you err, nephew. I was meticulous in my methods. We all know the unpleasant effects that slapdash stilling can have." Bailey's chest tightened as she thought of Vincent.

Garrett's lips twisted and he paused. "I tried white rum, and Brazilian cachaça, and overproof rum—everything. I'm no fool. I know what the recipe calls for. But in this case, as in most of life, older is better.

"Dark rum, not light. The conventional recipe, like you, Zane, was errant. I was forced to bide my time as a fresh, pure batch came through the pipeline, as it were. I had to wait longer still as the rum aged in charred barrels. But by my calculations, the time has come, and in approximately"—he shook a watch from his sleeve—"twenty minutes—"

Bailey had no time to think either. She shot out her hand and her old fashioned–powered telekinesis followed suit. Garrett's glass wavered, toppled, and tumbled to the floor, shattering.

"*Party foul!*" Sorensen said, throwing his arms in the air, delighted.

The others stared. A moment ago the Long Island iced tea had been a dose of aged rum away from glowing and, presumably, granting immortality. Now it was just a dark stain on a concrete floor, garnished with glass shards and a lemon slice.

Looking disappointed but perhaps not surprised that no one joined in on his joke, Sorensen retreated and slapped Garrett heartily on the back.

"Hey, don't sweat it, old pal. What were you drinking? We'll get one of the bartenders to—"

"An old fashioned." Garrett looked up, not at Sorensen but, with cold anger, at Bailey.

"Done," Sorensen said. "I'll—"

"Not for me, you imbecile," Garrett snapped. "The girl. She's had one."

"You're done, Garrett," Bailey said.

Still in shock, Zane managed to glance between Bailey, his uncle, and the broken glass. "Bailey—you—" he croaked. "That was it."

"Sorry," Sorensen said, "but I feel like things have just gotten *crazy* intense here. What's—"

"Shut up, Bowen," Garrett said. "Ms. Chen. I assume, given your financial situation, that a cab from Ravenswood would've cost an exorbitant amount, rendering you at the mercy of the Chicago

Transit Authority. Assuming further that you came here immediate-ly, which I imagine you didn't, I would posit that you have less than ten minutes left of psionic potency."

Bailey said nothing. Technically he was wrong, but he was still right. In fact, thanks to her small body mass and lack of fat, she probably had even less time than that. Already she felt the magi-cal warmth cooling around the edges. "Ten minutes is more than enough to stop you."

Garrett nodded. "I can't dispute the veracity of your conten-tion," he said. "So instead, I proffer this counterquery: is it sufficient time to stop *her*?"

"Stop wh—"

A blunt object clocked Bailey on the back of the head. She reeled forward, her vision filled with cascading stars. She tried to marshal her psychic powers and catch her fall, but someone caught her first: Zane. The red lining of his cape flared around them as he pushed her upright. His face was pale. Two feet away a figure with bowed head crouched like a tiger, wearing not a costume but a bartender's outfit: black McNee's T-shirt and white towel tucked in a belt. Bailey didn't need to see the face to know that Mona and her thick-soled boots had been the one to kick her down.

"Babe?" Zane said weakly. "What are you—"

But before he could finish, he and Bailey were under attack.

CHAPTER EIGHTEEN

Mona bounded forward, but Zane was rooted where he stood. Fortunately, Bailey's mind was already in high gear.

"*Move, you dapper idiot!*" She shoved him aside and gave Mona's bootlaces a telekinetic yank, but it wasn't enough to topple her. She rolled forward and, with a low sweep of her leg, aimed a kick that Bailey barely jumped over.

With everything she had, Bailey pushed back. This time Mona slammed into one of the four giant stills; a metallic clang rang through the loft like a cathedral bell.

Garrett was already receding into the darkness. Bailey tore after him.

"Bowie, get the other bartenders up here!" she yelled. "I'll explain later!"

"But—"

"*Go!*"

Garrett had disappeared. From the quick rattle of footsteps, it sounded as if he'd taken to the catwalk. With shaking hands, Bailey snapped open her purse, gestured, and lauched her projectile— a billiard ball swiped from the abandoned Long & Strong, where she'd fixed her old fashioned. But Bailey's mind was too frazzled to keep the ball on target, and it caromed off one of the catwalk's rails.

"*Bailey!*"

She had barely caught the ball before Zane tackled her to the ground. A whip of water lashed out where they'd stood, and Mona, who'd surrounded each of her arms with a long liquid tendril, wound back for another strike.

"Come on!" Bailey scrambled to her feet, pulling Zane behind a still as a second lash cracked from Mona's arm.

"What the everloving *fuck*." Zane was breathing hard. "What the hell is she doing?"

"I don't know," Bailey said.

"This can't be happening," he said. "I saw it. The Long Island iced tea. But . . . Garrett—Mona—she wouldn't—"

"Newsflash, Zane. It can and she did." Bailey poked her head out in time to see Mona shoot a shard of ice toward them like a glittering arrow. Mentally she swatted it away. "Do you want to keep sitting here and saying it isn't?"

"*I'm going through a lot here, okay?*" he said. "My uncle and my girlfriend are trying to, I don't know, kill us. Why would they even—"

"Because I was right." Bailey dumped her purse and sent another pool ball—the sixteen—careening off the metal fixtures criss-crossing the huge open space, distracting Mona until Bailey could track down Garrett. "Your uncle's taking over, and he's bringing people down with him. First Vincent, then us. If he gets that drink, this place will be swarming with tremens." She was practically shouting over the clang of flying icicles hitting the stills and the roar of the machinery. "The Long Island will pull them here, and the drunk people downstairs will be a buffet. There aren't enough bartenders to stop them. And your uncle, the man who made this all happen, will be un-fucking-touchable."

"Shit."

"Yeah." Bailey sensed the sixteen ball wobble. "I've only got a few minutes left in me. Get downstairs. Make sure Sorensen evacuates the place. I guess I can hold them off—"

"Mona and Garrett? They're two of the best bartenders in Chicago."

"And what would you do about it if you were here?" Bailey snapped. "You're sober, which is synonymous with *useless,* so if you want to help, come back with something in your system. I'll cover you."

And then, for good measure, she kissed him.

Zane blinked when she pulled away. "Bailey?" he said. "What the hell was that?"

She smiled bittersweetly. "That was for me. Go."

He nodded.

She nodded back.

Then together they surged out from behind the still.

Icy hail flew at them from every direction. Bailey ducked, gesturing at their point of origin, and her six remaining billiard balls zoomed in that direction. Instantly her temples throbbed. Controlling multiple flight paths felt like her brain was juggling pieces of itself.

Zane turned when she slowed, but Bailey squeezed her eyes shut and plowed on. "Keep going!"

Above them, someone ran in the catwalk; Bailey's head ached all over again.

Zane threw himself past her and his long legs carried him quickly across the industrial floor. Mona adjusted her angle of fire. Bailey intercepted the shards, but as she sent the ice veering off course, she lost her grip on one of the pool balls, which skittered to the floor. Gritting her teeth, she redoubled her efforts to maintain control, but it was almost impossible while also shielding Zane.

Of course, Bailey realized. That was the whole point. Mona was trying to split her focus.

Well, Bailey thought, *two can play that game.* She eyed the tiny figure rushing across the catwalk and listened for footsteps beneath the whine of the machines, did some hasty telekinetic math, then let the striped eleven ball fly. As a second round of ice shards flew forward, the ball shot straight through the railings and clocked Garrett with a skull-rattling *crack*, loud enough to distract Mona.

The shards faltered, then fell like hail.

Bailey had already launched herself at the nearest staircase. She bounded up the steps, risking a glance down as she climbed. Mona sprinted across the floor, her dark eyes locked on Bailey, but behind her a not-magician's cape flashed just as the elevator doors slid shut.

Hope fluttered in Bailey's chest. Zane would be back with reinforcements, and maybe even another drink for her. And once the rest of the bartenders showed up to fight, Mona and Garrett would lose. All Bailey had to do was last until that fight could begin, which . . .

Easier said than fucking done.

Sprinting onto the catwalk, Bailey called her pool balls and set them orbiting around her like tiny moons, a rotating shield. From this high, she could finally see where Garrett was running. At the other end of the catwalk were more stairs that led down to the collection tanks, where he could dispense a second round and mix again. If he got even a few moments alone, it was game over.

But Garrett had taken a pool ball to the head, and Bailey had a lead on her pursuer.

Mona seemed to read her thoughts. Rather than vault for the stairs, she pulled back one of her water whips, lashed it at a catwalk railing, and swung swashbuckler-style directly into Bailey's path.

"Chen." Mona landed softly, the cresting water around her glowing in the light.

"Mona," Bailey said, because she still had no idea what Mona's last name was. "You're . . . a surprise."

She tried to shoot the eight ball forward, over Mona's shoulder and toward Garrett, but Mona smirked, held her arms wide, and summoned the water into an immense, glittering wall. The ball smacked and fell, scattering droplets.

"Let him drink, Chen," Mona said.

"No way in hell."

A gush of water surged forward, but this time Bailey was ready. She knocked a billiard ball straight into Mona's wrist, and the water fell limply to the floor.

"The first one he made's probably called a whole delirium on this place. If he makes another, then who knows what—"

"*I* know," Mona said, shouting over the machines. "I know what will happen. That's why it needs to." Her voice was even, but her arms and hands were tense with the effort of holding the water wall in place.

"What?" Bailey glanced again at Garrett. He was up again and hobbling toward another flight of stairs that led to the valves at the bottom of the stills. "Why?"

It wasn't a debate. Mona windmilled her legs into an aerial kick, water surging around her. Bailey panicked and fired off two shots, but Mona dodged them, grabbing the railing and swinging out of the way before a crushing torrent smashed Bailey face-first into metal.

Gasping, Bailey struggled to push back against the overwhelming pressure, but the heavy water was everywhere, clogging her eyes and ears and throat as the billiard balls clattered to the ground. She was losing power. Losing air. Losing the fight.

No. Think, Bailey.

Right. She could think her way out.

Telekinetically, she grabbed her own ankles and pulled as hard as she could. The jagged floor tore at her skin and grated her orange dress like cheese. But a moment later she was out from beneath the water, coughing and scrambling to get back on her feet. Her dress clung heavily, and with a little burst of psychic effort she shoved her sopping hair out of her eyes. She needed an advantage, and fast. She'd wasted so much time, and another magical swirly would suffocate her.

Suffocate. That was it.

Mona surged another whip of water, but Bailey hit it with a telekinetic hammer. She was too weak to wrest control from Mona, but she caused a decent backsplash, drenching them both. Bailey blocked her mouth with a forearm, but Mona wasn't ready and for a second she coughed. That was all Bailey needed.

With a vicious slash, Bailey willed Mona's towel, now freshly wet, to rip out of its belt loop and plaster itself over Mona's face. Mona attempted to claw it off but the heavy cloth cut off her air. Bailey clamped down as hard as she could and commanded the towel to knot itself behind Mona's head. The twin water whips immediately fell inert, splatting through the perforated catwalk floor and onto the concrete below. Barely pausing, Bailey turned, planted a foot, and with a door-breaking kick launched Mona down the nearest flight of stairs.

Ahead, Garrett had reached the floor near the collection tank. He'd produced another glass and started to mix.

It was too far for Bailey to run—and judging by how viciously her scraped-up skin stung, she was almost sober. But not quite powerless. She grabbed the nearest railing and jumped over the edge.

Air whistled past her ears as she directed all her mental power into flinging her body forward like a shot put. *Shoot for the moon,* she thought, dazed. *Even if you miss, you'll land on concrete and smash into a bunch of bloody, dead bits.*

But she didn't miss. She didn't stick the landing but kind of hit the ground running. Pain ricocheted up her leg, but she couldn't give two shits if it was broken. She was alive, and she was already fantasizing about giving Garrett a heroic punch in the jaw and declaring something like "Garrett, I'm cutting you off."

Ooh, that was pretty good.

"Garrett, I'm cutting you—ah!"

She stumbled on one of the loose pool balls—not enough to lose balance but enough to distract Garrett. It wasn't a pithy reach-for-the-sky moment, but it worked.

"Oh, Ms. Chen," Garrett said, lowering his glass. "A victim of your poor education."

Bailey hobbled forward, wincing. "I was Vincent's best student."

He smirked. "I was referring to UPenn."

Fury twisted Bailey's stomach, but the pain in her leg kept her from thinking of a rejoinder.

"You thought you'd get out there and change the world." He laughed mirthlessly. "I've held this city together with my own hands for the better part of fifty years. I've seen fellow Tribunes come and go, each more idiotic than the last. All enter this office with hopes of changing things, only to become co-opted by it. And I know now what you and your little brat barback friends can never appreciate: it's not the new blood that makes the best changes. It's the old guard. And with this cocktail, I'll devote my endless lifetime to the service of Chicago. Assuming, of course, that it will in turn serve me."

"That's not service!" Bailey yelled. "Even Vincent could see that. Even after he—"

Garrett's expression flickered, and the revelation hit Bailey like a slap across the face.

"*You*," she said, her voice shaking. "You tampered with Vincent's gin. You blinded him."

Garrett scowled. "A necessary measure. A fire-breathing anarchist like Vincent Long had no business with a Long Island iced tea. Men like him wish to break things down, but not to build something in the absence their efforts create. He was an old man, but he never grew up. And neither, apparently, have you."

Vincent's voice wafted into her head: *The grown-up who says they know what they're doing is a grown-up who's lying.* She smiled, and that was when she knew she wasn't a grown-up. Not yet.

Because she knew what to do.

Bailey lunged for Garrett's throat with all her bloodied, banged-up might. She was wounded, woozy, and short, but he was old and, well, even shorter.

Before she could strangle him, a cold, wet tentacle wrapped itself around her wounded ankle. Bailey fell onto her stomach, banging her head on the concrete floor as a heavy boot planted itself between her shoulder blades.

"Stay down, Chen," Mona said. "Garrett, do it now."

Bailey thrashed, but orbs of water clamped her hands, instantly hardening into ice. Her arms were pinned, and she began shivering from the cold.

She twisted her head up to see Garrett carving out a perfect lemon slice with a silver pocketknife.

"Garrett!" she yelled as he jammed a straw into the glass and stirred with a flourish. "People will die!"

Like he hasn't considered that. A dull amber glow blossomed in the glass. Garrett hesitated—barely half a heartbeat—and then brought the Long Island iced tea to his lips and drank.

Bailey cried out, and to her surprise the ice shackling her suddenly melted.

"We have to go." Mona seized her by the back of her dress and pulled her to her feet. "Up. Now!"

"What—"

A discarded billiard ball rocketed straight at Mona. Bailey whirled just in time to see Zane, hand outstretched, sprinting up from the elevator bay with ninja Bucket behind. The ball flew too fast for telekinesis—Zane must have drunk a screwdriver for super-strength—or for Mona to parry it.

But Mona didn't dodge. Instead, she stomped her foot and held

Bailey close while a purple bubble of energy erupted around them. The ball smashed into it and shattered like glass as circular ripples radiated outward along the shield.

Up close, Mona smelled like sweat and tequila, and for a second the eyes of everyone, including Garrett, were on them.

Bailey jerked out of Mona's arms. "How—"

Manifesting two drinks at once was impossible. But Bailey realized she was the only one still staring at Mona. Everyone else was looking up to where the windows of the Sears Tower's top floor—tempered to resist every element the upper atmosphere could throw at them—had shattered. And from those jagged holes, tremens—an uncountable number of tremens—bled inside.

The Tequila Slammer
A potable to instill protective properties

1. *In an old fashioned glass, pour one and a half ounces of tequila and a quarter lime's worth of juice.*

2. *Layer one and a half ounces of ginger ale on top of the tequila.*

3. *Cover the mouth of the glass, lift it, and slam down the glass to mix the ingredients.*

4. *Drain the glass before the ginger ale stops foaming.*

The tequila slammer is difficult to prepare. The ingredients must be properly layered or the slamming effect will be spoiled. Because tequila slammers are consumed rapidly, like a shot, this ingestion provides further risk for a bartender looking to enter the field; the sudden spike of alcohol in the bloodstream means that, if improperly prepared, a tequila slammer will render the drinker incapable of metabolizing magic for as long as an hour.

Though the tequila slammer was invented in Mexico (where it is known as a muppet or *mópet*), its creator is unknown. The drink was brought north in the mid-1960s by vacationing American bartenders who had observed locals using it to great effect against the tremens that often haunt resort towns. The shield it projects was—and remains—ideally suited to the defense of drunk and irate tourists, who are usually less inclined to obey lifesaving orders while on vacation.

FIG. 92—*Agave tequilana.*

FIG. 93—The blue agave plant, the source of tequila, is pollinated by the endangered *Leptonycteris nivalis* (Mexican long-nosed bat).

GINGER ALE.

FIG. 94—*Zingiber officinale.*

Though American apothecaries first brewed a variation on ginger ale *circa* 1851, the modern version, distinguished as dry ginger ale, did not arrive until some fifty years later in Canada. It was initially slow to take hold, but its popularity exploded during Prohibition, when it could be conveniently used as a way to hide stockpiles of illicit spirits (along the way improving the flavor). Ginger ale was also useful as a steadying ingredient. Much the same way that carbonation and ginger root settle an upset stomach, the combination can also tame more chaotic liquors like tequila, another quality that proved useful during Prohibition, when bartenders were forced to use subpar and unreliable products to carry out their fieldwork.

CHAPTER NINETEEN

All at once Bailey saw three ways to die.

In one corner was Garrett Whelan, a grudge-holding old man who'd just drunk his way into godhood (or something like it) and who was more than a little pissed off at her.

In the other corner was the impossibly powered Mona, her friend until ten minutes ago, enemy until fifteen seconds ago, and now . . . something else entirely.

And in every other corner or otherwise were the tremens, life-drinking skinless demons who thankfully didn't hunt in packs, except for the times they decided to be total assholes and do exactly that.

Mona stomped again, and the energy shield around them collapsed. She shoved Bailey aside and took off running. With a gesture, she peeled the stagnant water puddle off the concrete and re-formed it around her arm. Zane and Bucket moved to intercept her, but Mona threw her water arm to a railing like a grappling hook and hauled herself over their heads and onto the catwalk. Barely settling on solid ground, she lashed out again, swung herself over the giant stills, and disappeared.

Meanwhile, the tremens, dumb and nearly blind but certainly hungry, scuttled down the walls.

"*What the fuck just happened?*" Bucket turned to face the swarm, swatting his ninja mask out of the way.

"Hell if I know!" Bailey grimaced against her ankle pain. "Please tell me you brought me a drink!"

Zane pressed a glass into her hand: smoky whiskey and sweet, sharp citrus. Another old fashioned. "Drink up. We need you."

Bailey chugged. Standing before them, Garrett Whelan appeared radiant. His skin was still spotted and sagging with age, but it also glowed with a golden aura, as if he'd swallowed an industrial-strength lightbulb.

"Chicago requires none of you anymore." His voice boomed as he flexed luminous fingers. "From now until the day the swamp upon which it lies swallows it again, it will have *me*."

He thrust out a hand. With a blisteringly bright beam of energy, he blasted two tremens whole, leaving nothing but angry scorch marks on the wall behind them. The oncoming delirium wavered, but only for a moment. Then it surged again, more fervent than ever.

"Yes!" Garrett cried, hurling another blast of magical energy into the skinless horde. "Come to me and find yourselves lacking! Chicago is mine, and your touch will no longer sully its streets!"

Zane and Bucket looked on, stunned and still. Bailey wiped her mouth in frustration and pitched her empty glass against the wall.

That made the Alechemists move.

"We have to do something!" Bailey said.

"What about Mona?" said Zane.

Bailey felt a stab of indignation, but it disappeared when she saw Zane's face: panicked and pained. She couldn't imagine what he was going through. "Mona's gone," she said. "She fled. Like a coward."

But even as she said it, she didn't believe it. The woman who could kick any of their asses—even sober—was no coward. Of all of them, Mona stood the best chance of surviving the delirium, and she'd probably relish the chance to annihilate it.

Garrett clapped his hands, and a crescent-shaped wave of golden energy spun from them and scythed through three tremens at once. They instantly burst into clouds of foul smoke, but still more rushed to fill the gap. Even with Garrett's formidable powers, he couldn't hold back the tide forever.

She looked from Bucket's panicked, de-ninjaed face to Zane, who appeared considerably more resolved.

"We can't leave him," he said.

"He'll be fine," Bailey said. "*We* aren't immortal now."

"But the delirium," Bucket said. "Who's going to stop it if we don't?"

"Who's going to stop it if we're dead?" Bailey snapped. She was still stuck on Mona. Maybe she knew something they didn't.

"Zane, we're going!" She clutched his elbow, but he didn't budge. His face was . . . reverent. There was no other word for it.

"It's the Long Island iced tea, Bailey." He blinked, awed, as if the room weren't flooding full of demons. "It's . . . beautiful."

That was what was holding Zane back—his thirst. He was staring past Garrett to the stills. He was doing the math in his head. Deciding if it'd be safe to make a break for it. Build his own drink. Finally get his own glassful of grand panacea. If ever there was a time, it was now.

She took his hand and squeezed it hard. "Zane."

"Uh, guys?" Bucket nodded at Garrett. "He's getting brighter. Is that a thing Americans do?"

"You can't," Bailey said, and she tugged on his hand a second time. "Not now."

He glanced down at their hands. Then back up at her. Then back at the stock of supplies. And then she felt his hand relax in her grip.

"Thank you," he whispered.

"Oh, yeah, just ignore the Canadian," muttered Bucket. "Old

guy's *literally* getting lit and—"

"Uncle Garrett!" Zane called, newly urgent. "We've got to fall back!"

"Not a chance!" Garrett crowed, easily blasting away another tremens. One finally got close enough to try latching on to him, but the old man dodged nimbly and dissolved the creature with a touch of his hand. He'd once been a man internally illuminated; now he looked like pure light.

"But Uncle Garrett—"

"*Boy,*" Garrett said sharply, and a crack formed on one of Zane's eyeglass lenses. "Your inconsequential dabbling in the deeper arts of bartending betrays your lack of greater understanding. You have before you the privilege of watching a master at work. I suggest you take the opportunity. Gratefully. And you, Ms. Chen," he added, gathering more golden energy into his hands, "I will deal with you momentarily."

"Seriously, what the hell?" Bucket said. "Did I drink a martini or—"

But before anyone could answer, Garrett Whelan exploded.

Light—bright and hot enough to singe hair—detonated across the concrete floor. The impact nearly blew Bailey off her feet, but by then the engine of her psychic powers had revved up again. She pushed back against her own body and steadied herself, her eyes burning behind their lids. Bucket threw himself to the floor, his shouts lost in the roar.

Zane tumbled past them.

Bailey opened her eyes to a squint just in time to see the blast pick him off his feet. Bucket was too slow to reach him, but Bailey wasn't. She visualized herself grabbing Zane by the foot. The psychic strain was immediate, but he hung horizontally, inching forward as Bailey fought to pull him in against the current of the explosion. She couldn't let this beat her, couldn't let him go.

"I got you!" Bucket, who had anchored himself to a metal trap-door handle, grabbed Zane's other ankle with his free hand, and together he and Bailey pulled, just enough to keep Zane from slamming into a concrete wall or, worse, flying out a broken window.

"*Uncle Garrett!*"

Zane's scream reached Bailey, but Garrett—the man at the eye of the storm—was gone. Bailey watched in fascinated horror as his clothes dissolved, and then the skin beneath it, and then the muscles, until she could make out only the faint black outline of Garrett Whelan's bones before they, too, turned to dust.

A short moment of silence was quickly followed by a fearsome, blinding *crack!*

Stinging light surged in every direction, filling the massive two-story room. Heat and pain buffeted Bailey from all sides, and at last she felt her grip on the ground release.

She was falling.

Her eyes flew open. *Why am I falling?*

Another *crack!* and then a crumbling sound.

Oh, duh, she thought. *Because the floor's collapsing underneath me.*

They plunged downward: Bailey and Zane and Bucket and machinery and debris, rushing toward the Apex floor with alarming speed.

Bailey desperately grasped for the mental strength to slow the fall. It was working: the air rushed past slower, chunks of concrete flew sideways and out of range even as pain threatened to devour her from the very center of her skull.

Just before impact, she jerked their three bodies horizontal as hard as she could. Bucket went spinning off to the side, but she and Zane took hold of each other and skidded across the marble.

Crunching thuds of concrete sent shock waves across the floor. Panic clutched at Bailey's chest, but no one was there to get flattened; the bar was empty. She jumped to her feet and flung out her arms, slowing the concrete pieces and mentally cradling them to rest.

"Bailey!"

She looked up and saw the twisted chunk of a distilling vat plummeting toward her. Zane rushed to her side and caught it, his screwdriver-induced superstrength halting the stainless steel meteor with barely a bend in his elbows. It was light enough for him to lift but too big to hold, so he shunted it aside, skipping it across the marble. It gouged deep lines in its wake.

Before Bailey could thank him or even form a complete sentence, wet drops began spattering down over them.

"Is it raining?" Zane squinted at the wreckage above.

"The sprinkler system," Bailey said. The floor was littered with charred furniture, discarded bits of Halloween costumes, and broken glass and concrete. But mercifully no blood.

"Sorensen got them all out," Bailey said. She couldn't quite believe he'd been useful in the end. "There's nobody h—"

"What the hell happened up there?"

It was Trina, her Statue of Liberty costume singed and her spiky crown askew. Her torch hung together in two barely connected pieces, like an oddly shaped set of nunchaku.

"Garrett Whelan drank until he exploded," Bailey said. She looked at Zane, but the truth was that she didn't really know *what* had happened, and she doubted Zane did either. "And then the rest of the stuff happened," she finished lamely.

"You didn't see him?" Zane asked Trina. He glanced around as if expecting his uncle to pop out of the debris.

"No," Trina said emphatically. "All I know is that you left to head back upstairs, that guy in the Napoleon hat told everyone to get out, and a fuck-ton of tremens started climbing outside the windows."

"Yeah," Bailey said, "sounds about right."

"I was mixing something while everyone was trying to cram into the elevators, but right when they broke through and started for me, the whole ceiling fucking collapsed." Trina said. "Took all the bastards out at once."

"Guys!" Bucket called. He limped into sight, his black ninja costume covered in soot and dust.

Zane indicated his bum leg. "Are you okay?"

"Nothing sweet-ass health care can't fix," Bucket said. He held out his wounded leg to Bailey's own busted limb. "Hey, now we can be limp buddies!" He considered his words a moment. "Or a totally different term. A better term. A cooler term. Like—"

"Comrades-in-legs?" Bailey offered.

"No," said Bucket, "I was gonna say—ugh, dammit, yours is way better." When Trina giggled, he eyed her for a moment. An easy grin crept onto his metal-studded face. "We meet again, Ms. of Liberty," he said, smoothing his mohawk. "You're from France, eh? Because it just so happens I'm from a French-speaking province with an ardently separatist history."

Bailey smiled, but Zane didn't seem to have a laugh left in him. He had a faraway look in his eyes, as if still in shock. She took his hand and wove her fingers between his. "Hey," she said, "we'll be okay. It's over."

"He's—he was my uncle, Bailey," Zane said. "I can't just shake it off like you can. That's a superpower you're born with, not one you can build in a Collins glass."

She could hear Trina whisper to Bucket: "What are they talking about?"

"I'll explain later," he very audibly whispered back. "There's kind of a lot of subtext."

Bailey could think of nothing to say. It had been too much too quickly. Maybe a golden platitude could set Zane straight after everything he'd lived through, but she sure as hell hadn't learned it in business school. Or anywhere else, for that matter. So she just stood next to him, running her thumb along the curves of his hand as the sprinkler system rained down on them.

"When did this happen?" said Trina, nodding at them.

"Not totally sure," said Bucket. "They're better about it than a lot of the couples I've met."

"So, what now?" Trina said, surveying the wreckage that was Apex.

"Yeah," said Bucket. "I hate to be That Guy, but if Garrett's gone, then I'm out a job, and the immigration people won't be into that. Also, neither will the cops when they show up."

Hearing those words brought Zane back to life. "Right," he said. "We have to get out of here."

"How?" Bailey glanced toward the elevator bay, where the doors were warped and bent.

"Magic," Zane said.

"Oh, right," Bailey said. Even after fighting demons and shooting electricity from her fists and watching a man spontaneously combust, she forgot that sometimes there really was a magic solution.

"The bar's smashed, but the booze in the storage room should still be intact," Trina said. "We'll get out of here with white Russians."

"What do those do?" said Bailey. She couldn't remember the entry in *The Devil's Water Dictionary*.

"Well," Trina said, "they're kind of my specialty since I'm a dessert gal. And they—"

Bailey glanced up. Maybe because looking up at people had become a habit. Maybe her survival instincts—weak as they were, though they'd gotten her this far—prompted her to. Whatever the reason, she managed to catch sight of something large and pinkish unfolding from the ruined ceiling.

"Tremens!"

It got Trina first. A sticky tentacle wrapped around her leg and jerked her knees. Zane leapt forward, fists up, but the tremens tightened its grip and flung Trina into his path; together they crumpled to the floor. The tremens darted on top of them, its ring of black teeth glinting as it prepared to feed.

But Bailey was ready. The moment its mouth opened, she flung her arm and sent a chunk of concrete debris straight down its gullet. The tremens stopped midbreath, its tentacles flailing. Bailey relaxed a tiny bit, waiting for it to explode and die, but it didn't. Choking and gasping, the beast rounded on her and pounced.

She couldn't get out of its way—her ankle was too weak—but she realized that she could move it out of hers. Training her focus, she gave the tremens a telekinetic shove in the flank, then V-stepped aside like a matador. The tremens whooshed past and slammed against the wall. It shuddered and bucked, its visible muscles working to dislodge the obstacle in its throat.

Bailey pushed the concrete back down. It was sick and brutal; she'd never killed a tremens so slowly. Behind her, Zane was up on his feet, but when he jumped forward, Bailey stuck out a hand to stop him.

"No," she said. She could feel the tremens's throat muscles relaxing and giving way, its thrashing growing more feeble, and it oozed to the floor as whatever vital force animated it slowly drained away.

"Bailey—"

"It's fine," she said. "It's dying."

Something rammed against her knees, and Bailey buckled to the floor.

"Bailey!"

She felt a tug around her ankles, dragging her forward across the slick marble. Her vision was speckled—she'd clocked her head—and her hair was a wet curtain on her face.

A trail of red followed her.

Whatever was tugging stopped, and Bailey felt a rush of gratitude. Fireworks exploded in front of her eyes, and with the pain of her ankle, the throbbing of her skull, and the exhaustion of staving off the apocalypse, she just wanted to sleep. She was spent. Above her, the tremens heaved and inhaled, its disgusting lips convulsing around the concrete, and Bailey shuddered as the deep, gnawing ache bloomed inside her. A choking tremens wasn't a harmless one; it didn't need to breathe. And she'd driven the creature into such a frenzy that it wasn't merely drinking her life essence away; it was trying to shotgun it like beer from a punctured can.

Dimly, Bailey knew she should fight back. But she'd already saved Chicago. She'd saved Bucket. And Trina. She'd saved Zane. She'd finally actually done something that mattered. So if this was the way it was going to end—

"No!"

With a bone-rattling slam, the tremens shot backward and into the wall. Zane had struck it, and he bounded over Bailey and toward the wall to land another blow. From over Bailey's head, someone lashed out with a thin whip of water that snapped against tremens flesh—Trina with her mojito. Bucket ducked and rolled to their side, a torrent of fire erupting from his outstretched hands.

Scorched, bruised, and broken, the tremens exploded.

Bailey gasped like she'd just emerged from the bottom of a deep pool. The night air was cold and harsh in her lungs, but she was still alive. She sat up wincing and blinked.

"You guys saved me," she said dumbly.

"Of course we did," said Trina.

"No matter what," Zane said, his gray eyes shining, "you're one of us."

"Duh," said Bucket.

Bailey smiled through watery eyes. "Thanks."

That seemed as good a time as any to faint.

The White Russian
A libation to induce a certain lightness in the feet

1. *Fill an old fashioned glass with ice.*

2. *Add one and a half ounces of vodka and three-quarters of an ounce of coffee liqueur.*

3. *Float three-quarters of an ounce of fresh cream on top..*

4. *Stir slowly until mixed, and serve.*

The White Russian's invention is credited to Vivienne Vandenberg of the Andere Vrouw in Rotterdam in 1938. A longtime skeptic of dairy products in general, Vandenberg initially dismissed as frivolous the effects of what became her most famous creation. However, her partner (in life and love as well as in tending bar), Coby Vandenberg, quickly realized the potential of a cocktail that allowed its drinker to walk on air—the closest any known drink has gotten to full-on flight—and she convinced Vivienne to refine the recipe.

It proved prudent. The Vandenbergs' innovation greatly improved bartending oversight in Rotterdam, allowing drinkers to more easily descend from the Witte Huis, an eleven-story building that served as a lookout to seek out tremens activity. In the prewar years, Rotterdam boasted one of the lowest tremens-related fatality rates in Europe, although it did suffer a subsequent spike in memory modifications, as bartenders unused to aerial navigation often wandered into plain sight by accident.

CREAM.

Prior to the addition of cream, the combination of vodka and coffee liqueur was served under the name "Black Russian." Vandenberg's invention of the White Russian came one afternoon when she was entertaining a visiting delegation of the Belgian Cupbearers Court. One of the delegates, not understanding that the coffee liqueur he was being served contained no actual coffee, stubbornly refused to even taste it until it had been lightened to the degree to which he was accustomed. Etiquette demanded that an official meeting could not begin without all present sharing a drink, immediately bringing the Dutch and Belgians to a standstill. Vandenberg, just as stubborn as her Flemish counterpart, fetched a pitcher of cream from the café next door and proceeded to empty it into the delegate's glass. The request having been filled in letter, if not in spirit, he had no choice but to drink the result. To this day there is no historical consensus on what surprised him more: the degree to which he enjoyed the flavor or the fact that he had just bumped his head into a rafter.

FIG. 103—*A cream pitcher.*

CHAPTER TWENTY

Bailey awoke on a sofa and remembered nothing.

Well, not *nothing*. She remembered taking on Mona and Garrett and fighting what had possibly been a ton of tremens at the top of the Sears Tower. She definitely remembered sort of strangling that last one, right before she almost died and the Alechemists came to her rescue. In fact she remembered a lot more than nothing. The only thing she didn't remember was how she'd gotten there.

And she didn't even know where *there* was.

At first glance, it seemed like a normal enough living room. The floorboards were narrow and laminated, like the ones in bowling alleys. The white walls looked as if they'd built up an inch-thick coat of paint over the years. An old brass radiator stood in the corner. But the floor was covered in woven straw mats enclosed by dark wooden frames. The coffee table was surrounded by cushions that looked as if they were meant to be knelt on. And everywhere she looked, she saw stacks of comics and DVDs.

She picked up the nearest DVD and looked at the cover. A drawing of a frowny young man with physics-defying spiky hair stared back with impossibly big eyes. She couldn't read the title; it was spelled out in neon green kanji characters. Next she grabbed a comic: big-eyed, small-mouthed girls in sailor outfits, all posed dynamically with various weapons. This title was also in kanji, though at least it had an exclamation point and a large capital X at the end to help her make some sense of it.

Bailey's heart sank. If she was where she thought she was, she'd much rather have let the tremens kill her.

All the posters on the walls were for anime series. The book-shelves overflowed with manga. A pair of decorative katana hung crossed on the wall, and the lamp on the table next to her was shaped like a leggy cartoon girl with cat ears.

Right on cue, the apartment's owner, carried on quiet shoeless feet, appeared in the doorway. "*Konbanwa*, Tokyo Rose," said Trent, bowing. His dirty blond hair was ponytailed, his neck afflicted with a patchy beard. "Welcome back to the land of the living." He beamed and flashed her a little peace sign. "I was wondering when you'd come out of it. Thought you'd take up my couch forever. Not that that'd be the worst thing in the world."

Even if Bailey hadn't felt like she'd been dragged from one end of Chicago to the other by a semi, Trent still would have been too damn chirpy. *No wonder he's a barista,* she thought.

"What am I doing here?" she said. "Where are my friends?" And with annoyed resignation she added: "And I'm Chinese."

"Your friends went out to kick tremens ass after they left you in my care," he said. "Whenever someone's taken a walk on the wild side and had trouble walking away, me and my java-slinging breth-ren get to play Florence Nightingale."

He unceremoniously pulled the blanket off her. She recoiled instinctively, then berated herself for upsetting her injured leg. Except she felt no pain. She was still wearing her shredded dress from the night before, but her cuts had healed, too.

"Coffee," Trent said. "It'll cure what ails ya. Unless what ails ya is insomnia."

"Good," Bailey said, rising. "Then I can—ah!" The moment she tried to stand, the apartment started spinning, as if she were still in the grip of a tremens. She collapsed back onto the couch.

"Easy there, Bailey-chan," he said. "That tremens took a good drink of you. I spent most of the night just healing the physical damage. I needed you awake before I refueled your animus reserves. Hang on."

He disappeared into the kitchen. She heard a machine whirr and buzz to life, and the smell of coffee hit the air. He reappeared soon after, carrying a steaming mug. "Drink it slowly," he said, handing her a cappuccino topped with a perfect tuft of foam. He'd sprinkled powdered cinnamon over top in the shape of a cross, like on the side of a first-aid kit.

Bailey eyed it. "This coffee can heal me?"

"That cappuccino can replenish your stores of innate magic, and then some . . . if you drink it slowly."

"What happens if I drink it fast?"

"Then you burn the roof of your mouth, and I'll have another thing to fix."

She drank slowly.

Bailey's dizziness receded as she sipped. Despite its warmth, the drink cooled her insides like a balm. And though she never would've admitted it to Trent, it tasted damn good. At last she put the empty cup aside with a contented sigh, stood again, and instantly regretted it, falling back with a yelp.

"*Gomenasai*," said Trent, bowing. "Coffee doesn't work as fast as booze. It'll take awhile until everything's completely healed." He brightened. "But hey, while we wait, I'll throw on some episodes of *Ultimate Frisbee Fighter Gengoro X*. I just got it in the original Japanese."

Too weak to escape, she had to suffer through fifteen minutes of Trent's running commentary on the first episode before her salvation appeared.

"Now here's something interesting," said Trent, who was almost certainly about to tell her nothing of the sort. "In the Filipino dub,

Kazemaru was made into a woman and her name was changed to—wait, hang on." He pulled out his phone. "Hello? Yeah, she's right here."

Bailey reached for his phone, but he waved her off.

"I don't think she's really ready for . . . Well, why don't you come up? We're watching *Ultimate Frisbee Fighter* . . . " His voice trailed off. "All right," he said, the color draining from his face. "I'll send her down." He hung up and turned to face Bailey. "Zane and his friends are downstairs waiting for you," he said. "I'm so sorry to interrupt the episode, but they really insisted that—"

But Bailey was already on her feet.

Fighting residual dizziness, she took her time going down the steps. She'd just survived hell and more. The last thing she needed was to fall and crack her head open. But she felt flutters in her gut the whole way down. On the one hand, she was excited to see Zane. On the other, every single thing had changed overnight. They hadn't undergone this much interpersonal turmoil in a twelve-hour period since the Fight.

When she reached the street, Bailey wasn't greeted by a scarecrow-thin modster in an old suit, or a punk stereotype with a Canadian accent, or a redhead in a puffy coat. Her welcoming committee was a severe-looking black woman with dangling dreadlocks. She stood smoking a cigarette as the cold November wind rippled her long coat.

"Hello, Chen," said Mona.

Bailey immediately tried to turn and run back inside, but the door had slammed shut. For a wild moment she thought Trent was somehow in league with Mona, but then she realized he must not have known about Mona's betrayal. He probably thought she was still one of the Alechemists.

Frantically her eyes raked across the building's list of tenants, looking for Trent's name. But a hand covered the directory, and suddenly Mona was next to her, filling Bailey's nostrils with secondhand smoke. "I won't hurt you," she said. "I'm here to talk."

"How can you expect me to trust you?" Bailey said, trying to sound more angry than afraid.

"I don't," Mona said dispassionately. "But you know if I wanted to hurt you, you'd be hurt. I wouldn't have let you see me coming. So walk with me. Please."

So they walked.

"Do you know why I'm here today, Chen?" said Mona. "Why I sought you out?"

Bailey cast about for a retort that was brave and pithy and just a little angry. "Because you suck."

Dammit.

"Bartending is like any other discipline," Mona said. "A distanced perspective is necessary to fully understand every aspect of it. Garrett . . . Zane . . . even Vincent: they all were too close. Too stubborn to take a wider view. But not you. You're good, but you're still coming into this as an outsider. And you're wondering why I stood with Garrett. Why I wanted to get you out of there. And you saw what happened to him."

Something niggled at the back of Bailey's brain. "Why'd you let us go there in the first place if you just wanted us to get out of the way? For that matter, why'd you let Garrett mix the Long Island at Apex? All those people would've been killed if we hadn't been there."

"But you *were* there," Mona said. "And he wasn't mixing at Apex."

"Okay, so technically it was the distillery *above* Apex," Bailey said. "Same diff—"

But no, she thought. It wasn't the same.

"The distillery," Bailey said. "Garrett's explosion destroyed all the equipment."

A shadow of approval flitted across Mona's face. "The Long Island iced tea is too dangerous for anyone to possess. When you accused Garrett in front of the Court, I realized the threat he posed. I approached him, offering him Zane's breakthroughs. When Garrett took them and didn't back away, I knew what I had to do. And I did it."

A pang of bitterness hit Bailey. "So everything that happened up there . . . it didn't matter. I could've just stayed home, and everything would've played out just like it had."

Mona shook her head. "You showed me where to look. And you didn't know what you were walking into when you showed up at Apex. You just showed up anyway, ready to go to bat for a bunch of people who hated you. That's not nothing, Chen."

Bailey stayed silent. But now she was confused. Was this a pep talk?

"Garrett got his wish." Mona went on. "His legacy will serve the Cupbearers' Court forever . . . as a warning. They'll cover it up, of course, and I doubt most bartenders will ever even hear about it. But now they know what will happen if one of them tries to seize ultimate control again."

"But they aren't the only ones trying to mix it. I mean, you saw Zane. You were there when he almost did it."

Mona stared at her calmly.

"What did you do?" Bailey said. "What did you do to stop him?"

Another fleeting smile of approval. "A thumbprint on the inside of the glass," said Mona. "The residual oils from my fingertips were enough to throw off the balance of the Long Island's composition and render its magic inert after the initial reaction. Simple and undetectable once the first liquid is poured."

"So without you, Zane would've succeeded? He'd cracked the code?"

"He's certainly smart enough," said Mona.

Everything was lining up in Bailey's brain. "And you've been with him for over a year. How many other times has he come close?"

A third approving grin, this one showing the tiniest sliver of teeth.

"What if he'd found a way to succeed anyway?" Bailey pressed on. "What if he found a way to outsmart you?"

The smile faded. "That would've been an . . . interesting day," she said, her voice distant. "Have you heard of Hortense LaRue?"

"That's like asking if I've heard of George Washington," Bailey said. "I read the *Dictionary* backwards and forwards."

"Then you know her last deed in the Court's history was the apprehension of Tom Collins," Mona said. "After that she dropped off the earth. Except some say she didn't. Some say she was the first person after the Blackout to re-create the Long Island iced tea. And that after she did, she realized no one should ever make the same mistake."

"*Some say?*" Bailey echoed. "Do you have any proof?"

"No," said Mona. "But you know why." And the moment she said so, Bailey did.

"She wouldn't have wanted proof," Bailey said. "The best way to keep a secret is to make sure no one knows you're keeping one. But then, how would *you* know it?"

Mona took the last drag of her cigarette.

Bailey suddenly remembered their strange chat in the alley. *Those things will kill you.*

And Mona had shaken her head. *No, they won't.*

Realization dawned in Bailey's brain. Her spine tingled. "Mona," she said carefully, "when Hortense LaRue made that Long Island iced tea, did she drink it?"

"I couldn't say," Mona said. "But if she did, she probably regretted it." She dropped her cigarette and ground it under her toe.

"Why are you telling me all this?" Bailey said. Instinct told her she should be afraid, but for some reason she wasn't. If anything, she was too calm.

Mona looked down at her. "Because I like you, Ch—Bailey." Her voice softened. "Because even if you don't trust me, I trust you. And because I don't believe we're done with each other. I want to be your friend, Bailey. I very much do. But I also want you to appreciate what it means to have me as an enemy."

Bailey shivered.

"That's all," Mona said, as if it they were wrapping up a business agenda. Bailey looked up and realized with a start that they were standing at the corner of her block. Her parents' block.

"This is where I leave you." Mona held out a hand for Bailey to shake. "But not for good."

Bailey had no idea what the hell to say. All she did was shake Mona's hand like they were actual grown-ups, nod, and start down the path to her house. She didn't look back, but it didn't matter; she already knew that if she did, Mona would be gone.

"Bailey!"

Bailey froze. She'd been planning to lie, to rehearse how best to explain her prolonged absence to her parents. But now there they were, bursting through the door wearing bathrobes and very concerned expressions.

"Um," Bailey said as her dad crushed her to his flannel-covered chest. "Hi."

"We were so worried, Beetle," he said. "When you didn't call—"

"Where have you been, young lady?"

Her mom never called her young lady unless Bailey was in deep, deep shit. As her dad disentangled himself and marched inside to the couch, Bailey racked her brain for an explanation. Halloween shenanigans provided a convenient cover, but they couldn't excuse everything. And she imagined downtown had probably been chaos last night. It was a miracle the city wasn't on some kind of high terrorism alert after what had gone down in the Sears Tower.

"Well," Bailey said, "here's the thing." She desperately began concocting a G-rated version of the night's events that still technically counted as the truth. "I guess you've noticed I've started staying out later and later. Hanging out with a new group of friends. Um, drinking a lot." She took a deep breath. "And I know that on the face of it that seems really irresponsible, but the thing is that for the first time in my life I feel like I'm doing something important, and I want you guys to know that you can trust me ... "

She fully expected to have been cut off by now. But her parents weren't yelling. In fact they were kind of smiling at each other.

"Beetle." Her dad set his ACCOUNTANTS DO IT WITH BALANCE mug on the coffee table. "Of course we trust you. We understand."

That was the last thing she expected to hear. "You do?"

Her parents exchanged a look. "Didn't you ever wonder why there are no pictures of your father and me from before we got married?" her mom said.

Bailey had to admit the thought had never crossed her mind. She shook her head. "You were both in San Francisco," she said. "You met at a concert. Hit it off. Got married. Then I happened."

Her mom shook her head. "Not quite." She nodded at the computer in the corner, where Bailey's dad had called up a photo. "This was where I met your father."

Bailey didn't know what to expect—a young professionals' mixer, a college reunion, maybe even a tasteful bar. She definitely hadn't expected a black-and-white photo of a graffitied concrete basement, the floor littered with crushed beer cans. She hadn't expected to see a crowd of sweating young men and women with leather jackets and patched jeans, moshing furiously while three tattooed rockers wailed away on instruments.

And yet there it was.

"Regular Puke," said her mom, pointing to the band. "They

broke up two weeks later. But your dad and I didn't."

She clicked to the next photo, and Bailey's jaw all but hit the carpet.

Her dad was a tiny nightmare, the cuffs of his loud plaid pants stuffed into combat boots. He wore a black T-shirt with a red anarchist *A* sprayed on it, and his hair detonated from his scalp in spikes that were the burnt orange that Asian hair took on when bleached. Her mom had a short crew cut Vincent would've envied, topped with a lopsided black bowler hat, and she wore a spike-studded leather jacket and short ruffled skirt. They held each other so tight that even with the grainy quality of the image Bailey could make out the depressions where her dad's fingers sank into her mom's jacket.

They couldn't have possibly looked more in love.

Her mom paged through some of the other pictures: herself, age twenty-whatever, hiding from the rain under a black umbrella shaped just like her bowler hat; Dad, leaning against a wall and giving the camera the finger as he smoked a cigarette; Mom, hunched over and screaming into a microphone—

"Holy shit," said Bailey. "*You* were in a *band*?"

"Language, young lady," her mom said. "And no, my roommate was." Her smile could've run the length of a football field. "I just stopped by for practice once, and they got a picture of me goofing off. No, if you want a shocker . . . " She clicked to the next picture. A younger version of her reclined on a leather bench as a man etched a stylized rose into her forearm. When Bailey's eyes flickered to her inkless arm, she said, "I got it removed when you were less than a year old. No way you'd remember it."

Bailey's mind sagged from all this new information. "So you and Dad—"

"Were cool a long time ago. Well, your mom's still pretty great," Bailey's dad said, smiling at his wife. "Beetle, when we were growing up, falling in line was important. And we both came from Chinese families, where that was important no matter what decade you were living in. We both needed out of it. We needed the time to be selfish."

"We were some of the only Chinese kids in the SF punk scene, if you can believe it," her mom said. "We were bound to meet eventually."

They smiled at each other, and for once Bailey wasn't grossed out.

"The point is," her mom said, "I remember how long it took for me to realize I'd grown out of my parents, not the other way around. It's just a normal part of life."

"But you're so normal *now*," Bailey said.

"First comes love, then comes marriage, then comes Bailey in the baby carriage," her dad recited.

"We shuffled the steps around," her mom said. "But we did go through those phases, too. And it wouldn't be fair of us to deny you the chance to explore and try things and make mistakes."

"Wouldn't be very punk rock either," said her dad.

"Anyway, Bailey, we know we raised a smart girl. You'll find out what you're supposed to do eventually." Her mom squeezed her shoulder and eyed her ripped-up dress. "But maybe take it easy on the partying, huh?"

Bailey opened her mouth but was interrupted by an urgent buzzing in the depths of her battered purse. She rummaged through—where the hell was her phone?—and when she finally found it, the screen lit up with a familiar picture.

Zane Whelan calling

Her parents seemed to know enough to give her privacy, and she fumbled to answer it. "Hello?"

"Bailey?" he said. "Where are you? Trent said you left with me, but obviously you didn't and—"

"I'm here," Bailey said. "I mean, I'm at my house. My parents' house." Whichever it was. Maybe it didn't matter. "Where are you?"

"On our way to Nero's," he said. "Need a ride?"

Before she could answer, a loud squeal of tires and a sonorous car horn melody sounded like...

"Was that 'O Canada'?" Bailey said incredulously.

She heard someone in the background shout: "Tell her she's damn right it was."

"You're both yelling right in my ear!" someone else yelped. Trina. Bailey laughed.

"Yeah, so . . . " Zane said. "We're outside. You'll, ah, know which car."

She sure did. If Bucket's vehicle had been painted white, it would've been a classic kidnapper van—huge and window-less. Mercifully it wasn't white—at least, not entirely. The driver's side was painted like the Canadian flag—a white field emblazoned on each end with a bold red bar and an obnoxiously huge maple leaf in the middle. It was stupid and magnificent, and Bailey was thrilled to see it. Them. The whole car.

"Nice," Bailey said as she jogged over.

"Wait till you see the other side!" Bucket called.

"Or the license plate," Trina added from beside him.

Bucket cheerfully threw the van, whose Quebec license plate read "P4RDN ME," into reverse and proceeded to execute a not quite expert U-turn in the middle of the street, with only minimal screaming from Trina. When he'd righted the van, the passenger side revealed a sprawling mural of a beaver punching a bald eagle in the face.

"This is the stupidest van I've ever seen," Bailey said as she climbed inside. Trina was riding shotgun, so the only seat was in the back next to Zane. Which was just fine with Bailey.

"Thanks," Bucket said, not insulted in the least. "When the

van's a rockin'—"

"Speaking of rocking, I hope you have a noncrappy stereo system," Trina said, and she plugged in her phone as they trundled off. "And I hope you like Orange Banana."

"*Tch,*" said Bucket. "Do I like Orange Banana? I only went to high school with a guy who dated the bassist's ex-girlfriend for a few months. No big deal."

Bailey wasn't really listening. She'd taken the seat next to Zane, not skipping the middle seat like when they were kids, and once she'd buckled up he put his arm around her shoulders. Not just to rest; he was really holding her. Simple as that.

It was going to be all right, Bailey realized. It really was.

"So, what now?" Zane said from above her. Even though the air was thick with Canadian Japanese metal from the noncrappy stereo system, she was close enough to hear him just fine.

Bailey considered what to say. Then, suddenly bold, she took his hand and held it.

"Bailey—"

"Don't."

"No, I have to." Zane sighed a sigh that ruffled the top of her hair. "I fucked up. I should've listened to you, I was an idiot not to, and I said and did a lot of really shitty things along the way. I'm sorry for all of them, and I wish the English language had a stronger word than *sorry*, so I could use that instead. I was kind of the worst person in the world."

It had rushed out of him, like air from a suddenly punctured balloon. She smiled. "Yeah," she said, threading her fingers through his. "You really were, weren't you?"

He blinked, taken aback. "Not what I expected you to say."

She shrugged. Their hands looked good, linked together on top of his knee. "I care about you a lot," she said. "Stupidly a lot. But that doesn't change the fact that I almost died for you, and so did a lot of others. I accept your apology, Zane. I even forgive you. I think."

"Thank God."

"But maybe you should listen to me more often."

"Maybe we should just not not talk ever again."

She shifted enough to see him smiling, but then he hung his head. "No. In seriousness," he said, "I'm sorry. I do want to do better."

"Okay. Good." Bailey leaned back into his chest. "So tell me what happened after I was knocked out."

As it turned out, a lot. After busting the tremens, Bailey was out cold, and the Alechemists had rushed her north to Trent's ("In this?" Bailey said in disbelief. "This is a terrible ambulance."), then returned to the field to do some clean-up and mass memory modifications.

"It was nasty, but we got it under control. Sort of."

Zane pulled out his phone as a visual aid: the *Chicago Tribune* site showed a bombed-out Sears Tower splashed across with the headline TRIPLE-DISTILLED TERROR AT TOWER. Despite the alarmist headline, the content of the article claimed the source of the destruction had been a massive malfunction in the distillation equipment. The article went on to state that the Department of Planning and Development only now seemed to be realizing that a high-rise distillery was a horrible idea. Curiously enough, none of the officials whose signatures appeared on the approval paperwork could even remember signing off on it. Garrett's work, to be sure.

"And no one caught a picture of a tremens or anything?" Bailey took the phone, incredulous.

"Nope," Zane said. "Sorensen convinced everyone to go to this underground nightclub he owns two blocks away with the promise of free drinks—"

"Mixed by yours truly," Trina said with pride. "We convinced them the oblivinum was a kind of exotic Canadian liqueur."

Bucket beamed. "That part was my idea."

"And the thing about being underground," Zane said, "is that the cell reception is terrible."

"Ah." On a whim, Bailey thumbed to a stock market tracking site and saw that the values on all of Bowen Sorensen's publicly traded companies had fallen precipitously in the past day.

"That was a long time coming anyway." Zane was reading over her shoulder, and when he spoke she could feel his warm breath on the back of her neck. "Divinyl was doomed. Records are out. Cassettes are back in." He grabbed his phone, then pulled up a new app and pointed to the screen. "This is the newest app: Kickassette. It makes all your modern audio files sound exactly like those old tapes."

Bailey stared at the interface—an image of two tape reels spinning in unison—for a long moment. And then she threw back her head and let out the kind of unhinged, hysterical laugh that seemed to come only at the end of a very, very long day.

"That's not even the best part," Zane said. "This is." He tapped a display of a tape recorder button, and a moment later the strains of For Dear Life's "Dark November" started to play, just loud enough for the two of them to hear.

As the familiar lyrics and chords drifted to her ears, something unknotted inside Bailey. She'd spent so much of the past two months running from her old self, but for the first time she felt maybe she didn't have to. She'd been a boozy demon fighter and Zane's bitter enemy and a really awkward kisser, and all those things were contradictory and messy and totally okay. What mattered was the future, and she still had plenty of that left. It was the same bubbling excitement she'd felt the last time she'd heard this song, when they were just Bailey Chen and Zane Whelan, fresh from a show and still young and stupid enough to be excited about what was to come.

"We're here!" Bucket wrenched the wheel for a jerky parallel park and turned, smiling, to the backseat.

His face fell. Bailey and Zane were kissing.

"Oi! None of that in my van!"

Zane lifted a hand and flipped him off. Bailey pulled away, no doubt blushing brilliantly, but kept her expression as serious as she could.

"Shut up," she said. "Let's get some damn pancakes."

They burst into Nero's with a clatter and settled into their regular booth.

"I'm hungry enough to eat a moose," Bucket said. "Which, actually, I've had before. Not a whole one, though. It turns out the antlers—"

Trina, who was sitting next to him, mashed a hand into his face to silence him. "You're more charming this way," she said. She turned to Bailey, ignoring Bucket as he pretended to gnaw on one of her fingers. "So what now?"

Certainly seems to be the question on everyone's mind, Bailey mused: not the future or the insanity of the immediate past. Bailey had some witty answer, but she lost it when she glanced out the window. Across the street, two men were out on an afternoon walk: one pudgy and black, the other much older and taller. He wore a green military jacket over his tight black T-shirt, and Bailey knew beneath that jacket she'd see arms covered in old tattoos.

The two of them held hands, their interlocked fingers swinging like a pendulum between them. And in front, barely restrained by his leash, a schnauzer puppy with an already impressive beard trotted along.

As the three of them turned the corner and walked out of sight, Bailey smiled. *We did it,* she thought. *Happy retirement, boss.*

"Now," Trina declared, "I'm ordering me some bacon."

"It's not *real* bacon," Bucket muttered.

Trina rolled her eyes. "You know what I meant."

"Well," Bailey said, tearing her eyes away from the disappeared Vincent, "I guess it's back to the job hunt for ol' Bailey Chen." She nudged Zane in the ribs. "You're getting this meal, right?"

"Mine, too," Bucket said from behind his menu, "seeing as all of us are now without a home bar."

"Well, actually," Zane said, "here's the thing. I kind of own the Nightshade now. Since Garrett . . . "

Everyone fell quiet. Zane cleared his throat.

"Anyway. I'm gonna be a good owner. Build its name and cred back up from nothing if I have to. But I'm going to need staff."

Trina leveled a look at him.

"*More* staff." Zane corrected himself.

"I accept!" Bucket said, slapping down his menu. "You won't regret it, boss."

Inspiration struck Bailey. "What you need," she said, "is an assistant manager."

Zane frowned. "That sounds . . . . corporate."

"Think about it," said Bailey. "Chicago's a mess right now. And if the Court has any hope of staying relevant and maintaining control, then you need to step up, Zane. You're the only one who can keep everything from going to shit again. You're the only one who—"

Who almost made the Long Island.

Zane fiddled with his napkin-wrapped silverware bundle, but he nodded.

"So you need help on the home front," Bailey continued. "You need someone who's good with numbers. Preferably someone with a business degree."

"And a minor in demon slaying?" said Zane.

Bailey grinned. "Couldn't hurt."

Diana finally showed up, bringing along four Americanos. Bucket and Trina went to take a sip, but Zane waved a hand.

"Wait. Hang on." He lifted his mug. "To Garrett. Rest in peace."

Bailey suspected that if there was an afterlife, Garrett was unlikely to rest, peacefully or otherwise, but she raised her cup all the same. So did Bucket.

"To Vincent," he added.

"To Chicago," Trina said.

"To you guys," Bailey said, then thought better of it. "To us. The Alechemists."

With a gentle *clink,* they brought their mugs together.

"Cheers."

The Long Island Iced Tea
The impossible elixir

1. *Fill a highball glass or a Collins glass with ice.*

2. *Pour in half an ounce apiece of tequila, light rum, vodka, gin, and triple sec.*

3. *Pour in two ounces of sweet and sour mix.*

4. *Finish with a dash of cola. Stir gently until very cold.*

   1 oz lemon juice
   1 oz gomme syrup

5. *Garnish with a lemon twist and a straw and then serve.*

The official position of both *The Devil's Water Dictionary* and the Cupbearers Court is that the Long Island Iced Tea does not exist. This legendary drink of the pre-Blackout days, the grand panacea of bartending, has long been sought by ambitious bartenders who were both metaphorically and literally thirsty. And yet in those centuries of striving, there are no records of its successful manufacture. Even Hortense LaRue, the art's paragon, told the Court that her failure to synthesize one was her second-greatest regret (for details on her greatest regret, see *MARTINI*).

Rather than reading more on this subject, a bartender's time would be better spent putting down this book, fixing him- or herself a drink, and doing terrible things to the first tremens he or she finds. Please do so now.

This paragraph and those that follow assume that you, the reader, did not put down this book, but instead kept reading. Very well. As you wish. ←

this book is awfully sassy.

Despite the total evaporation of codified bartending knowledge post-Blackout, legends persisted of a drink that could violate all known laws of magic by infusing its drinker's animus with enough alcohol to make said drinker equal parts magic and man. Such a being would be able to manifest more than one magical ability simultaneously, withstand greater amounts of pain and damage, and even cheat death.

The legend drove many bartenders to quest after the secrets of its manufacture. A loose recipe was decoded from pre-Blackout fragments, but all attempts to mix it ended in tragedy—always for the one mixing it, and usually for anyone else who happened to be on the same city block that day. The Court ultimately declared it to be an impossibility; today, its attempted manufacture is an infraction of the highest order. Still, even the strictest law cannot deter unauthorized attempts. Therefore, it is the advice of this book that bartenders restrict themselves to mixing only the mundane version of this drink, which, while not an elixir of immortality, does taste rather pleasant.

However, the writers of *The Devil's Water Dictionary* find it likely that if you did not stop reading earlier, and indeed looked up this recipe at all, you are disinclined to listen to reason and will endeavor to create a Long Island Iced Tea of your own. To which we say again: Very well. As you wish. You're an adult.

God I hope not.

ACKNOWLEDGMENTS

The hardest part about writing the acknowledgments for a book I authored is finding a way to stretch the words, "Great job, Paul!" See, that's the thing about this book: I wrote it all by myself, because I'm the greatest. If there's anyone here to acknowledge, it's definitely just me, and me alone. It's an unfortunate side effect of being, as you might recall, the greatest.

I mean, who else am I supposed to thank? My editrix, Blair Thornburgh? As if. "You were completely crucial to making this the best book it could ever be" is a sentence that definitely won't appear in these acknowledgments. And I certainly wouldn't go on to express my unending gratitude to her for believing in me and my ideas, as well as giving me the chance of a lifetime.

In no way will I thank my agent, Jennie Goloboy, for all her enthusiasm and shrewd creative input. I won't thank her for her unfailing support and excellent career advice, either. She's been an invaluable partner and friend during this entire enterprise, but come on, people. Let's not forget who this party is for.

I guess it'd be customary to thank my mom, my dad, and my brother Timm, but they don't get a shout-out just for always supporting this crazy little ambition of mine. They don't need credit for all the books they gave me to instill my deep love of reading. They might've sat quietly so many times and let me work out story issues aloud, but it's not like I'm about to nominate them for sainthood over it.

Who else? My beta readers Matt Brauer, Cal CaDavid, Ron Corniels, Dustin Martin, Connor McCrate, Natalie Neurauter, Colin Thorpe, Matt Willems, Leslie Wishnevski, and Andrea Zevallos? The people whose feedback kept me humble, and honed this narrative into something that belongs on a shelf and not in a shredder? The people whose kind thoughts and honesty kept me going during the times when I just wanted to roll over and call it a day? Fuck 'em.

Katie Locke might think she's getting a whole paragraph here, just because she gave me a graf in one of her own books. But if she thinks I'm going to thank her for all the times she tempered my Slytherin cunning with her Ravenclaw wisdom, or for all the super-poutine inside jokes spawned by our daily gchats, she'll be sorely disappointed.

I'm not about to thank the women and men who work in the service industry. Your customers suck and your pay's a cruel joke, even though you're the duct tape that holds the world together and the grease that keeps it running smoothly. If this book is for anyone, it's for you. But I still won't thank you, because I was the one who wrote the book while you were all out doing things that really mattered.

I will thank Mira. She's my roommate's cat, and she spent most of my drafting process lying quietly in a nearby sunbeam. It was the single most profoundly inspiring thing I've ever seen.

And finally, I won't thank you, dear readers. I probably should, because you're the people who've allowed me to live my dream. But if there's one thing I suck at, it's being humble.

Okay, see that last sentence right there? That was me, being humble.

And I nailed it.

PAUL KRUEGER *is a fantasy writer and cocktail connoisseur whose work has appeared in the Sword & Laser anthology. He lives in Los Angeles.*